Beacon
Book 2 in the Ronos Trilogy

TYLER RUDD HALL

This is/for Curtis
BE

Printed in the United States of America.

The characters and events in this book are fictitious. Any similarity to real persons, living or dead, is coincidental and not intended by the author.

BookLocker.com, Inc.
2013

First Edition

Also Written by Tyler Rudd Hall

The Ronos Trilogy
Catalyst: Book 1 in the Ronos Trilogy
Beacon: Book 2 in the Ronos Trilogy
Book 3 (Coming fall 2014)

King and Wakefield
The Death of Jonas Wakefield (Short Story)

BEACON

Book 2 in the Ronos Trilogy

For Dad,
Thanks for helping me see my potential.

Table of Contents

If you knew your potential,
nothing could stop you from reaching it.

Chapter 1
Always Awake

Sneed didn't go by Sneed anymore. To him, that name represented who he used to be: a man who was so addicted to a fabricated reality that he didn't know real from make-believe. He got so disconnected from the real world that he was unrecognizable to his family and friends and ended up on the street covered in his own filth. At the time it didn't matter to him because he was living life through his Imp. What happened in his false reality was the only thing that had mattered.

He wasn't like that anymore, though, and he didn't want to be constantly reminded of it. He didn't want to be Sneed anymore. Several days after he and the only man in Passage with an Imp used a mobile dead zone to take down General Zinger's space yacht, Sneed brought up the idea of using a new name.

"I didn't think Sneed was a good name anyway," said the only man from Passage with an Imp.

"It's a character from one of my books," said Sneed. "It's not my real name."

"Then what is?"

"Quentin Lenoch."

"Not much better, but I can go with that if you need me to."

Life in Passage was easy for Quentin. Small town life suited him. His stories were still hugely popular so he didn't need a real job; he could live off of royalties. His fans had long ago written him off for producing any new material or answering any of their questions. No one expected anything from him, but his stories kept selling.

After Quentin delivered Mac's message to the only man in Passage with an Imp and helped take down the space yacht, he didn't have anywhere to go, so the only man in Passage with an Imp offered his own house.

"There's a spare bedroom you can use until we hear from Mac again."

"Thanks," said Quentin. There was a little hesitation before he asked his next question. "If I'm going to stay here then I should probably know your name. When people around town ask me where I'm staying I need to be able to give them an answer without telling them you have an Imp."

"Use the name they use," said the only man in Passage with an Imp.

"What's that?"

"Smith. No first name."

"That's what Mac said. But what's your real name?"

"If you need to, you can add a *Mr.* in front, but that's it. If it's good enough for the other people in this town then it's good enough for you."

Passage was a village made up completely of Luddites. No one there had an Imp and most didn't trust people who did. Imps were the cutting edge of technology. It was three computer chips surgically implanted before babies turned a year old, one chip in the brain and one in each eye. Imps acted like a computer that could be accessed through thoughts. The computer chips in the eyes projected images that only the person using them could see. It was the ultimate hands free device. Memories could be recorded. Anyone anywhere could be contacted at any time. Luddites didn't like Imps because they were worried about the government, military, big businesses, or in most cases all three, were using Imps to collect information and control the population.

As much as Quentin had heard that Luddites were suspicious and unfriendly, he never found any evidence of that. He didn't have friends instantly, but he wasn't expecting that. Of course he wasn't expecting to have to wait very long for Mac to return, but days turned into weeks and Quentin needed something to do to occupy his time. Perhaps to get him out of his hair or to help him integrate more with the community, Mr. Smith set up a book club for Quentin to host. This worried Quentin until he realized that they meant books on paper. He was so worried about getting lost in an electronic world that he wouldn't do anything else. He was happy to host the event, and sooner than expected he was considered a resident of Passage. This only happened because there was a large section of the population of the village who had a love for the written word. They recognized that Quentin was one of them both because he had no Imp and because he was a writer.

Quentin hadn't seen Mac for almost a month. As the days went by and there was still no word from Mac, Smith looked more and more worried. There were no updates. Not even the news had any reports on Mac. The space yacht incident was being passed off as an accident and no names were mentioned. Wherever Mac was, the military wasn't desperate enough to use the media to find him yet. That was good, but both Quentin and Smith were anxious to know more about what happened at Northgate and whom they could trust. Northgate, a city of ten million people, had been completely destroyed by a mysterious ship. Mac had gone off to find who was responsible.

The update came one day in an unexpected form. Quentin had thought he was alone, but while he was reading the book

club selection, *The Pursuit of Happiness* by Eric O'Brien —
the best chicken-related story Quentin had ever read — a
creaking noise came from the kitchen. Someone was coming
into the house. The back door's hinges were loud enough to
be heard from all over the house, but Mr. Smith said he
wasn't going to be back until later that night. Passage was
becoming more and more friendly. Quentin thought maybe
there was an unspoken "mine is yours" rule that he didn't
know about.

Not worrying too much about it, he went to see who was
there. As he walked down the hallway he heard rushed
whispers but couldn't make out the words. It sounded like
there were two men sneaking around. His suspicions were
confirmed. The one leading the way into the building was an
older man with red hair. The red hair, more brilliant orange
than red, hid the age that the crow's feet around his eyes
betrayed. He was tall and lanky and had big ears. The other
man was a foot shorter and at least a foot wider. Not that he
was extremely overweight, he wasn't scrawny like Orange.

They stopped moving when Quentin came into the room
and waited for him to speak. The longer the silence went on
the more suspicious Quentin became. They clearly did not
have a good excuse for being there.

"It's not what you think," said the shorter man.

"Quiet," said Orange.

"We didn't do anything wrong — that he knows of
anyway."

"I said be quiet."

"What's going on, guys?" asked Quentin.

"We are looking for someone," said Orange.

"Well, you found someone."

"And who are you?"

Quentin could see what was going on here. It was obvious that whoever these two guys were they were as suspicious of him as he was of them, and it was more than them being worried about being caught in the act of coming uninvited into someone's house.

What kind of shifty friends does Mr. Smith have? "My name is Quentin Lenoch."

"You don't live here then," said Orange.

"How do you know Mr. Smith?"

"We have mutual friends."

"I gave you my name. What are yours?"

"I'm Michael," said Orange. "We'll come back later."

The two men turned to leave but the unnamed short man stopped them and said, "I'm getting a message on my Imp. It's from Mr. Smith."

"What did he say?" asked Michael.

"He asked if we are here because of...you-know-who."

"Is you-know-who Mac Narrad?" asked Quentin.

At the sound of Mac's name Michael pulled out a gun that had been tucked in the back of his pants. It happened so fast that Quentin didn't have time to flash his life before his eyes. Michael took a couple steps towards Quentin and kept the gun aimed perfectly between his eyes.

"How do you know Mac Narrad?" asked Michael.

"I'm a friend."

"That's not really answering my question."

With a gun pointed at him, Quentin didn't feel like he had any other option than to tell the truth. "I met him in McAllister in Australia. I was disconnected and he helped me. Mr. Smith gave him a way to get rid of his Imp so that he couldn't be tracked and I was able to get rid of mine as well. He asked if I would come here and deliver a message to Mr. Smith."

"How did you get rid of your Imp?"

"We burned it out of ours eyes with surgical glasses. It sounds worse than it is. There are no side effects. Do you know Mac?"

"I think you're overreacting, Michael," said the short man who looked very nervous about the escalation of the situation.

"Where is Mac?" asked Michael.

"I don't know. I'm waiting for him here. We haven't heard from him in a while."

"How long?"

"About a month."

Michael looked like he didn't know what to do. He kept his gun up and didn't look away from Quentin, but he didn't want to pull the trigger. He didn't fully trust him. The three men stood there in silence for a moment. The silence was broken up by the sound of a hover car door opening and closing and then the front door of the house opening and closing. Mr. Smith came in the door moving quicker than Quentin had ever seen him move before. The old man didn't look fazed at all by the gun and simply walked over and tore it out of Michael's hand.

"What do you think you are doing? Killing someone isn't going to help you hide, idiot," said Mr. Smith.

"Who —" Michael didn't have time to finish his question.

"I'm Mr. Smith. You are Jace Michaels and Scott Ryder. This is Quentin Lenoch and all four of us are on the same side so there's no need to point weapons at each other."

"Why should we trust you?" asked Jace, the man who hadn't lied all the way when he posed himself as Michael.

"You were right to think that what you did for Scott would be something Zinger didn't want the public to find out, but that's only because he thinks he can still find you two.

You need to get rid of your Imps. Not you Jace — I know you don't have one."

"How did you know that?"

"Doesn't matter. Scott, you understand you need to get rid of your Imp if you don't want to end up back in prison, right?"

"You understand that I can't do that. What if Lynn tries to call me? I need to be online if I want to talk to her again," said Scott.

Mr. Smith nodded his head. "That's fine. I can throw them off the scent then. We'll see how long that lasts. The military can be fooled, but that's 'cause those guys are mostly idiots. It's the independent Imp detectives you'll have to worry about, but I have a friend who can lend a hand there. Scott, you'll have to give me additional access to your Imp so I can set everything up."

Quentin held up his hands. "Hold on a moment. Can someone fill me in on what's happening here?"

Mr. Smith obliged. "Mac and Jace were part of the Northgate recovery team but then they found out that there was something more going on. The entire city had been destroyed but it might not have been aliens that were responsible. While they were looking for Mac's family and for the truth about who was behind the attack, they found out that there were two people who might know more about what was really happening — Lynn and Scott Ryder. Mac went to get Lynn. Jace here went to get Scott. From the looks of things, Jace did his part and came back to meet up with Mac."

"Okay. So what evidence do you have, Scott?" asked Quentin.

"I was the manager of a munitions factory. It's possible we made the weapons and ammo that destroyed Northgate," said Scott.

"That's a start," said Quentin who had no idea that Mac had already figured out that the military was behind the destruction of Northgate. General Zinger orchestrated it to get the people of Earth to more actively support the war against the alien invaders.

"You guys look like you've been through the refiner's fire. Why not come sit down and fill us in on how you got here," said Mr. Smith while he led them to the living room.

Both Jace and Scott walked with the weight of the world on their shoulders, as if they had been walking for a week straight and their joints were about to come unstuck from their bodies. When they told the story of how they got there, their slow movements were understandable.

Scott had been in prison, moved there from a loony bin after what had happened in Northgate. Not after the attack, but after the revelation that Lynn had survived and publicly called the war a fake. The government thought that it would be easier to keep an eye on him if he were in prison.

That left it to Jace to find a way to break him out even though Jace was being hunted down by the military for what he and Mac did in Northgate. The prison was deep within the Rocky Mountains, and to make a clean escape they had to run without technology and get to Passage as fast as they could. This was difficult with Scott having an Imp, but they were still able to make it. Now Mr. Smith could help them hide more effectively.

"That was a week ago," said Jace. "We meant to walk or take public transportation the whole way, but the hover buses don't come this far off the main highway so we ended up borrowing a car."

"Stealing. He means stealing," Scott said.

"So that car parked out back is stolen?" asked Mr. Smith.

"Yes," said Scott.

"I know. I'll get rid of it," said Jace. "I needed to find Mac first, or at least try to find out what happened. Have you heard anything?"

"No," said Quentin.

Jace looked anxious. He got up from the couch and started pacing the room. It was like he had been moving so quickly for so long he didn't know how to sit still. There had always been a plan for what to do next and now there wasn't. Mac was supposed to be there and he wasn't.

Mr. Smith tried to calm down Jace. "A friend of Mac's is a friend of ours. You two can stay here until he gets back — whenever that is."

Jace looked relieved, "That's great. But first I need to go ditch that car we borrowed."

"I'll walk out with you," said Mr. Smith.

The two of them left. Quentin looked down at Jace's still full glass of water on the end table by the couch. He hadn't taken a single sip. Scott saw what Quentin was looking at.

"He doesn't eat or drink much. When we were on the run it was him trying to find food for me to keep me going. I never saw him have more than a sip of liquid or a bite of a sandwich."

"For a whole week?" asked Quentin.

"That's right. I thought it was unnatural too, but he said he had training and that he would eat when they got to where we were going."

"But he hasn't," said Quentin. "There's a whole glass of water there for him and he didn't even think about drinking it."

Scott reached over from the other side of the couch and took the water for his own. "If it makes you feel better, I'll have his water. Don't let Jace get into your head. He does lots of strange things. I've never seen him get tired or sleep. The guy is always awake."

"He could have been sleeping while you slept. And a minute ago he was hobbling like an old man to get into this room."

"Right. I think he was putting on a show. He wants people to think he gets tired, but when we were on the run he didn't have time for theatrics," said Scott. "Don't get me wrong, I owe Jace Michaels my freedom, but the longer I'm with him the less I feel I really know him. He didn't have a firm grasp of the distance I was capable of covering in one day. He was always pushing me to go faster and farther. At first I thought it was because he was a military man and I've spent most of my life as a manager behind a desk and making sure a plant runs on schedule. But then it seemed like he didn't have any idea of what normal people should be capable of when running for their lives."

"Why are you telling me all this?" asked Quentin.

"You're a friend of Mac's. Jace hasn't let me out of his sight since we met. That must mean he trusts you. I think I only needed to vent about my traveling companion. You know how it is when you spend too much time with the same person."

Quentin nodded and asked Scott if he was hungry or if he needed a shower. Scott opted for the shower and was shown where the bathroom and towels were. Quentin said he would look around the house for something Scott could wear until they went out to get new clothes.

By that time the only man in Passage with an Imp came back.

"What do you think?" he asked Quentin.

"I think they are honest with what they've said. But I'm a little worried about what they aren't saying."

"Well put. They are fugitives after all. When I went with Jace to the car we didn't say much. He asked me about Mac, but overall wasn't too keen on communication. Before he drove off I put a tracker on the car so that we can see where he is going."

"Scott seems okay," said Quentin.

"I agree, but we'll keep our suspicions about Jace to ourselves. I have the tracker connected to my Imp so I'll let you know where he takes the car. Chances are he is going to dump it like he said he would and we will have nothing to worry about. This is only a precautionary measure," said Mr. Smith.

"Absolutely," said Quentin. "If Mac thinks Jace Michaels is on our side then who are we to disagree."

The next day there were other complications beyond Jace and his suspicious behavior. More people had showed up, most of them unfamiliar. There was one giant of a man with skin the color of night. His legs were as thick as Quentin's whole body. When he stepped up to ring the doorbell, his body barely fit in the frame of the door. He wore a buttoned-up white shirt and dress pants. Of the three people at the door his attire was the most formal, but it looked like the clothes were one size too small. His already impressively sized body was about to burst out of the shirt; buttons would have flown in every direction.

Next to him was a middle-aged woman with dark hair and pale skin. Either there was too much sun for her or she was a perpetual squinter. She had her arms crossed across her chest and did not look comfortable in the jeans and t-shirt she was wearing. Quentin pictured her natural habitat as a boardroom of some big company and her typical attire as a pant suit.

There was another girl standing there but Quentin couldn't really see her. She was standing too far behind the man. They didn't look like they were part of the military. Were they here to look for fugitives? Maybe they were bounty hunters.

"Can I help you?" asked Quentin.

"We are here for Mac," said the man. His voice was high for a normal male. With his body it was almost laughable, except that Quentin was worried about some kind of retaliation for laughing.

"There is no one here by that name," said Quentin. There was something suspicious about this group. The fact that they were looking for Mac didn't help their cause.

"We know, but there is no one at his house and he told us that if he was not there then we should meet here," the man said.

Quentin heard a tap on the wall to his side. That was Mr. Smith in the next room listening in. He was subtly trying to tell Quentin to get some names so he could run a check on his Imp.

"I don't know when Mac will be back. No one has heard from him in a while. If you leave your contact information I'll pass it on to him when he gets back," said Quentin.

"Where's his family?" said the man.

"They were in Northgate, unfortunately."

"We don't have Imps for Mac to contact us through."

"No one around here does. Tell me your names. I'm sure that will be enough."

"I'm Brock Burnson," said the man.

"I'm Sabriel Moreau," said the middle aged woman.

The girl behind Brock stepped forward and gave her name. She was a young girl. Still in her teens. Her hair was long but it was up around her head so she didn't have to fuss with it in the wind. Her eyes would have broken the heart of any high-school boy.

"My name is Janelle Stewart," she said.

Chapter 2
The Other General

Mac Narrad had taken out two alien collector ships all by himself. Anytime the military took out a collector ship it was at the extensive cost of human life. The young soldier that should have been hailed as a hero set to change the tide of the war was instead detained in a prison cell on one of the capital ships.

Detained was a stretch. There was never a moment where he felt like he was trapped. He was surrounded by humans. Actual humans, not emulated humans from the collector ships — the alien impostors that could disperse into a deadly swarm that could enter your body and tear it apart from the inside out. The aliens who pretended to be human walked at the same pace and rarely had facial expressions. Where Mac was now, everyone walked quickly, almost in a panic, and most wore an expression of concern, extreme fatigue, or both. The change that had taken over his body made him more powerful than any human on that ship. There was nothing stopping him from busting out of that cell and proceeding with his plans.

Mac had no need for food anymore. He was offered some but declined. It had been over a week since he had eaten anything and he wasn't the slightest bit hungry. He needed to make sure he couldn't starve to death. Because if he could starve to death, then so could Lynn. Trapped on Ronos, he didn't know if she was resourceful enough to find food on her own. Maybe if that was all she had to worry about she would be able to figure something out, but her last communication haunted Mac. The message came through mind speech. A new-found ability in addition to unprecedented strength and no need for constant nutrition that Mac and Lynn had acquired since they injected themselves with the liquid rock they found on the secret planet Ronos.

It's Raymond. I don't know how, but he's still alive. I can't get away from him. He always knows where I am. It feels like I've been running for hours.

If Raymond, the Military Intelligence Major who was obsessed with getting rid of Mac and Lynn, had injected himself with the power giving liquefied rock then he was going to be an impossibly deadly enemy. Forgiveness and logical thinking weren't his strong points. He would harbor anger against Mac and Lynn for escaping even though his being left behind was his own fault.

The cell they put Mac in was similar to the one on General Zinger's personal space yacht. It was a boring gray room with a cot and a scratchy blanket. No pillow. The door was more of a prison door. It had a slot for food. He hadn't been in the room for more than ten minutes when a plate of food was shoved inside.

Mac had never been a prisoner in the military he'd once served, but if this is how the prisoners were treated then there was nothing for them to complain about. Food so soon after getting captured was a treat, especially food of this quality. Roast beef, mashed potatoes, peas and corn, and a tall glass of refreshing beverage. He might not need to eat anymore but that didn't stop the food from smelling appetizing.

He needed to set up a timeline for Lynn. When he started to get hungry then he knew Lynn was in trouble. Mac ignored the food and lay down on the cot. In his mind there were only three things that he needed to do: go back to Ronos to save Lynn, find out where the aliens had taken Janelle, and then do whatever he could to win the war. The objectives were clear in his mind but he had no idea what he should do next. Getting to Ronos would be the easiest. The planet emanated a pull that attracted ships to it if they got too close. Getting a ship down to the surface would be nearly impossible though, because the planet was entirely covered in corrosive gas now. Going to save Janelle behind enemy lines would be even harder. Mac had blown his cover before he knew he even had it. Aliens didn't think humans had the ability to mind speak, but now they knew that Mac did so there was no way he would be able to sneak over and rescue her and the other captured emulated humans. Winning the war was the most vital objective, but Mac knew he wouldn't be able to do that himself and he knew he couldn't count on General Zinger, the leader of the Earth military, to help. Everything that Mac needed to do kept pushing at him to act, but he knew he couldn't until he figured out what he was supposed to do first.

The ideas kept swimming around in his head but it wasn't long before there was an interruption and his brain was assaulted with a thought message.

Is it true? Can you communicate with your mind now? said the unfamiliar male voice.

Mac opened his eyes and looked around. Nothing had changed. The floor was still covered in plates with uneaten food.

Who is this? asked Mac.

There was no answer but Mac had a general idea of who it could be. There were only two groups of people that could mind speak: aliens and people who had been changed on Ronos. The only two people that had been changed on Ronos were Mac and Lynn and the voice was a man's so it definitely was not Lynn. What were the aliens up to now?

There was no way for him to tell time anymore. He looked at all the food he had been given. The plates were spread out on the floor and all the food was cold. He also had fallen asleep so many times now that he had lost count. A week could have passed, or for all he knew it was a month.

No food came. Instead the door opened and a man walked in followed by two grunts in full body armor. Mac had no idea who was behind the armor or helmets. The man in front wore the uniform of a general. He was the Zinger of the front line.

The confusing thing about that was that the military hierarchy only allowed for one general. The General was the highest rank. He or she was the one that made all the decisions, the big decisions that would affect everyone. If there were two generals they would compete against each other and nothing would get done. There could only be one general and, unfortunately, that was General Zinger. Who was this guy?

He was tall and authoritative. His black hair was cut so close to the wood that you could only see enough to know it was dark and he was not balding. His eyebrows were mangy and his eyes were full of power. This was not a guy to mess around with. The grunts pointed their weapons at Mac. The general pointed his finger.

"I am General Roy, leader of the Earth military pushing back the invasion. Who are you and where did you come from?"

"My name is Spacer Mac Narrad. Former Spacer, I guess. I was a pilot and soldier in the Earth Military. I was assigned to the Northgate recovery but most recently I came from a military base on Ronos."

"I looked into that. There is no military base on Ronos. There isn't even a planet listed as Ronos."

"The only people that know about it are General Zinger and the people stationed there."

The General snorted at Zinger's name. Hopefully he had the same feelings about his obese counterpart as Mac did.

"Come in here," the general said to someone standing outside the door where Mac couldn't see.

Spacer Nelson Koyczan came in with his hands in front of him with restraints on. Before Mac had been put in the cell three men, Nelson, Ryan, and Cliff, had helped Mac get onto one of the alien ships and destroy it. General Zinger had meant for the alien attack to show Mac that the war was out of his control but instead it convinced Mac that he needed to make as many people like him and Lynn as he could. If one person could take out hundreds of aliens then thousands or millions would be an army that could save humanity.

"Yes, General Roy," said Nelson.

"Look at the food that he hasn't eaten," said the General.

"Yes, sir."

"Can any human go that long without eating food?"

"No, sir."

"Is this man a human?"

Nelson hesitated to answer.

The General got within an inch of Nelson's face. "I asked you a question."

"Sir, if he was an alien then why would he have saved our lives?"

"Yes. I saw the Imp feed. Mac Narrad, I've heard reports from dozens of soldiers that you single-handedly took out two alien collector ships. Is that true?"

"Yes, but I won't be able to do it again," said Mac.

"Why not?"

"Because there is only one of me and from what I hear millions of alien ships —"General Roy tensed up. Did they not have the real numbers? "— if I'm the only one out there then it will take too long. My skills are better put to use elsewhere."

The general smiled. It wasn't a good smile.

"I'm not going to let you do that. I don't know what you are really up to, and until you decide to tell me the truth you are going to stay in this room." He kicked at the plates as he turned around to leave. "This Spacer here who you've been indoctrinating was put in a cell like you. We needed to know if he was human. We withheld food and watched him shrivel. You on the other hand have gone without food for almost two weeks with no signs of starvation. No human can do what you do. No human can go that long without food."

Mac knew that he needed to get out of that cell and away from the front line. Of the three things he needed to do, rescue Lynn, find Janelle, and win the war, he decided the best thing to start with was the easiest. He would start with rescuing Lynn. That meant going back to Ronos, and he wasn't going back alone. Mac knew that eventually he would need to change as many people as possible so why not start with people that deserved it. People like Jace, Sneed, and the only man in Passage with an Imp.

Getting off the capital ship was going to be easy. Mac only needed to get to the docking bay. But before that he needed to break out of the cell. Getting up from his bed he went to the door and examined it. It was a heavy steel door with no window, but it did have the slot that food could be passed through. It wasn't meant to be opened from the inside, but with his superhuman strength forcing it open was no big deal. Through the small slot he was able to see how many guards were on the other side. There was only one that Mac could see. That didn't seem right. Didn't General Roy consider Mac one of the enemy? Mac had also proved that he was dangerous and powerful, way more than one guard could handle.

"I heard you messing with the door," said a familiar voice. "You ready to finally get out of here, or what?"

The guard had been standing on the far side of the room outside of the cell. The lighting wasn't very good. The only light source was a single bulb at the top center of the building. It left the corner where the guard was standing in darkness.

"Do I know you?" asked Mac.

"I'm almost offended, Mac."

The guard took a step forward and his orange hair and skinny body was fully illuminated. It was Jace Michaels. Mac couldn't have been more happy. Right when he needed an ally the man who helped him find his family in the ruins of Northgate showed up.

"Jace!"

"Not so loud. I'm the only one here for now. The others will be back soon."

"What about the cameras? They'll see us talking."

"You know they don't use cameras. They rely too heavily on Imps. Neither of us has one anymore."

"Last time we met you told me the reason you didn't have an Imp was a secret. You ready to tell the tale?"

"Do you still trust me?"

"Yeah."

"Then let's get out of here."

"You don't think they'll notice the empty cell?"

"Not right away. I don't think General Roy understands what you are really capable of. They only check the cell every five hours when someone puts more food through that slot."

"How much longer until the next round of food arrives?"

"One hour. We should wait until after then before we get out of here," said Jace.

"Agreed. We'll need to get Nelson and Ryan out of here as well," said Mac.

"Why? More people will slow us down."

"They only helped me because the only other choice was being collected by the aliens."

"Sounds like they were looking out for themselves."

"They disobeyed orders and took a chance on me saving everyone. They shouldn't be punished for trying to do a good thing. Plus, they might be useful to us."

The sound of approaching footsteps signaled the other guard's return. Mac started to close the food slot on his cell door but Jace had one more thing to say to him.

"I won't be able to answer you directly, but you can still communicate with me through mind speech. I need to know everything you know about Ronos."

Mac closed the slot and went back to his bed. Jace was right. They each needed to know everything the other person learned after they parted ways in the Earth Space Port (ESP). Lying on his bed he reached out to Jace in his mind and started telling him about the pull that had trapped the *Terwillegar* in orbit and how a HAAS3 had destroyed the ship and almost destroyed the shuttle he, Lynn, and Raymond had been on. Then he told him how they had crashed into the cave system full of the corrosive purple gas that slowly ate away at the shuttle. They couldn't get out of the cave unless they went through the gas and they couldn't get through the gas without burning alive. Raymond figured out that the gas was lighter than air and thought he could crawl to safety. He left the shuttle crawling along the cave floor. Too bad he left before Lynn figured out that the gas didn't burn a certain kind of rock and that if they injected themselves with the liquid form of the rock they not only survived the gas but became super charged by it.

That's why I can go weeks without eating, why I have super strength, and it's also why I can mind speak, Mac said in his head, but he paused when he realized the implications.

His mind went back to the first time he learned that he could mind speak. It had been on an alien collector ship. They had plucked him out of space thinking he was one of them, but when he had spoken out loud instead of using mind speak they knew he was human. While the aliens discussed what to do with him he noticed that they weren't saying anything out loud and realized they were telepathic. Mac focused on one of them, a massive black guy who had muscles that Mac didn't even know existed, and kept thinking *My name is Mac. What's yours?* The two of them were able to make a connection but only after concentrating and focusing their energies. The alien confirmed that they had tried to communicate with humans this way before, but it hadn't worked. The only reason that Mac had been able to was because he had been changed on Ronos.

This led back to another simple truth. There were only two types of people that could receive or talk in mind speak. If Jace could hear everything that Mac was saying, then Jace had to be an alien.

That was the reason Jace didn't have an Imp. That was the reason he was so sure that it wasn't the aliens who had destroyed Northgate. That was the reason he was willing to help Mac find out the truth. Jace and his alien race needed to know who was responsible for, or rather who had the capability of, destroying an entire city. The ginger was nothing more than a spy who found someone with the same goals as he had.

If the alien talking to Mac really was an alien emulating Jace then he wanted nothing to do with him. Being in a different room from Jace helped Mac hide the shocked look on his face. He stood up and started pacing the room aggressively. After everything that had happened, he was no more than a pawn for the enemy. He had helped the enemy reach its goals. They used him. The more he thought about it the more he believed that there was no chance Jace actually went to get Scott. Mac had also told Jace to meet him in Passage. Had he unknowingly put Sneed and the only man in Passage with an Imp in danger? Out here on the front line there was no way for Mac to warn them. They could be dead right now because of the alien pretending to be Jace.

For the first time it really struck Mac that Janelle wasn't the only one who was taken by the aliens. There were millions of people abducted. There were creatures from all over the galaxy — even other galaxies for all Mac knew. He didn't know how long the alien menace had been collecting people and using them. Wherever Janelle was, the real Jace Michaels was with her. His body was being emulated and being used to control Mac. Janelle and Jace needed to be freed. They all needed to be freed. But how was Mac going to do that? After all the commotion he caused destroying two of their ships there was no way he was going to be able to go rescue anyone. Somehow Mac had to send someone else with his abilities to the enemy side. That meant he first had to get back to Ronos. Maybe he could take Nelson and Ryan with him.

An hour passed. No more food was given to Mac. Why would they? General Roy had already told him what they were trying to accomplish with the regular gifts of delicious dishes. Instead when the time came for more food, several soldiers came in and cleared away all the plates and slammed the door closed without saying a word to Mac. Once they were gone he got off his bed and went to the door, holding his ear against it trying to hear what was going on in the room on the other side. The door was too thick. He could hear people moving around but he couldn't tell how many there were.

Now that Mac suspected Jace was an alien, he didn't have to rely on him and probably shouldn't. But Mac also now knew something that Jace didn't and maybe that could be used to Mac's advantage. Maybe instead of Jace using Mac, Mac could use Jace. Mac had no idea what Jace's end game was anymore but that didn't matter. Jace was going to help Mac, Nelson, and Ryan get out of there.

The food slot opened and Jace spoke from the other side, "You ready to get out of there?"

"Absolutely," said Mac.

The door opened. The two men looked at each other, each with a smile on his face. Neither of them was sincere.

"It's good to see you again," said Jace.

"You too. How did you get out here?" asked Mac.

"I came out here looking for Scott Ryder."

"What?"

"Yeah, you didn't think General Zinger would keep someone like that on Earth did you? Scott got moved off planet as soon as Lynn's video about Northgate being an inside job went viral."

"Okay, but how did you cross the line without the appropriate paperwork?"

"I'm a military intelligence officer. I can get the paperwork if I need it."

"Right. Let's get the others and get out of here."

"Others?"

"Nelson and Ryan."

"You sure you want to take them with us? It might make things harder."

"I'm sure," said Mac.

Jace thought about it for a moment. Then he laid out his plan for Mac.

"You can't wander around the ship without getting noticed. But I can. So I'll lead you to an air duct that will take you to the docking bay." Jace handed Mac a key card. "Use this to get into one of the shuttles. You wait there and I'll bring the other guys. Then we can get out of here. But we need to hurry."

"Why?"

"Well, for starters, the guards only check the cells every five hours but this *is* the General's ship. It was transferring supplies and personnel when they picked you up but now they are going to their hiding spot in the Valbetus asteroid belt. Piloting our way through there without being caught is going to be nearly impossible."

Mac looked at the key card. He didn't know what to think about what Jace was telling him. If Jace was an alien, did that mean everything he was saying was a lie? If Jace was an alien, why didn't he kill Mac for what he had done? Two collector ships had been destroyed because of him. Giving his head a shake he decided to worry about the big questions after they had escaped the front line. As long as Jace was still helping him escape he would go along with his plans.

"Okay, show me where to go. We'll get out of here and I'll take you all back to Ronos with me," said Mac.

"That's exactly what I want to hear. Follow me."

Mac was crawling through the air ducts as quietly as he could when the ship started rocking back and forth. Warning sirens wailed. They were loud enough that Mac could pick up speed without drawing attention. He followed Jace's directions and after half an hour of crawling, during which the alarms rang for ten minutes, he kicked open a vent and emerged into the docking bay. Men were running all over the place. Red lights flashed. The ship was under attack. Mac needed a place to hide.

He moved to a small ship with an interplanetary drive and went inside to wait. The ship reminded him a lot of the shuttle he, Lynn, and Raymond were trapped on in the caves on Ronos. It was a little unsettling at first, so Mac forced himself to focus on the differences. There was no dangerous goods compartment. The door between the front of the ship and back was a smaller swinging door as opposed to a large sliding one. The control room was bigger with more storage space.

The *Bears Paw* shook violently. The attacking alien ship wasn't messing around. Mac was tempted to strap himself in so he didn't end up hurting himself but didn't put his thought into action soon enough. After a thunderous attack, the capital ship rolled enough to send the smaller ship he was hiding in toppling on its side. Not being strapped to anything, he flopped around inside free to make contact with whatever else wasn't strapped down as well as every wall, the ceiling, and the floor.

Mac groaned from underneath heavy metal boxes containing military rifles. They spilled out onto him from a storage compartment. He hit his head on a chair and was now half in it half off it. He was dizzy but still didn't feel any pain. There was something different, though. He searched for why he felt like that.

While tossing around and falling into things he cut open his arm. The wound captivated him, repulsing and inspiring him at the same time. The gash was deep but the blood was reluctant to flow out. It was that same blood that gave him his power. He squeezed the meaty part of his forearm where the cut was to try and coax some of it out. There was a little bit, but not much. It was a different shade of red. Mac had to keep reminding himself that he was still human.

The blood gave him an idea. There was no way he would be able to sneak behind enemy lines to find Janelle and the other captors, but someone else could. Until Mac spoke, the aliens thought he was one of them. All anyone had to do was avoid talking out loud and, if they could mind speak, then they could go wherever they wanted. The alien ships were controlled by mind speech.

Could giving someone his blood enable them to mind speak? It was worth finding out. The sirens turned off indicating the attack was over. The *Bears Paw* had escaped the threat. Mac sent a new message to Jace.

Before you get Nelson and Ryan, ask them if they know a sympathetic doctor they can bring with them. It's important.

Chapter 3
The Unsympathetic Doctor

While Mac waited he noticed the return of the same strange feeling he got every time he sat still and turned his thoughts inward. It was so subtle that it was impossible to detect otherwise. Everything around him had to be still. His eyes had to be closed. Usually he felt it as he was trying to fall asleep. It was a pull. On Ronos, embedded in its crust was a machine situated over a chasm that released the gas that forced him to inject liquefied rocks into his veins. The colossal machine reached out to ships in space and pulled them towards the planet against their will. Once they were close enough there was no escaping unless someone knew the secret to get off Ronos.

He could feel the pull coming from that machine, that beacon. It wasn't so much that he knew which way to go. The pull was prompting him to keep moving. It left him uneasy and feeling constantly out of place. Would he feel the Ronos pull for the rest of his life? If he calmed himself enough and quieted his mind so that all that was there was the pull, would he be able to guide himself to Ronos?

There wasn't time to try. The door to the ship opened up. The door was on the roof because the small ship had settled on its side after the attack. Looking down on him was Jace, Nelson, Ryan, and a new face.

Mac brought his arm up to shield his face from the extra light. The new guy must have been a doctor because he took one look at Mac's arm and ordered the others to lower him into the shuttle.

"Great, the biggest guy here wants the rest of us to carry his weight," said Nelson.

Mac made eye contact with Jace. *Can you give me some time with these guys? I'd like to explain things to them. I'm going to tell them the truth about what's going on. Northgate, Ronos, what I can do. You go find a way to get us off this ship.*

Jace nodded and left without saying anything to the others. Mac wondered how they convinced the doctor to come. Nelson and Ryan were supposed to be in cells, not out wandering the ship.

The new guy landed with a thud beside Mac. He was thick and tall. He had a medical bag with him. Mac wasn't sure what was all in it, but he was curious what the doctor would have to say about the injury.

"I am Dr. Pilgrim. Can I take a look at that arm?"

He didn't wait for an answer. He reached out and took Mac's arm. The ship's power source wasn't working properly since it flipped over, so the doctor called up to the others to throw down a flashlight. The other two jumped down and shone lights on Mac's arm.

"I guess I shouldn't have expected something normal from you," said Nelson.

Under the glare of the intense flashlights the peculiarity of the wound was fully revealed.

"There should be more blood than this," said Dr. Pilgrim. He looked around on the floor as if the blood was a pen he dropped. If only he could find where it was before someone kicked it away.

"I'm pretty sure it's the wrong shade of red as well," said Nelson.

Bleeding out wasn't going to be an issue. There was a little blood showing but it wasn't dripping out of the wound or anything. He could almost feel it healing itself. Without exposure to the gas it took a little longer.

"Nelson, tell him what you saw me do to the swarms and the collector ships," said Mac.

Nelson laid out the story of how Mac wasn't affected by their swarm attacks and how he was able to take out two of the ships almost single-handedly. In one day Mac had gained more knowledge about how the aliens worked than anyone had since the war started. Anything else was a guess based on poor judgment compared to what Mac knew and was able to do.

When Nelson couldn't remember details Ryan filled in the blanks, but Nelson had been around Mac more. However, Ryan was able to finally confirm that Cliff had died trying to prevent the destruction of the *Skyrattler* during the battle with the alien ships.

While Nelson spoke the doctor bandaged up Mac's arm. With every new bit of information he gave Mac another look of disbelief. There were some things that only Mac saw or experienced—the emulators, the conversation with the leader, and the mind speaking. When the story was over Mac posed a question.

"Do you believe what we're saying?" asked Mac.

"I'm not an idiot. I know what's going on here. You are the one responsible for my nephew here being locked up in a cell."

"Nephew?"

"Nelson Koyczan. He's my sister's kid."

"I told you, Phillip, it's not what you think," said Nelson.

"As soon as they know you are outside of your cell they will overload your Imp and then I get to say 'I told you so'," said Phillip. "When I'm done here I'm turning you all in."

Mac explained more. "Do you know why the aliens take people instead of killing all of us."

"No."

"It's because they need our bodies. What we see when we go over to their ships isn't who they really are. What they really look like are those swarms that attack us. They use our bodies to emulate us because they can't maintain the cloud form. Do you understand?"

"Yeah, sure," said Dr. Pilgrim as he continued to work on Mac's arm.

"You don't seem like you're listening."

"I'm a doctor on a ship that recently survived a brief but deadly skirmish with an alien collector ship. Two decks were breached and there was one fire. I have a medical wing full of dead and dying people. With my Imp I'm able to be in two places at once. Patch you up, talk my idiot nephew out of AWOLing or whatever it is he is doing now, and giving instructions to a nurse on how to keep a man from dying. Sorry for being distracted."

Mac spoke quicker, "When I destroyed the emulator generators on the ships the aliens couldn't hold their forms anymore. Even the swarm forms. Every single person who was collected by them, whether they were soldiers or the people who were taken five years ago when this war started, are being held captive and copies of their bodies are being used by the aliens," said Mac.

"Do you know where the captives are?" asked Dr. Pilgrim.

"No."

"But you're the only one who can go get them, right. You're the only one who can use that mind speak you were talking about."

Mac looked at the three of them very seriously, making eye contact with all of them before continuing.

"If I can make you like me, will you go and find where they keep their prisoners and free them?"

Dr. Pilgrim scoffed. "That sounds like passing the buck."

"I can't go back because they would recognize me. They know I'm not one of them. But they only realized it once I started talking out loud. If you guys were to sneak onto one of their ships and wander around without talking, no one would challenge you. Humans don't have the ability to communicate with their technology so they won't suspect you."

"It's a suicide mission," said Dr. Pilgrim.

"How would you make us like you?" asked Nelson.

"You aren't doing it, Nelson," said Dr. Pilgrim.

"If we free the prisoners then we will be dealing a critical blow to the enemy. How can we not do this?" said Nelson.

"Then we take it to the general. If it's that big of a deal then we need to let him know so that we can give it the best chance we've got. We don't have the military authority to create missions. No matter how vital they are."

Nelson shook his head. It didn't make sense to him, "But that's the reason for all the secrecy on the front line. When one of us is taken they learn everything that person knew. The more people we tell the less of an advantage we have. If only we three go then no one will know where we went or why we went. The aliens will have no idea that there are humans among them. If we tell someone on this ship and this ship gets collected then our mission is blown."

"General Roy needs to know everything that is going on so that he can make the best decisions to win this war," said Phillip.

"General Roy thinks Mac is an alien. There's no way he would listen to what he says. We can't risk telling anyone what we're doing, like the general can't risk assuming something that acts inhuman is a human. We've lost too much to compromise. And he's not going to believe anything Ryan or I say," said Nelson.

"You're talking like you already made up your mind," said Dr. Phillip Pilgrim.

"I have," Nelson said. "Mac, how are you going to make us like you?"

Mac held up his arm. "It's in my blood. If I give you some of my blood it might make you like me."

"Might?"

"It's not something that's been done before. I got this way by injecting something right into my bloodstream. It's possible if you had some of it flowing through you that the same thing would happen."

Nelson looked to his doctor uncle for confirmation. Ryan was looking at Mac's arm; his face was pale. Was it a fear of needles or one of the other million things that could go wrong?

"It's not possible. Do you know your blood type? Is it compatible with ours? Do you know how to get on one of the alien ships? Do you know how to get around on one of those ships? Do you know which ship the prisoners are being kept on? Do you know the culture of the aliens? What will make us stand out from the others? What will help us blend in? What if we need to sleep? What if we need to go to the bathroom? There a million things wrong with this idea and only one good thing," said Phillip.

"Even if that one thing is ending the war?" asked Nelson.

"That's a jump."

Phillip stood up. No blood had seeped through the bandage so he felt confident that his services were no longer needed. He was leaving. He reached up to the doorway and pulled himself up. It was a bit of a struggle and his swinging legs almost clipped Mac in the head. Once the doctor was at the top he looked back at the three people in the ship and said.

"I can't pretend like this didn't happen. Go to the brig like you're supposed to. Make sure you go in the same way you came out so no one notices and pray they don't review our Imp feed. I've already contacted the General on my Imp for a private meeting. You secrets are safe for now, but I need to tell him this plan. If it's a good plan then he will support it. Not everyone will know about it. Telling the General will be adding another person into the circle. If I check back in an hour and you aren't in the brig then I'm blowing this all out of the water."

Dr. Pilgrim left. Mac didn't object with what the doctor had to say. It didn't matter if they went to the general because the general wouldn't believe them.

"What do we need?" asked Nelson.

Mac looked to Ryan, "Are you in?"

"Yes. I'd rather die doing something that mattered then getting slaughtered on another useless mission."

"Come on, we haven't even done anything yet and you're already ready to die," said Nelson. "Mac, what do we need?"

"I'm not sure. That's why I wanted you guys to bring a doctor," said Mac.

"Sorry about that. My good uncle Phillip isn't one to jump to make a change to his routine. The only reason he joined the military was to keep me out of trouble. He had a perfectly profitable private medical practice back on Earth. His storming off doesn't mean that he's out forever. Once I make the change he will come along for the same reason he enlisted."

"See if you can find a first aid kit or a med pack or something," said Mac.

They couldn't stay there anymore. They helped pull each other out of the ship and looked around for what they needed. The docking bay was empty now, at least from what they could see. There had to be a soldier nearby in case they were attacked, but right now the three young men were alone.

Mac wasn't sure how long Jace was going to be away, but he wanted to make sure that Nelson and the others were transformed before he came back. It was important that Jace, who Mac suspected to be an alien, didn't know that there were other humans on the *Bears Paw* who could mind speak.

"Over here," said Ryan.

Mac and Nelson went over to where he was pulling a med pack off the wall. Inside was what Mac wanted: a syringe. He would do it the same way it had been done to him. Except his own blood would have to substitute for the melted rocks. What's the worst that could happen? He had no idea if mixing blood would have any negative consequences, but if it worked it would be faster than flying to Ronos and doing it the old fashioned way. They found a tourniquet and tied off Mac's uninjured arm.

"Try and find a vein," said Mac.

"Are you sure this is going to work?" asked Ryan who was holding the syringe.

"No."

The confession didn't deter him. Ryan found a vein and plunged the needle in. He pulled back but no liquid came out.

"That's...different," said Ryan.

"You must have missed it," said Mac.

"Dude, your arm is super vascular. You can see the needle in the vein. The blood won't come out," said Nelson.

"Try again," said Mac.

Ryan took the needle out and inserted it again. Not in the exact same hole but the results were still negative. Mac started undoing the bandages on his other arm. At least he had seen blood come out of there so he knew it was possible.

"Give that to me," he said taking the syringe.

The wound was a couple inches long and deep into the muscle. It didn't hurt. When he looked at it, it was like looking at someone else's arm. There was a little bit of blood on the bandages but not as much as there should have been. He lodged the needle into the bloodiest part of the wound and pulled back on the plunger. Blood started dripping into it. The more blood he took out the weaker Mac felt. The syringe was barely even an eighth full and he felt like he had been hit in the face by Zinger's meaty fist. He must have looked it too. Ryan reached for the syringe.

"Let me hold that," Ryan said and continued to pull back on it to fill it with more blood.

The more he pulled back the worse Mac got. It was starting to look like he was in actual pain. His new blood was meant to stay in his body. Taking it out was more painful than it should have been. He wanted more than anything for it to be over. He wanted to give up but he knew he couldn't. He couldn't think of any other way for it to happen. The color drained from his face. The whiteness was shocking.

"Maybe we shouldn't do this," said Nelson.

"We almost have a full syringe," said Ryan.

Mac couldn't say what he was thinking. One syringe wasn't going to cut it. They would need two. Three if Nelson was right about Phillip changing his mind.

"There we go," said Ryan.

He pulled the needle out and it felt like someone pulled a corkscrew right out of his arm. Mac could have sworn the flesh was torn, but when he looked at his arm it looked almost exactly the same. The only difference was there was less blood. A lot less. How much had been taken out?

Ryan held up the sample to investigate it closer. It wasn't red and certainly didn't look like something that should be injected into a human. He offered it up to Nelson first.

"I'm having second thoughts," said Nelson.

"Me too," said Ryan.

Mac didn't want to hear that. "Take two more samples. Take them to your doctor uncle and see if you can talk yourselves into doing the right thing."

Easier said than done. Ryan put the needle back in while Mac grimaced. The second sample was magnitudes more difficult to procure. After one small sample it was almost like all the blood in Mac's body was gone. Either that or it was hiding. He couldn't believe how difficult this was.

"Sorry," said Ryan as he plunged in deeper to search out the life-changing blood.

Mac almost passed out. His legs started twitching. He had no control over their movements. It felt like he was dying. This was a bad idea. He was wrong. Going to Ronos would be easier.

He had never felt so light headed. His eyes rolled around in his head and he was unable to focus on one thing for very long. The more blood they took from his body the more he twitched uncontrollably. By the time the second sample was drawn, Mac was ready to die.

"We aren't going to do anymore. You won't survive another one," said Nelson.

Mac agreed, but he also knew that it would take more than two people to go save all the captured humans. The doctor was essential. Who knew what state the prisoners would be in? He reached for the last syringe and handed it to Ryan.

"And what if it kills you?" asked Ryan.

"If I pass out then take me to Dr. Pilgrim," said Mac.

"That's not really a solution to the problem," said Nelson. "Do it. Quickly."

Ryan didn't say sorry this time. He stuck the needle into the cut and tried to get something out of it. The arm with the cut in it was now completely numb. No pain. No feeling of any kind. Mac hoped it wouldn't be like that forever. Maybe when he got back to Ronos it would heal itself, but he hoped it would happen before then because he didn't know when he was going to get back there or even how he was going to do it. One step at a time. Right now he needed to focus on not dying.

That part of the plan wasn't going too well either. He looked down at the needle and couldn't see any blood in it. That didn't mean there wasn't any in it. It meant Mac's vision had gone so fuzzy he couldn't see details or color anymore. The edges were darkening.

Nelson moved close to Mac's face and said something but by then it was too late for Mac. All he could do was smile at how lame it was that he was going to die by his own foolish plan. Accidental suicide wasn't something he had ever aspired to.

Dr. Phillip Pilgrim walked back to the infirmary after he met with Mac and the others. As he walked he realized he should have at least taken Nelson with him. He had never met Ryan before and didn't really care what he did, but he suspected his nephew might go through with the crazy plans of the young soldier with mind speaking abilities and blood that didn't act like blood.

They were all too young. Nelson was only 20 years old. The man named Mac didn't look much older, physically anyway. Phillip could see something in his eyes that said Mac had already seen enough to fill a lifetime. The doctor had always suspected that all the young, malleable soldiers were sent to the front because they were better at taking orders without thinking.

Phillip was old enough to qualify for a midlife crisis. Some people back home even said his joining the military was a midlife crisis in action. "He's bored and looking for adventure." If he had been there when they said it, instead of hearing it through the grapevine, he would have put them in their place.

He struggled since the beginning to keep up with all the kids. After signing up he barely met the minimum physical requirements for deployment. The reason he was sent to the front line was his skill as a medical practitioner. The way it was phrased made it feel like a compliment, but once he got out here he realized that why he was here had as much to do with his age and maturity as it did his skill at healing. Everyone around him was a hot-headed youth. To find someone level with him he had to go high up the ranks and those men were few and spent most of their time away from full combat. Phillip was on war ships sent to fight so that he could bandage up the young guys who hadn't thought about the possibility of dying until they saw people around them ripped apart in swarm attacks.

He had become a surrogate father to dozens of young men; maybe it was more of a reluctant step-father because he didn't want to be their sounding board while they talked about how they wished they never signed up or how much they missed their girlfriends or their fallen comrades. The only one he was there to help on a personal level was his nephew, Nelson Koyczan.

Nelson never regretted anything, or if he did he never spoke openly about it. He had been out here for a few years and he had seen friends die. There was sadness but never regret. Despite some of his obvious juvenile tendencies, like running off to sneak around enemy ships based on unconfirmed information, he was one of the more mature young soldiers. Phillip was proud of him but wouldn't say that out loud. That would feed his nephew's ego in a bad way. If he praised Nelson for being the best of the immature kids then Nelson was more likely to do immature things. That kind of praise would be saved for a birthday, wedding, or funeral. Whichever came first.

The one hour deadline he had given his nephew hadn't even come close to expiring before Nelson and Ryan came rushing in carrying Mac's limp body. The infirmary was already bustling with wounded men. There was already chaos all around without these kids adding to it.

"What did you do?" asked Phillip as he directed them to put Mac on one of beds.

"We were taking blood samples and then he passed out," said Nelson.

"How much blood did you take?"

Nelson held up three vials. The first two were full, the third was only half full, but none of them looked like they had blood in them. The liquid inside was almost black. If a color had to be assigned to it, then it was closer to a dark purple than red.

"That's not blood," said Phillip.

"It's his blood," said Nelson. "You saw that cut on his arm. His blood doesn't act the way ours does."

"You realize that makes him less human. And that we're at war with aliens."

"We need you to try and save him, okay?"

Phillip hooked up monitors and tried to figure out what was wrong with Mac. Normally he would have passed this on to one of his underlings, but he wasn't ready to let the secret of Mac and Nelson working together out yet. There was still hope he could change his nephew's mind. Even as he thought that, he wondered what the odd-looking blood they had extracted was all about. Mac was so pale he might as well have been dead. Phillip didn't understand how taking two and a half small vials of his mutant blood would take such a toll. There should be tons more blood than what he was being shown. Curious, he pricked Mac's finger. It didn't do anything but make a hole. What if the doctor put as much normal blood in him as black blood was taken out?

"Give those to me," said Phillip.

He didn't wait for Nelson to comply. He checked the measurements on the samples and then added them together. If Mac was human then he shouldn't have a problem with getting some universal donor blood pumped back into him. If he died then at least he wouldn't have to talk Nelson out of doing something stupid.

There was no point in pumping Mac full of blood even though he acted like he needed several pints of it. He would put in as much as was taken out. He went to the back of the infirmary where the blood bank was. He grabbed a bag of what he needed and brought it back to the bed. Carefully he injected the same amount that was taken out. The color was returning to Mac's face.

"Is it working?" asked Nelson. He talked quietly so that the other doctors and patients that were running around wouldn't be able to hear what he was saying. Phillip followed suit.

"I think so," said Phillip.

"I guess he's more human than you thought."

Phillip looked at the sample vials he had in his hand. Nelson read his mind.

"We should at least see what they can do," said Nelson.

"It doesn't seem like it did this Mac guy any good," said Phillip.

"That's only because we tried to take it out of him. He could still do lots of other things. Lots of good things for other people. I thought that's what you were all about. Helping other people."

"How do we know this won't kill us?"

"We don't. But we have to try. If it gives us the same abilities as Mac has then it will be worth it."

Phillip didn't feel like that was a solid argument. It was more the rationale of a young cowboy wanting to be the hero. Would there be any convincing him otherwise?

"There is so much more at risk than injecting ourselves with this stuff. You know that right? What are we going to do once we get over there?" said Phillip.

"They won't see us coming. We will have the advantage. All we have to do is not talk and we will be okay. This has never been done before. They aren't prepared to defend against this," said Nelson.

"As far as we know."

"Doubt will only make this harder. If we go in with a negative attitude then we are sure to fail. We need to confidently go and do our best."

As if all it takes to survive is to do our best, Phillip shook his head. That kind of thinking was going to get them all killed. The last place he wanted to go was behind enemy lines, to a place that no human ever came back from, with two kids that were so eager to be the heroes of the war that it didn't matter what happened to them.

There was no talking them out of it. He turned his back to his nephew and Ryan and walked to his office adjacent to the infirmary. Mac was stable now. No one would pay him any attention. Nelson and Ryan followed Phillip. Once the door was closed Phillip injected one of the samples into his arm. Might as well get it over with. If he ended up dying then at least Nelson would know not to do the same.

The blood left the needle much more easily than it entered. It flowed into his veins and up to his heart. He could feel its progress through his body. As soon as it got to his heart the organ started beating spasmodically. Phillips eyes got wide and he collapsed to the floor.

"You okay?" asked Nelson.

"Give me space," said Phillip.

He felt like he was going to explode. It was like overdosing on adrenaline. He needed to stay still, curled up on the floor because if he moved he thought he might not be able to stop moving. He would have to run and jump and yell at the top of his lungs until he died. It was like having all the energy in the world but being afraid to use it.

Nelson and Ryan stood over him for a few tense minutes. They weren't sure what to do. Should they go get one of the other doctors?

Phillip started moving. After the new blood had mixed with his old blood and had circulated throughout his body he started to calm down and feel more normal. He still felt different, but he no longer thought he was going to explode with energy.

"How was it?" asked Nelson.

"I can't explain it. You'll have to do it yourself to feel the full effect."

Nelson reached for one of the two remaining samples. Phillip stopped him.

"I don't think you need to take the whole thing. It'll mix with your other blood anyway. We need three more equal samples."

"Three more? But there's only the two of us."

"I'm not going behind enemy lines by myself with two kids to watch out for."

Chapter 4
Kilkenny

Phillip realized the risks of adding another person to their mission. The more people that snuck behind enemy lines, the greater the chance they would be discovered. Had he put his head on straight he would have done the mission by himself and left his nephew and Ryan behind but it was too late for that now. They had all changed and none of them would be able to avoid suspicion for long. Their Imps stopped functioning when they injected themselves with Mac's blood. Soon someone would try to look for them or send them orders and then realize they weren't on the Imp system anymore. They needed to leave as soon as they could. Nelson and Ryan managed to sneak back into their cells. Phillip went to find the last member of their team.

Most soldiers suspected Jazlyn's age hovered around fifty, but when asked, she would say "twenty-nine" with a smile on her face. Most of the men were fine with imagining her as a twenty-nine- year-old.

Her smile wasn't only there when she lied about her age. It was there all the time. It was the biggest most sincere smile that anyone had ever seen. It wouldn't have been out of place back on Earth where there were still things to smile about. But out on the front line where soldiers were dying every day and no one knew if the next meal was going to be their last, Jazlyn's smile as she served the meals was enough for them to avoid going mad with stress.

Phillip didn't doubt for a second that her smile was the reason she was put in charge of the food on the ship. Every day she interacted with almost everyone onboard and they were all the better for it. He'd have been lying if he said he hadn't had extra meals most days so he could have an opportunity to talk to her one more time. But it was different for him. He didn't feel like he fit in with any of the young guns he was surrounded by. Sure there were some senior officers that were the same age or older, but they didn't run in the same circles as he did, and unlike Jazlyn they wouldn't talk about how the pancakes that day were so fluffy they would melt in his mouth.

When he told Nelson who he was recruiting Nelson rolled his eyes in a way that reinforced his immaturity. Did twenty year olds really roll their eyes with such proficiency? Phillip had to resist the urge to poke the kid in the eye for being so stupid.

His nephew said the only reason that Phillip wanted Jazlyn on the mission was because he wanted to be with her. It was true — kind of. Phillip wasn't going to deny it. He had been married before but his wife died young and he had never dated anyone else. There had never been anyone he was interested in. He'd never felt the stirrings again.

And despite the smile she gave to everyone, Jazlyn actually hated her job and was looking for a little adventure. She had confessed this to him before.

"I thought that serving on the general's ship we would see more action," said Jazlyn while ladling soup into Phillip's bowl. Her voice was authoritative when it needed to be, but right now it was in a wispy whisper. She didn't want people to know she wasn't satisfied with what she signed up for.

"The general needs to stay alive. That means keeping out of the action and hiding in an asteroid belt. Besides, this ship has been attacked a bunch before. Were you asleep this morning when we got rocked?" said Phillip.

"But nothing ever changes down here except for the masticators. I keep serving food while you guys fight the war."

"You want to fight?"

"I signed up to fight."

Phillip had been impressed by her enthusiasm. It's true that even the people with menial jobs like cooking and organizing and making sure the ship runs were all trained soldiers, but he had always figured that Jazlyn was someone who liked to cook and maybe even asked for this job. He had never thought of her as a soldier before.

The day she told him she wanted to fight he had taken a step back and really taken her in. She was fit. There was nothing in the kitchen that ever slowed her down because it was too heavy to lift. The only thing that really gave her age away were the wrinkles on her face and hands which was the only exposed skin she ever had. Her hair was short and white, but it was the kind of white that made people think she dyed it that color the way young people often do. Even if she was over fifty, she still wouldn't have hair that white. Phillip wasn't convinced she really was in her fifties, if only because he was in his forties and wanted her to be closer to his age. She went to the training room and kept up to the military standards like everybody else did. She was a soldier. That's what Phillip told Nelson and Ryan. They didn't look convinced, but Phillip had assumed the leadership role of their mission and decided he was the one who would make all the important calls. Jazlyn's maturity and the fact that she didn't look like a typical soldier would help her avoid suspicion once they got to the other side.

"I was trying to call you," said Jazlyn when Phillip approached her in the cafeteria. She was cooking a pot of thick and chunky stew.

"Really?"

"Yeah, this morning. I have a friend in the infirmary. Why were you avoiding me?"

Imps didn't malfunction. If you couldn't get a hold of someone they were either avoiding you or doing something more important. Phillip, Nelson, and Ryan, hadn't been able to use their Imps for the last hour. Phillip had managed to get someone to cover him in the infirmary for the rest of the day and Nelson and Ryan wouldn't be looked at too closely as long as they stayed locked up. But it was still only a matter of time before someone noticed.

"I have a new mission. Top secret," said Phillip.

"Really?"

"I'm supposed to pick one more person to come with us. Are you interested?"

There was risk approaching someone with an Imp and talking about the mission, but Mac had taken that risk and gotten away with it. Phillip had to hope that they hadn't made it onto a watch list or something. He also had to keep away from suspicious words but struggled to think of the kinds of words double agents would use. If anything bad happened he didn't want Jazlyn to get in trouble, so he wasn't going to tell her anything important until after she got injected.

"Am I interested? Oh sure, I'll overlook the fact that a doctor is leading the mission, that they are letting the cook — who may or may not be an old woman — go, and the fact that you have the strangest look in your eye — like you are alive for the first time and have no idea what to do with yourself…Absolutely I'll come with you."

Jazlyn didn't need any more information. That's how desperate she was to get into the action. Phillip smiled. Now at the very least he would have someone to talk to while they went off on their suicide mission.

Mac woke up in a bed in someone's private quarters. There were no pictures on the walls and no decorations. He had no idea where he was but he could hear voices coming from the other room. He threw off the covers and swung his feet out and under him. That action alone took most of his energy. Giving up his blood like that was not something he was going to do again. He wasn't sure he could, even if he wanted to. Having no idea where he was or how long he had been out of it, he needed to touch base with Jace again.

Jace, I don't know if you found a way off the ship but we need to meet up again.

Mac didn't know where to tell him they should meet. He decided he should first find out where he was. As he took a couple steps away from the bed he realized that maybe he didn't need Jace. Mac wasn't going to take the alien with him; he only needed his help to get off the ship. If Mac could manage to do that himself then he could ditch Jace at the front line.

Staggering out of the bedroom and into the living room, Mac felt like he knew who was there before he even got in. He could tell that there were two people in the room: Dr. Phillip Pilgrim and an older lady. He could feel them there without seeing them.

Dr. Pilgrim greeted Mac with a smile. The woman was smiling as well. They both had energy that could barely be contained.

"We did it. We injected your blood into our system," said Phillip.

"It worked?" asked Mac.

Phillip and the woman looked at each other. They weren't sure how to measure the success, but Mac knew that it did work. The reason he could tell they were in the room was because they had his blood flowing inside of them. It was still part of him and he could feel it wherever it was. Nelson was still Nelson but Mac could feel his influence inside of him as well. He could also tell that Nelson and Ryan were back in their cells. How they managed to sneak out of and then back into the cells without anyone noticing he had no idea. Maybe Jace had helped them. It was an intrusive feeling to think that there was a part of Mac inside of four other people now, and he wasn't sure how the others would react if he told them. He wasn't even sure if they could feel it. Why was Dr. Pilgrim willing to go on the mission now? Was it because he saw the light or because he now had a little bit of Mac subtly influencing his decisions?

"We were measuring the success by our still being alive, but then we figured we should get you to teach us to mind speak," said Phillip.

"Absolutely," said Mac. "I'll tell you everything I know about the swarms, collector ships, generators, emulators, and the people they emulate."

"You have a friend over there?"

"Yes. I need you to bring her back, along with everyone else they took."

"Okay, how do we get over there?" said Phillip.

"We have to wait for the aliens to attack. Doesn't that happen all the time?"

Dr. Pilgrim and the woman now looked worried. The woman — who introduced herself as Jazlyn Oliver — filled Mac in.

"We are in the Valbetus asteroid belt. It's one of the safest places on the front."

"Why would the General bring me here if he thinks I'm an alien?" said Mac.

"Two reasons. One, you are supposedly in a cell and have no idea we are in the asteroid belt and two, there is a prison ship coming here to take you away" said Phillip.

"Okay, then what we need is a ship to get me back to Earth and another one for you guys to get back behind enemy lines. How do they not know I'm out of my cell?"

"We don't know. But you've been out for almost a day and no one has raised an alarm."

To Mac it was obvious that Jace was doing something to keep the attention away from where Mac was supposed to be. Maybe the human impersonator was the one guarding the empty cell. It didn't really matter how Jace was able to pretend the cell was occupied as long as no one was looking for Mac.

"You're a doctor. How are you getting away with not having an Imp?" asked Mac.

"I have today off and I told everyone that I'll be logging off of all nonessentials while I relive some memories back home. That's pretty normal out here. People like to escape. I told them to leave messages with me. It's easy enough to read messages on a terminal. Responding to them will be okay at first, but people will get suspicious when they see none of my answers are going through an Imp."

Mac nodded. They didn't have a ton of time to plan out every little detail. The longer they stayed on the *Bears Paw* the more likely others would learn about their plan. The more people who learned about their plan the more likely the aliens would be able to find out about it. The asteroid belt may be the safest place on the front, but that didn't mean that soldiers weren't being transferred from ship to ship all the time. Word would travel. The circle of people had to be kept as small as possible.

Jace could not be in that circle. Somehow Mac had to leave separately from the group, but at the same time do whatever he could to get them to the front line.

"When does the prison ship get here?" asked Mac.

"Two hours," said Dr. Pilgrim.

"Okay. You guys need to get caught and go on the prison ship. Once it is clear of the asteroid belt take over the ship and use it to get to the other side of the war."

"How are we supposed to overtake a ship without any weapons?"

"If you're like me now, then you are a weapon."

Now that the plan was set for Nelson, Ryan, Phillip, and Jazlyn to get caught, it was easy to think of a way to sneak Mac into the docking bay. All he needed was a distraction, and since those other guys were going to end up in the brig anyway, they went to the opposite end of the ship and started setting things on fire in a wild rampage.

Sirens went off and everyone started running around. No one took note of the young man in an ill-fitting uniform — Phillip didn't have one his size — running towards the docking bay.

In the docking bay something caught his eye. It was a ship design that he had never seen before, and he thought he had seen everything. It must have been something developed on this side of the information barrier so no one on Earth had seen it yet.

What he saw was a ship with two modified hyper drive engines — but that didn't seem possible to him. Wouldn't it overheat? One hyper drive by itself had a cooling period and was never running at full speed. The only way it could was if it was on one of the big capital ships like the *Bears Paw*. On capital ships it didn't matter how much heat it had because the ship was big enough that you could build an effective heat barrier without affecting the rest of the ship. But on a small ship like this, one was already too much. It could never operate at full capacity without the crew inside of it being burned alive when the hyper drive engine overheated. So why would they put two on one ship?

Maybe it was an unmanned ship. Mac went for a closer look. A rollaway staircase led up to the cockpit. He saw through the window that it had two seats in it like a normal ship that size would. Markings on the side said it was named the *Kilkenny* and the type of ship was an HD22. Easy enough to figure out. The military wasn't very creative with class names. The HD stood for hyper drive. The first *two* meant there were two hyper drives and the second *two* meant that it was a two-seater. The ship was thirty feet long, but from what he could tell only the first quarter of it was meant for the pilot and copilot. The rest was either machinery or a heat barrier, which still didn't make sense to Mac. It wasn't enough to stop overheating.

He climbed down the stairs and went to the back of the ship where the twin engines were. The ship was longer than it was wide, another strategy to keep the possibly overheating engines as far from the pilot as possible. Still thirty feet wasn't enough, even for one engine.

The two engines were fitted onto the underside of the ship. The way the *Kilkenny* sat they came up to Mac's chest. He examined them as closely as he could without tools. They had what looked like extra armor on them, but when he took off one of the panels to get a look inside he saw that it was actually an advanced cooling system. There must have been a tank of cooling liquid somewhere on the ship that would constantly feed into the engine.

It was a good start, but still mostly ineffective. Mac opened another panel to follow some of the wires and found the answer that he was looking for. The wires led to a timing mechanism. It was something that he had seen before. Quickly he moved to the other hyper drive engine to see if it had a similar device on it. His suspicions were confirmed and what he saw made him want to fly that ship so bad he forgot that he was in the middle of a war zone.

It was ingenious. One engine would run until it got too hot then it would shut down and switch to the other engine. The ship would never lose full speed. Before one engine could overheat the other one would kick in. This small ship could potentially go the same speed or almost the same speed as a capital ship. It would be faster than any ship this size should be able to go. The engineering behind the timing had to be perfect. If it was off even a little bit the crew would cook.

"Good choice," said Jace from behind Mac.

Mac spun around, startled by the voice.

"Don't worry," said Jace. I made sure the room was empty. Where are your friends?"

"They aren't coming."

"Good. I locked the door behind me."

"Where is Scott Ryder?" asked Mac.

"I couldn't find him. He's somewhere on the front line, but it's past the level of clearance that I have."

"It's kind of amazing that you have any clearance over here. On Earth you are a fugitive and a deserter. If you went on a military ship there you would be arrested immediately," said Mac, doing a little fishing and hoping to expose Jace's lies.

"I'm lucky there is an information barrier. No one here knows I'm wanted."

"What about the ship that brought you here?"

"What?"

"Only military ships bring troops to the front. How did you get on a military ship without getting caught?"

"I was careful. Why are you asking all these questions?"

"You know why. Are you ready to tell me why you don't have an Imp, or is it still a secret and I should continue to blindly trust you?"

The energy in the room shifted dramatically. Neither man was smiling now and for a couple tense minutes neither of them moved or spoke. Mac guessed that Jace was going over all his lies trying to think of a way to keep the two of them on the same side, but there was nothing that could be said to accomplish that goal.

Jace took a tentative step towards Mac and the *Kilkenny* and said, "We are on the same side of this."

"That's not what it feels like anymore."

"Remember Northgate. I defected with you. I helped you find your family. I helped you escape. You were being surged and I saved you."

"Because you don't have an Imp."

"That's right."

"Why don't you have an Imp?"

"I'm not here to hurt anyone. I can explain everything, but we need to get out of here first."

"Why? What's wrong with explaining things to me now?"

"We don't have time to talk now. We need to go. The *Kilkenny* is fast, but not so fast we won't have time to talk on the way to Ronos."

Jace sounded like he really wanted to go to Ronos. It reminded Mac of the alien leader who had been emulating Janelle. She had said that all the aliens could feel the pull of

Ronos and they were all heading there. Jace sounded like he wanted to get there first.

"You can't come with me," said Mac.

Jace took another step towards him. "What are you talking about?"

"I don't trust you anymore."

"Mac, stop it. This isn't something you need to do."

Mac went to the rollaway staircase and started walking up it backwards. There were two seats in the *Kilkenny* but Mac had no intention of taking anyone with him. Once he was far enough away he would send a message back to General Roy that Jace was an impostor. Maybe that would garner some goodwill with the general. Mac had a feeling he was going to need at least one friend in the military before this was all over.

"I can only say it so many times. We are on the same side. Do not treat me like an enemy," said Jace.

"Then stop acting like the enemy. You don't have an Imp, aliens don't have Imps. You can mind speak without having to be changed on Ronos, aliens can too. You are telling me that you need me to take you to Ronos, the same place that an entire alien fleet is trying to get to. You can feel its pull but you can't pinpoint its location, so you need the help of someone who has been there."

"Mac, you don't understand how important it is for me to get there. I can help you win this war."

"You're going to help me kill your own people?"

Jace closed his eyes and put his head down. If he were human it would have looked like he was sad or maybe even crying, but to Mac it looked like he was calling out in his mind. As Mac thought this the emergency changed from a fire set by Phillip and Jazlyn to an alien attack. Battle stations were called. The lock on the docking bay was overridden and soldiers streamed in. Some hurried to the HAAS3's to fly out and meet the enemy, and a couple others went to the shuttle that was on standby to blow up the cache of explosives that would destroy the *Bears Paw* to take out the collector ship.

Mac ran up the last few steps and got in the cockpit. Before he closed the cockpit door he looked down at Jace.

"We'll see each other again, and then you'll know your mistake," said Jace.

"I won't help you get to Ronos."

"We'll see."

"There is a collector ship attacking us. The only way they could have found us was if you helped them. You tell me you're on my side and then you go and help the aliens destroy the most important ship in the human fleet."

Jace didn't put up a fight, which was weird. He was desperate to get to Ronos but not willing to fight Mac to get there. That didn't make sense but Mac tried not to think about it. Jace was an alien. That meant he was would do things that a normal human wouldn't do.

Mac studied the ship's control panel. It was pretty standard. He wouldn't have too much trouble operating it. He turned it on. It was louder than he thought it would be. Were both engines on already? All he was doing was idling. Carefully he used the control stick to lift off the ground. He didn't want to make the wrong move and charge full speed into one of the walls.

The HAAS3s were all powered up and ready to leave the ship. The docking bay door opened. Instead of the black of space there was only brown rock. Not only were they hiding in an asteroid belt, they were hiding inside of a massive asteroid. The HAAS3s took off and Mac followed close behind them. His terminal crackled to life as a message came through.

"*Kilkenny* what are you doing? You are not authorized for departure," said some random communications officer.

"Put the general on. I have something he needs to hear," said Mac.

There was a pause.

"Who is this!" demanded General Roy.

"Former spacer Mac Narrad. You weren't letting me go so I had to take things into my own hands," said Mac.

"Bring the ship back and we won't be forced to take action."

"No, you *do* need to take action, but not against me. Everything I told you is true. I know of a way to save us but I need to go back to Ronos to do it. The action you need to take is against Major Jace Michaels. I know you have your own way of finding out if he's an alien or not, but the only way you'll get rid of him is if you find his emulator generator."

Mac could hear all kinds of commotion on the other side of the conversation. He wished he had opened a video channel with them instead of only audio. Everyone was talking at once.

"That's impossible."

"He's lying. Why should we listen to him?"

"Is that true?"

"We can't trust him."

"Someone find me Jace Michaels." That was the general's voice.

Jace could hide on that ship forever. All he had to do was take human form — however often he needed to do that Mac didn't know — in a place where no one could see him.

"Hey, is anyone there? I need to tell you something," said Mac as he followed the HAAS3s through the asteroid and out into the Valbetus belt. No one answered. "Hey!"

Finally the communications officer got back online.

"Major Michaels doesn't have an Imp. We can't locate him."

"I know," said Mac. "Has the general been briefed about the emulators we discovered during the last attack? Not the attack on the *Bears Paw* but the one where the *Skyrattler* was destroyed."

"Of course."

"The only way you are going to stop Jace is if you take out his emulator generator. You need to search the ship."

"Copy." He passed the message onto the general.

"I have something else I want to tell General Roy. Can you put him on?" asked Mac. There was a pause.

"This is General Roy."

"Have I earned some trust?" asked Mac.

"You need to come back to the ship so we can have a real conversation."

That wasn't what Mac had hoped for. The statement was laced with sarcasm. He debated saying what he had planned to say. He wanted to tell the general about Nelson and the others and the plan to find the prisoners and rescue them, but then he realized that it might not be a good idea to broadcast that. He decided he would keep that on the down-low but he would still try and help as much as he could.

It was also hard for Mac to concentrate on the conversation. They were in a fairly dense area of the belt and flying would have been difficult in a HAAS3 but flying the *Kilkenny* was even harder. The ship was incredibly fast and that was more unhelpful than anything in an asteroid belt. Mac was constantly changing direction and dodging asteroids. He stuck close to the big rock the *Bears Paw* was hiding in. There was a collector ship on top of it working at cracking it open. It looked like a beetle with hundreds of arms beating against a rock. Two dozen HAAS3s buzzed around it trying to shoot off the arms that were working at breaking the asteroid apart.

Communication with the *Bears Paw* was cut off. They had bigger problems to deal with. Mac would do what he could. Nelson and the others needed to get on that ship but not at General Roy's expense. The aliens would be able to learn too much from him. Mac found the *Kilkenny*'s weapons and let loose a volley that eviscerated one of the collector arms but the alien ship didn't slow down.

A crack formed in the asteroid and the *Bears Paw*'s hull was exposed. Collector ships could cast a powerful light on anything mechanical and disable it. Once the hull was exposed the lights came on and the ship was incapacitated. The HAAS3s were not effective, and it was only a matter of time before they were swatted out of space. The only thing the *Bears Paw* could do now to defend itself was to order the shuttle in the docking bay to blow the cache of explosives and destroy the ship before the collector ship could get to it. Mac waited, fully expecting it, but it didn't happen.

What's going on down there? Mac asked Phillip.

The shuttle failed. It got taken out or something.

Well, then it looks like you are going to the other side sooner than you planned. Whatever you do make sure you protect the general. If the aliens learn his secrets then more people will die before we can end this war.

We will. You should get out of here, said Phillip.

Good luck.

We're all going to need some luck.

Chapter 5
Inside

Instead of doing everything he could to survive or to try and find a way off Ronos, Raymond had spent the last several weeks trying to kill Lynn. That wasn't even the most terrifying aspect of Lynn's life right now. The most terrifying thing was the way that Raymond looked now.

His eyes were a deep menacing purple, almost black color. They had a slight glow to them and were the only part of his body that did. Not like Lynn who had the glow all over. Half of his face was burned off revealing muscle tissue and horrible looking scabs. His right hand and arm looked the same way. There was a long deep gash on the side of his neck that was surrounded by burn marks. When he yelled at her with his real voice it sounded like someone was strangling a rodent. Luckily he could mind speak like she and Mac could.

He had obviously been changed somehow, but it was not the same change that Lynn and Mac had experienced and he had not changed quick enough to not get burned by the gas. The worst part of it all was that no matter where Lynn went on the planet Raymond always knew where she was. He kept calling out to her in mind speak saying, *I can feel you.*

She went to hide in the mountains and he had found her and tried to bury her in a landslide. The rocks would have crushed her old body but now it only trapped her for a moment. Then Raymond showed up and tried to remove her head from her body with a rock. She had escaped into a cave where it was easier to hide. Unfortunately it was also the only place where she couldn't reach Mac with her mind speak.

That was worth it as long as Raymond didn't find her. She walked deep into the cave system and found a place where she could hide and sleep in peace without Raymond there trying to murder her.

The noise of someone nearby woke Lynn up. She wished she could turn off the revealing glow that she had going on. Both she and Mac glowed purple when exposed to the Mac Gas on Ronos. Now that the whole planet was covered in the gas she was constantly glowing. That would only help Raymond find her more easily. The cave had split off into two different paths and she was lucky that the footsteps, probably Raymond's, were going down the other one. It sounded like he was dragging one of his legs. She had smashed one of his legs with a rock to get away from him last time. Maybe Raymond didn't heal himself like she and Mac did when exposed to the gas.

She followed him, staying close enough to hear which way he was going but far enough away that he couldn't see her glow. As they got further into the cave they got closer to something familiar. Lynn wouldn't have to worry about her light being seen because the cave was being illuminated by the red pulsing light that came from the pull machine which acted like a beacon. It attracted nearby ships to the planet and then trapped them in orbit. Now she knew where she was and how to get out of the caves without getting lost — unless there was more than one beacon. She was confident that it was a one of a kind thing.

The tunnel she was following Raymond in was only as wide as she could stretch her arms and the ceiling was only a couple of inches above her head. She ducked anyway because it wasn't smooth and she had already bumped her head a couple times.

Ahead of her she could hear Raymond jump down into the massive cavern that looked like it was built around the pull machine. They must have been high up because when he hit the bottom he cried out like he was hurt. Lynn was able to run to the edge to spy without worrying about being seen. Raymond was too distracted.

It was about ten feet up. With an already broken foot or leg it would have been a horrible fall. He was now dragging himself with some determination. Where was he going so desperately?

The beacon took up most of the cavern. It was a massive gray metallic disk that was twenty feet high where it wasn't broken. The blinking red light was in the middle of the disk and was so big that Lynn and Raymond could have fit inside of it. She and Mac suspected that the pull machine was a ship that crash landed years ago. It was broken in several places; longer jagged fissures stretched out on the hull and some were so deep they cut through the entire ship. Despite that destruction it somehow still had power to keep blinking that light and pulling ships to Ronos against the will of their captains.

She had no idea how the ship got there but she knew that an ancient alien race had to have stumbled onto it because the cavern was covered in carvings that looked like an ancient alien alphabet. But she was no linguist. All she knew was that nothing natural could cause carvings like that.

What was Raymond doing here? Lynn stayed by the ledge where he jumped down. She would wait to see where he was going before she jumped down to follow him. It was weird standing by the ledge while close to the beacon. She always felt like she was about to fall off. To combat the feeling she laid down on the ground, but it still felt like she was being slowly dragged into the cavern. It wasn't actually happening, but she felt like it was. It was a psychological pull.

Raymond was painfully pulling himself along the cave floor, crying out each time he had to exert extra energy to pull himself to wherever he was going. Lynn looked for where that might be. There was a pool of dark water against the wall. He was heading in that direction, but was that his destination? Maybe it wasn't water. Maybe it was liquefied rock.

You tried to kill me, Lynn, Raymond said in her head.

She didn't know if he knew where she was or if he was calling out to her wherever she was. Not wanting him to hear her she answered back with mind speak.

I was defending myself. You almost killed me with a rock slide you caused, said Lynn.

You left me to die.

Raymond, we are the only two people left on the planet. We need to stop fighting and work together to find a way out of here, Lynn said, even though she had no idea how they would figure out how to get off the planet.

You haven't won, said Raymond like he never heard Lynn. He was bent on destroying her. *The gas heals you so you think you're invincible, but I too have tapped into some healing powers found in the caves you left me to die in.*

Raymond pulled himself up to the pool and then dragged himself into it. It wasn't deep enough to cover his entire body. He was face down in it. It looked like he was drinking it. As he splashed she could tell that it was liquid rock. Disgusting. She couldn't imagine what it tasted like.

I was running in the cave, looking for a way out, said Raymond. *The gas had already eaten through parts of my protective suit and was starting to burn my skin. The pain was so bad I was running madly to get away from it when I tripped and fell into a pool of black liquid. The pool stopped the burning and I found out that if I drank it then I could leave the pool without fearing the gas. As long as I have enough of the liquid in my system then I'm as powerful as you are.*

Lynn spotted the difference immediately. She had the upper hand because she would always be exposed to the gas and Raymond would always have to come back for some liquid rock if he didn't want to get burned. It was still possible for him to get burned. She would never get burned for the rest of her life.

I know you are watching me, said Raymond. *I can feel you wherever you are.*

Why do you want to kill me? Lynn asked again. She still didn't understand how he could be so irrational.

You burned me. You're the reason I'm like this. You abandoned me. I'm going to kill you and then I'm going to kill Mac.

Mac isn't here anymore.

He'll come back for you and I'll be here waiting for him. You'll be a headless corpse somewhere in these caves.

Lynn's solution was simple. She needed to get as far from the liquid rock as she could. That meant getting out of the caves. If there were more pools in the cave then she didn't want to be anywhere near them. She considered going back to the ocean.

While she was thinking about this she had stopped looking at what Raymond was doing. An unfortunate mistake. Imbued with new strength and energy he broke off a stalagmite and threw it like a spear at the opening where Lynn was hiding. His aim was off and the rock struck right below her. Now she was falling down to the cavern floor.

Lynn sprawled out on the ground while small bits of rock rained down around her. Nothing she couldn't handle. The real tribulation came from Raymond, still soaked in black liquid, charging her where she fell. He jumped in the air with the intent of landing feet first on her face. If he couldn't cut off her head then he would have to be content with irreversible damage, he hoped anyway.

He never got the chance. Lynn rolled out of the way and got to her feet running. Raymond caught up to her easily. Reaching out he grabbed a handful of hair and pulled her to the ground. In his other hand he held a rock. Lynn wondered if his plan was to simply hammer her head until it didn't exist.

Being tossed to the ground by her hair would have been excruciating before but not anymore. The only weapon nearby was the one Raymond was holding so that's what she went for, disorienting him with a full strength punch to the forearm. The rock dropped. While he was distracted by the attack she picked it up and smashed him in the head. He flopped over as she got up, but he wasn't dead.

You cannot defeat me while I'm this close to a healing pool.

"I don't want to kill you."

The rock you used to cave in my skull says differently.

He was already running back to the pool of liquefied Lynn Rock. His path wasn't a straight line because of the rock bashed against his head, but that wouldn't delay him for long. Lynn needed to get out of there or find a place to hide.

She started running as fast as she could. Before she knew it she was at the machine. There were enough hand holds that she could climb up to the top and start running towards the giant pulsating red light in the middle of the machine. That light got bigger and bigger the closer she got to it. It was big enough that she could fit inside of it. But that wouldn't be a good place to hide.

You only have two options, said Raymond. *Die now or die later.*

Aren't you open to – Lynn didn't get the chance to finish her sentence. As she ran over the top of the ship a hatch opened and she fell inside a dark hallway. The hatch closed behind her so that she was completely at the mercy of the light her glowing body was giving off.

The sudden drop had startled her. "Where am I now?" In the dim light she couldn't see where the passage ended in either direction. Lynn knew that she was inside the pull machine, but she wondered how she had opened the door and why it closed behind her.

She held up her hand to cast more light on the ceiling. There was a doorway there but no hinges or knobs. She didn't know how she was going to get back out. Not that she wanted to. Raymond had found where she had fallen in. In anger he was pounding on the doorway which had to be thick because the noise he was making was merely a dim banging sound. No doubt he was also screaming at her either in mind speak or out loud in his new unholy voice.

After a few tense moments she decided she was safe, from Raymond at least. Now she was inside of an ancient alien spaceship that doubled as a pull machine that had no immediate safe exit. At least she wouldn't have to be subjected to the mental ramblings of the man who wanted to kill her.

Then she made the connection. The ship had opened up to her when she thought *Aren't you open to...* Of course it had only been in passing and not directed at the beacon, but she had been screaming it in her mind and broadcasted it instead of sending it only to Raymond. Broadcasting mind speech required less concentration that sending a message to a certain person did.

Slowly Lynn backed away from where Raymond was pounding on the door, careful to keep her thoughts empty of mind speak in case she accidentally activated another part of the pull machine. She needed to get her bearings. Leaving the would-be murderer behind, she found a place to sit and calm herself. She sat on the ground with her back against the wall. Having barely woken up she wasn't physically tired, but mentally she was exhausted. Being trapped here wasn't what she wanted. How was she going to get off the planet? If Mac did make it back then how would he get down to the surface to help her escape? It felt like there was no hope. She wished that she could go home.

The Ryder family moved around a lot, but no matter where they were, *home* was always the same place for them. Her father was a teacher and could have easily stayed in one place for a long time, but he didn't like doing that. Every few years he would change jobs. He would teach advanced calculus at a university and then get a job teaching Shakespeare to junior high kids. His moods changed and his family followed him.

The only people who remembered their real home were her parents — she had no siblings. Until she was eight she never questioned this imaginary home but one day it clicked and she asked her dad.

"Where is home?"

"Home is where you were born and where you lived until you were almost three years old," her dad said.

"How come I don't remember?"

"It's hard for babies to remember things. Don't worry. We might go back there someday."

Might. That was the word that stuck out in Lynn's memory now. She knew what that meant. They were talking about the power of Grenor; the place where she was born.

Another memory came to her. The moment when she realized what the power was.

She was at a cemetery with her father, the patriarch of the family, the one with all the keys to all the secret doors of knowledge. Six feet below, in a wooden coffin was Lynn's best friend. Lynn was ten. Her friend Clair was nine. They were living on the west coast of North America. Clair had drowned in the ocean three days previously. She was the closest thing that Lynn had ever had to a sister.

The 'sibling conversation' always went like this.

"Why don't I have any sisters?" Lynn would ask.

"Because we would have to go home first to have her," said her father or mother.

"Why? No one else has to do that."

"We aren't like everyone else."

As she got older the language and persistence changed. It could morph between an honest question and an outright accusation followed by an argument. Being a teenager is rough on everybody.

The conversation at the grave site was different.

"Can we do it now?" asked Lynn as she reached up to grab his hand. Her eyes were dry but only because she had been crying for three days straight and now she was dried up.

Her father played dumb even though he knew exactly what "it" meant.

"What do you mean, dear?" he asked.

"Change what happened so that Clair can still be alive."

Her dad exhaled. He had been expecting this for a few years now and after this untimely death he suspected it would be today. He crouched down so he was at eye level with his daughter. With a prayer in his heart that she would understand, he started to explain it to her using questions so that she could build a mental bridge to the solution herself.

"You know we can only use it once, right Lynn," said her father.

"Well…yeah. But why can't this be the once?" asked Lynn.

"Why can't we save Clair?"

"Yeah. Why not?"

"What if we saved Clair? What if we used our power to go back and keep you two from…uh…going to the ocean that day?" He had to stop himself from saying 'sneaking out of the house.' There was no need to remind Lynn that this could have been avoided by listening to her parents. The tombstone would serve as a reminder for that.

"Yes, let's do that, Dad."

"But what if tomorrow Mom dies in a hover car accident. We won't be able to help her because we've already used our power to save Clair."

Lynn sniffed and looked down at the ground. The hope she had that her dad might give in was gone. Although the salty discharge from her eyes had run out, the liquid in her nose had not. She sniffled. She was sad because she would never see her friend in this life. He was sad because his daughter was starting to lose her innocence. The responsibility of the power of Grenor was starting to bear down on her. It meant looking the other way when horrible things happened while you waited for what could be the worst thing.

Because when you only have one shot at a second chance you have to wait until all hope is lost before you hit the reset button.

When Lynn asked her father when they would use their power to change things, her father wanted to give her that answer. He wasn't sure it would mean anything to her right then, so he avoided giving the real answer for a few more years.

"I don't know, but I hope you aren't the one who has to use it."

Chapter 6
The Other Side of the War

Phillip and Jazlyn were in the middle of causing chaos on the *Bears Paw* when the collector ship showed up. Security personnel were snapping restraints on their hands while a fire crew tried to douse the blaze Phillip had started.

"Did you hear that?" asked Jazlyn?

"No," replied Phillip.

The *Bears Paw* security officer told them both to shut up.

What did you hear? asked Phillip.

Mind speak. I can hear it right now. You don't? said Jazlyn.

Phillip concentrated. All he could hear was what was happening around him. Nothing out of the normal, and certainly no mind speaking.

There's more than one of them, said Jazlyn, *and it's getting louder. There are a whole bunch of people talking at the same time.*

What are they saying?

Jazlyn had to concentrate and focus. Trying to pick out a single conversation in a storm of sound was difficult. She got enough key words to take an educated guess.

"The aliens found our hiding place. They're attacking," she said.

"What was that?" asked the security guard.

The ship started shaking violently. Everyone stopped what they were doing and waited for an update. Phillip wondered if they were getting something over their Imps. After a few seconds the announcement was sent out that everyone was to get to their battle stations because they were under attack. The security guard didn't even try to take Phillip and Jazlyn to the brig. He dragged them both into a nearby bathroom and used the restraints to tie them to the pipes under the wash sink. Neither of them struggled. Jazlyn looked like she was having trouble focusing on what was going on. Once the guard left Phillip used his new strength to break free.

"Come on. We need to go get Nelson and Ryan. This is our chance to get off the ship."

Jazlyn broke free and followed after Phillip.

"They are really close now," said Jazlyn. "I feel like they are right in my head now."

"Try to block it out," said Phillip.

"Do you know how to do that?"

"No. But Mac said we wouldn't be able to listen in on private conversations."

"Well, he was wrong, because I can hear everything that is being said on that collector ship."

Phillip and Jazlyn started running. They didn't get very far. The power in the ship turned off as the collector ship latched onto *Bears Paw* and started cutting into it. Sparks spewed out from the ceiling and the two of them were lifted into the air as gravity vanished. The shuttle in the docking bay must have failed because the *Bears Paw* didn't explode in an attempt to take out the human ship before the aliens could use it.

What's going on down there? Mac asked Phillip.

The shuttle failed. It got taken out or something, said Phillip.

Well then it looks like you are going to the other side sooner than you planned. Whatever you do make sure you protect the general. If the aliens learn his secrets then more people will die before we can end this war.

We will. You should get out of here, said Phillip.
Good luck.
We're all going to need some luck.

Soon Phillip and Jazlyn were floating through space in a brilliant white light. There were dozens and dozens of people streaming out of the capital ship, a lot of them screaming, some resigned to their fate. The *Bears Paw* below them was still mostly enclosed by the asteroid, but every exposed part of the ship had a tear in it and people floating out. Nelson and Ryan would be in there somewhere.

Phillip saw something strange. One part of the ship wasn't being attacked. There was a large black box attached to the hull. Before the collector ship tore open that part of the ship the arms detached the box and brought it into the collector ship. Phillip recalled the brief encounter the *Bears Paw* had on the way back to the asteroid belt. Maybe the aliens were able to sneak a tracking device onto the ship.

We need to separate ourselves from the group, said Phillip. He made sure Nelson and Ryan could hear. *No more talking out loud.* Phillip and Jazlyn were sucked into the holding area where they floated around with the rest of the crew members. General Roy was there and could be seen cursing up a storm. He was the general of the front line. How was it possible that he was captured? There was a laser in his hand but when he put it in his mouth nothing happened and he started cursing again.

I know how we can get to where the others are being held, Phillip said.

How's that? asked Jazlyn.

We follow where they take the general.

Circling the area where the crew of the *Bears Paw* were floating was a walkway. Looking down at the crew were two dozen humanoid-looking people. None of them were talking.

Some of them wore military uniforms. Some had casual clothes on. Others had purple skin. This confirmed what Mac had told them. The aliens took people from all around the galaxy and turned them into emulators. Mac described some weird looking creatures, but at least the emulators they were looking at now had two arms, two legs, and only one head. Some were a little abnormally colored but nothing too outrageous. Maybe the aliens didn't want to freak the new human captives out too much.

There were three dark purple people. They had no hair, and as far as Phillip could tell they never blinked. For the two minutes he watched them, none of them blinked. Now they were pointing at Phillip and Jazlyn.

Who are you? asked one of the emulators in a monotone baritone voice.

Jazlyn took the lead. *We are like you. We were sent to escort these prisoners. We were on the ship waiting for the attack. There is a man here who is the leader of their army. His knowledge will be very valuable.*

How many are you? asked one of the purple dudes. All three of them were standing close to each other but Phillip couldn't tell which one was talking. Could Jazlyn?

There are four of us, said Jazlyn. Then she turned to Phillip. *Do you see the others?*

No, said Phillip.

Call out to them. The aliens won't be able to hear you.

Nelson! Ryan!

We are being sucked up now, said Nelson. *See you soon.*

Jazlyn spoke again to the aliens. *The two others are still coming from the human ship.*

The three purple emulators didn't have to think about it for very long. There were several long metallic arms that came down from the ceiling to start sorting through the people who had been sucked up by the ship. One of the thin arms latched onto Phillip and then Jazlyn taking them out of the increasing number of captives and putting them next to the purple guys on the walkway around the opening in the alien ship.

Phillip resisted saying thank you. He wasn't sure it was the alien thing to do, and they needed to start acting like aliens. He looked at the others around him. They all kind of walked the same. Same speed. Same arm swing. Same foot first. He wanted to point it out to the others but he was nervous about the mind speaking. Everything was changing now that they were actually on the collector ship. All the rules and information that Mac had told him were lost now. He couldn't remember them. Perspiration started to form. Did the emulators sweat?

As soon as Phillip and Jazlyn were out of the mix and on the walkway the purple aliens left them alone and it was only a few minutes until Nelson and Ryan were there beside them. The four of them stood there nervously. No one was paying attention to them but they still didn't feel comfortable doing anything.

Where do we go? asked Jazlyn.

Don't talk! said Nelson.

We can talk to each other. They can't hear.

Are you sure?

We are humans who can mind speak and we are here to steal back the people you use to emulate, Jazlyn said while looking at Nelson. He looked like he was scared out of his mind. None of the aliens did anything to stop them.

All we have to do is make sure we don't talk to them and they won't bother us, said Jazlyn.

And if we do need to talk to them I vote Jazlyn be our spokesperson. She's the one who seems to be into this the most, said Ryan.

We need to remember that we have to act like the aliens. Look at how they move and act and try to play along, said Phillip. *We also need to follow these prisoners back to where they keep the others.*

Good idea, said Nelson.

Another arm came down and grabbed the general out of the mix. He was being very loud ordering the men around him to try and kill him. Two young guys who looked disturbingly happy about being told to kill their commanding officer were trying to beat the life out of him when the arm came down to rescue General Roy.

"Put me down! Get these things off of me," he said.

As soon as he was on the walkway he took off running but he had nowhere to go. There were no doors. Phillip remembered what he was told about everything on the collector ships being run by mind speak or something like that. The door could only be opened by mind speak.

The general ran and no one was in a major hurry to stop him. As he ran past the other four humans on the walkway, Nelson and Ryan stepped out and grabbed each of his arms to stop him from running.

"Stop touching me. Let me go," he said.

We are helping you. Stick with us, Nelson said to the general but it didn't work to calm him down. The general was still trying to find a way to escape but there were no doors and there was nowhere else for him to go. The purple aliens were all looking at him now. He needed to cool down.

Ryan stepped in. *Sir, you need to calm down. Everything is going to be okay. We have a plan.*

The general stopped struggling but he wasn't sure what to say. The other four undercover humans looked at each other. It looked like Ryan was the only one who could communicate with mind speech to normal humans.

It's better if you don't say anything. We are trying to do the undercover thing. Pretend like we are aliens, but know that we are human. If we talk like normal our cover will be blown so the conversation is going to be one-sided until we get some more privacy, said Ryan.

Phillip couldn't believe what he was hearing.

Ryan! Don't tell him you are a human! Phillip yelled in mind speak.

Why not? He's going to get himself killed.

But now if he gets emulated the aliens are going to know we are human and our mission will be busted.

Ryan didn't say anything. He realized what a colossal blunder he had made. The mission might be blown before it even began.

Maybe we should kill him, said Ryan.

We can't do that, said Jazlyn.

Why not?

You need me to give you a reason not to kill one of our own people?

Phillip spoke up, *You're both right. We can't kill the general, but if he's about to be emulated then we don't have a choice. We'll wait until we don't have another option.*

The general was a hero to a lot of people — maybe not to the young guys who had readily agreed to try to kill him — and he was strong and full of pride in what he was capable of. All of that was gone now. He walked with his head down and shoulders slouched. His muscular frame would do him no good now. He was powerless and pathetic and he knew it.

It's a means to an end, said Ryan to the general. *We know how to win the war.*

Who knew if they could find all the people being emulated or if it would make enough of a difference to win the war. All he really knew for sure was that they needed to try and that Mac desperately needed to find someone name Janelle Stewart.

The other aliens were okay with where Jazlyn, Nelson, and Ryan had corralled the general. The three purple guys were the ones in charge. The other dozen or so human emulators standing around were taking orders from them. No one had any papers or computer pads. There were no terminals. The arms above the prisoners floating in space responded to the thoughts of the aliens.

The prisoners were being sorted into two groups. Some were put with General Roy. Others were put on the far side of the walkway. Phillip couldn't figure it out. Mac said the prisoners were being used as emulators, so why would they need to be sorted into two groups? Were they going to two different ships?

None of the aliens showed emotion, and it was getting really hard for Jazlyn to keep her face the same way. She had more of a connection with the men who were being sorted than with Phillip, Nelson, and Ryan. She had met all of them and formed an emotional bond with several of them. It was hard to watch them get sorted, not knowing what was going to happen to them. Phillip couldn't know for sure, but she looked like she was sending comforting messages to all of them.

What do we do now? asked Nelson.

We wait and then go with the group the general is in, said Jazlyn.

Why that group? asked Phillip.

Because those are the ones that have been designated to be emulated.

What about the others?

I can't tell for sure, but I know they aren't going to be emulated. They keep talking about testing potential but I have no idea what that means. It might not be good. I don't know. Alien testing of any kind didn't sound good at all.

Maybe you shouldn't be talking to the soldiers. It's bad enough that the general knows, but if anyone else figures it out we could get busted, said Phillip.

I know. I couldn't even if I wanted to, said Jazlyn.

Why does it look like you are?

Right now I can hear a thousand different conversations. You can only hear what people are saying at you, but I can hear everything. It's all a little overwhelming and I'm trying to force myself only to listen to what is going on in this room.

Jazlyn's gift wasn't a good thing anymore if they were going to be constantly surrounded by other aliens talking to each other.

The walkway around the floating people was getting uncomfortably crowded. Some people from each group had already tried to sneak into the other group to be with friends. The aliens weren't having any of that. People who tried it were killed immediately in a swarm attack. It didn't happen very often. No one was talking except for the odd shouted question asking what was going to happen next. The alien's death glare ended any more questions from the offenders.

When the two groups occupied as much area as they could and had met in the middle where the purple guys were standing, an order was given and two doors opened out of the walls at either end of the walkway. The four undercovers made sure they were in the general's group.

What is the plan, by the way? asked Nelson.

Keep walking and see where we end up, said Phillip.

There were other aliens in the crowd even though they were hard to spot because they were using human emulators as well. The best they could do was try to see if they were wearing a uniform or not, but even then it wasn't for sure since the aliens had been harvesting soldiers for years.

The hallway right outside of the collecting and sorting area was long and gray with nothing in it. No doors. No people. Where were they even walking to?

This is what Mac described to us, said Nelson. *Everything is run on mind speak. This hallway is really lined with doors, but no one is thinking them open.*

Can you tell where we're going? Phillip asked Jazlyn.

She shook her head. Now that they were on the ship she didn't want to mind speak as much. Adding to the noise in her head wasn't what she wanted to do. There was no point in asking if she was okay.

Phillip was tall and he could see over most of the people in the group and he could see the end of the hallway. Only one of the purple aliens came with them and led the way. When he got to the end of the hallway he didn't even hesitate. The door didn't even look like it was there before it opened up and they all walked through it and into a large room. The walls were the same shade of gray as the rest of the ship. The room adjusted its size to the number of people in it. As more people came inside, the room became larger.

When the room reached its final size they noticed that the aliens had moved to the walls leaving the middle for the prisoners. The four of them lined up with the aliens. Everyone else looked really nervous about what was going on. No one dared to ask any questions. It was all so quiet. It was easily the most unnerving thing about the whole situation.

Phillip tried to calm himself down by telling himself over and over in his head that he was pulling off acting like an alien. The plan was working, so far, and as long as the general didn't get emulated they would be okay.

Some of the aliens left. The purple guy was one of them, but before he left he walked up to Jazlyn and said something. None of the others could tell what it was. There was strain in her eyes but the aliens weren't good at picking up on human emotions.

Then captain purple went to Nelson, said something and walked away. Nelson followed him.

Where are you going? asked Phillip.

Training. He said it was my turn for training, said Nelson.

Well you can't leave us. Try to get out of it.

How do I do that? Explain the situation to him?

We have to stick together!

We have to keep our cover. If it gets hairy I'll get out of there, but right now they don't suspect anything, said Nelson.

Phillip stood still for a second to go over his options. In the end he decided to let Nelson go. They could still mind speak to each other. If the purple aliens were taking Nelson with them then that meant they thought Nelson was one of them which meant the interloping humans were successfully blending in.

The door opened and the purple dude left with Nelson and some others. There were seven aliens left; well, seven including Phillip, Ryan, and Jazlyn.

What did he say to you? Ryan asked Jazlyn.

He said if anyone talked then we were supposed to kill them, said Jazlyn.

We aren't going to be able to kill anyone. Besides the obvious ethical reasons, we don't know how to swarm, said Ryan.

I don't think it's possible for us to swarm, said Phillip.

Ryan broadcasted a message to all the prisoners, and made sure the aliens couldn't hear it. *We will be moving you soon. Anyone who talks will be killed. No more warnings.*

Chapter 7
Thief

Mac felt like he had been traveling for days. Space traveling all alone did that. There was really nothing to see and no Imp to keep him occupied. The star charts told him he was getting near to his home solar system. Earth and Ronos were each about the same distance from the front line. The three destinations almost formed a triangle of equal distance to each point except that Ronos and Earth were farther apart. The fact that Earth wasn't on the way to Ronos did not make Mac think that Earth was safe from a full-on alien invasion. Earth was too close to leave alone and the humans would never stop fighting.

The closer he got to Earth the more ships he saw. They were mostly civilian ships which he hadn't been expecting. Earth had recently suffered a major attack. Shouldn't there be at least one capital ship patrolling the system? None of the civilian ships tried to contact him. It could have been because he was Impless.

It also could have been that they couldn't keep up to the *Kilkenny*. The ship was performing better than Mac could have dreamed. One engine would power all the way to full speed and then turn off. The other engine would kick in and go to full speed and then shut off. They would go back and forth like this the whole time so that each engine was never on for more than a few minutes and they were always running at full capacity. The cooling system wouldn't be enough to cool a full time engine, but it was enough for these two part timers sharing the load.

Twin hyper engines operating at full capacity and staying cool was something that no one had seen before. The small ship sped past everyone else.

As he got closer he realized he needed a plan if he was going to get to the only man in Passage with an Imp and Sneed. If Jace was an alien then he probably wasn't the only one who was wandering around on the human side of the war. The mind speaking didn't seem to have a limit for how far apart the two people were. He communicated with Lynn when they were millions of miles apart. Mac had to assume that every alien knew about him by now, and that meant he had to assume that any alien spies that were on Earth knew about him as well.

It also meant that Mac couldn't land his ship in Passage and knock on the front door. He also couldn't continue to fly around in this sweet ride without attracting unwanted attention. If his brother-in-law Chester was still alive he could easily ask him for a ship. He owned a large shipping company so he had access to tons of ships. He probably had one that the *Kilkenny* could fit inside. That would allow Mac to move around freely and not have to abandon his new favorite ship.

But as Mac flew closer to Earth he realized that was going to be a problem. There were ships everywhere. Most of them were holding orbit around the Earth, but there was still a good number that were orbiting the moon as well. Mac did a quick scan of the area. There were no ships going down to either sphere. The military must have cut everyone off. Why would they do that? Especially the moon since its inhabitants needed constant supplies in order to stay alive.

There was no way that Mac was going to be able to get down to the moon to steal a ship to get down to Earth. That would be a waste of time. Instead he put himself in orbit around the planet like most of the other ships. He put the *Kilkenny* on auto pilot while he tried to figure things out.

Once he was in orbit an automated message came over the ship's computer. He guessed it would have come sooner if he had an Imp.

"Please hold orbit until further notice. Due to an investigation regarding the attack on Northgate, no ships will be allowed down to Earth without direct military authority. This shouldn't last long. Thank you for your patience."

This was going to be a while. Mac couldn't wait for things to resolve themselves.

The *Kilkenny* was fast enough that Mac could outrun anyone who tried to chase him, but there were possibly millions of witnesses that would see him ignore the order to hold orbit while he zipped off to Passage. He couldn't fly straight there and hope there would be no consequences. Maybe he could go to another part of the planet and then slowly make his way to Passage. How hard was the military looking for him?

Mac didn't know what to do, but he felt sure he knew someone who did. The only man in Passage with an Imp would know what to do. If things had gone according to plan then the only man in Passage with an Imp would be expecting him so he should be ready with a way to not get tracked through his Imp. Mac used the *Kilkenny*'s computer to talk to him.

"Hello? Are you there? Can you hear me?"

"Yes. You know these connections are being monitored," said the only man in Passage with an Imp.

"I know. I need something?" asked Mac.

"I'm going to guess at what you need. Passage off planet?"

The only man in Passage with an Imp was trying to talk in code. Who knew if it would work, but Mac decided to play along. The man was really wanting to know if Mac was trying to get to Passage.

"Yes, of course. But no one is allowed off planet," said Mac.

"Really? Well, I heard that wasn't the case anymore."

"From who?"

"General Zinger. I think he's about to send out a message to everyone."

The only man in Passage with an Imp had obviously doctored something and had simply been waiting for Mac to show up so he could follow through with his plans.

"Once the order is given you are going to need to make sure you don't have any company when you arrive," said the only man in Passage with an Imp. Mac figured this was another hint. The only man in Passage with an Imp was telling him not to go straight to Passage in case he was being followed.

"Don't worry, I got speed on my side," said Mac.

"Good. The faster the better. I don't think you'll have time to go through the proper channels."

"I got that covered."

For a ship with an interplanetary drive the protocol for visiting Earth was to dock at the ESP and then take a shuttle down. There was no way that Mac was going to be able to do that. The space port was no doubt already at capacity and the wait time to dock would be longer than what Mac had time for. Larger ships didn't have to dock and could send down shuttles through a designated shuttle route, but smaller ships like Mac's would have to dock and then find a shuttle to take the pilot and passengers down.

He had no intention of docking. His ship was small enough that he could pass for a shuttle. When the word to go down opened he would go down with the shuttles. There would be too much traffic for anyone to notice him, or if they did, they would be unable to do anything about it. At least that's what he hoped.

The computer beeped indicating an incoming message. There was no video. It was only the voice of General Zinger. Mac didn't know who else would be fooled, but he knew that this was something the only man in Passage with an Imp had made himself from old recordings that he polished up. It wasn't anything official. He had skills, but he didn't have those kinds of skills. The message wasn't coming through the proper channels or anything. It was being broadcast over all the public channels so that every ship in orbit would be able to hear it. The blockade must have been going on for longer than Mac guessed, because it looked like the only man in Passage with an Imp was expecting people to listen to a concocted message from General Zinger without questioning its validity.

"Earth is now open to all ships. I'm personally sorry for the delay that we have caused. Be assured that it was for your own safety. In an effort to get you back on schedule we are instituting a temporary leave in typical procedures. For the rest of the day interplanetary ships will not be required to dock with the space dock or to take a shuttle down. You can simply send the Earth Space Port a transmission with your flight information and then proceed to your destination.

"Again, the blockade is over and sorry for any inconvenience. Safe travels to your destination," Zinger's voice said.

Mac loved it. He wasn't sure where the only man in Passage with an Imp got a recording of Zinger saying he was sorry but that didn't matter. It worked. The effects were almost immediate.

Everyone was moving at once to leave orbit and head to Earth. The military ships that were there enforcing the blockade were powerless to stop the rush of ships. Mac didn't bother letting the ESP know who he was or where he was going. He plotted a course for Passage. His computer beeped at him letting him know that there were too many moving obstacles — other ships flying through the atmosphere — in the way for the auto pilot to work effectively. Mac was going to have to fly the ship himself.

The order given to end the blockade started a rash of poor decisions. Everyone had been waiting for so long they had forgotten that there were more people flying around. It was only going to be a matter of time before ships collided and lives were lost.

Mac was flying the *Kilkenny* in every direction. His speed was used to fly past and around everyone but he couldn't go full bore without risking getting into an accident. In order to blend in he followed the crowd. It looked like there was a large group headed for North America near where Passage was. Most of those ships were bulky transport ships. As they got closer he realized that they were going to Northgate. The ships must have been full of supplies and relief equipment.

It was too late for Mac to turn back when he realized that going to Northgate might be a mistake. He wouldn't be able to sneak onto the base with the *Kilkenny*. There was no way that they would let him land or let anyone else land until they were verified. All the other transport ships were expected. The *Kilkenny* was not.

The transport ships started circling the airfield over the base outside of Northgate. The base had doubled in size since Mac had been there last. There were soldiers and ships going in every direction. Maybe some real work was being done to help the people in Northgate. Maybe the monsters were called back by Zinger so there would at least be a few survivors to report the monsters and thus confirm it was aliens that attacked Northgate.

Mac had a plan. He synchronized his flight path with one of the other transport ships. He picked one that looked like a large flying box, twice the size of a typical house. No one would see him from the ground. He briefly thought about landing the *Kilkenny* on top of the ship but wasn't sure he could do that without the people on the ship noticing. He could try something else though.

He opened the cockpit of his ship. The wind rushed past him but it wasn't unbearable. Mac didn't need to breathe so the rushing wind wasn't going to hamper respiration anyway. Poking his head out of the cockpit to look down, he judged the distance then quickly programmed another flight path into the *Kilkenny*. However, he didn't press engage. First he climbed out of the ship and held on from outside. One hand was holding him onto his ship. All he had to do was let go and he would land on the transport ship and then once it landed he could find transportation to get him to Passage.

But first he had to get rid of the *Kilkenny* which was going to be one of the hardest things Mac had ever done. Well, not really. He had recently destroyed two alien ships almost by himself, but the *Kilkenny* was such a sweet ride it was hard to let go. Mac reached over and pushed the engage button and sent his ship off on a new trajectory away from Northgate. He was hoping it would be enough of a distraction so that Mac could do what he needed to.

He let go of the ship as he pushed engage. Now he was falling while facing up at the sky. It shouldn't have been more than a couple seconds for him to land on the transport ship but it didn't happen. Mac saw it fly past him. It had shifted course and was moving in to land. Mac rolled over in the sky so that he was facing down. The ground was quickly rising to meet him. There was only one ship left between him and the ground. Mac wasn't sure if it was possible to change directions while falling. He kept his arms at his side and his feet together and tried to point himself at the shuttle so that he would hit it instead of the ground, but a few seconds later he realized it wasn't going to happen. Also, putting his arms at the side like that was making him more streamline and speeding his descent. If he was going to survive the impact he needed to spread his arms and legs out, create as much surface area as he could.

Once he did that it didn't really seem like he slowed down very much but it was the best he could do. He was almost at the ground. He was going to crash onto the far side of the airfield in what used to be a farmer's field. Before he could decide whether he was more likely to survive landing on his back or his stomach he hit the ground.

Everything went black.

Mac thought he might actually be dead this time. His ears were ringing. His vision was starting to come back but it was cloudy. There was a bright light behind the cloud. He figured that could only be God welcoming him back home. Well, it wasn't all bad. Mac figured he would at least be done with all the drama of being alive and trying to save humanity. Now he could be with his family. His only regret was leaving Janelle behind and still captive. Then he remembered Lynn. He felt bad about that as well, but there was nothing he could do. As much as he really wanted to save everyone he couldn't because he was dead. He had been humanity's best hope at surviving and he had accidentally killed himself. Considering a lot more humans were about to be killed by aliens in the coming days and weeks he would have to try and keep that on the down low on the other side of the veil.

His ears started working more. He could hear a low rumble. The white light was becoming more focused and spherical. Mac blinked several times. Did he still have eyelids? Did people have eyelids when they died? The rumble sound could still be heard so that meant he still had ears to hear.

The more he blinked the clearer his vision became. The light was the sun. The low rumble was the sound of ships landing in the airfield. Mac wasn't dead. Slowly and painfully he started to pull himself out of the indentation he'd made in the ground. There was nothing graceful about it. He sat up and rolled out of the Mac-shaped hole in the ground. The more he moved the more his head spun. The dizziness was overtaking him and he fell over in the tall grass. He kept his eyes closed to stop the spinning. With his hands he took an inventory of his body, feeling for blood and broken bones. There were none to be found. With his new body he was able to survive the fall, but barely. He felt like his arms were about to fall off and that his legs wouldn't respond to commands from his brain.

Deep breaths. He needed energy. He needed to focus. The *Kilkenny* was on its way to making a distraction. Mac needed to be ready. When he opened his eyes again the world had stopped spinning. Slowly he rolled over and lifted himself onto his feet. The dizziness returned but he fought it away. If this had happened on Ronos he doubted there would have been any negative consequences. The gas would have healed him. But the gas in his own body right now was limited and he couldn't do a lot of crazy things like jumping out of ships and smashing into the ground if he wanted to survive.

There was a fence around the airfield. Mac put one foot in front of the other and approached it. Chain link. He could easily climb it. When he started climbing he realized he was still in recovery mode and scaling the fence was more difficult than he imagined. There was a lot of fence rattling and grunting as he made it to the top. Then a loud thud and moan as he misplaced his hand and toppled over the fence and onto the other side.

"Hey, over there," someone said.

They had spotted Mac. He saw five soldiers with weapons walking over to him. Mac got up and started wiping himself off. He thought about giving a fake name and rank but then remembered he wasn't wearing a uniform anymore. The *Kilkenny* had some civilian clothes in it that were close to his size.

"This is restricted space. You have to leave right now or you'll be arrested," said the lead soldier. They all had their weapons aimed at Mac's chest.

"Sorry," said Mac. "I'll leave. But can I go out the front door?" Mac took a couple steps and faked a limp, "I twisted my ankle when I was coming over the top."

"Come with us. We will escort you," said the soldier.

They started walking through the airfield. As they passed the ships Mac looked around for the one he wanted to take him to Passage. There was a shuttle that would do the trick. He wasn't sure what kind it was. It looked like a tanker truck with no wheels. It probably held some kind of liquid. Maybe water because fresh water was probably hard to come by in Northgate now. The only real source was the river and it was too polluted to drink from. The tanker looked like a civilian ship. The logo on the side read Hall's Hauler, a private company. That meant the military wouldn't have any tracking devices on it.

But Mac wasn't going anywhere until his distraction started. He waited. It had been too long. Maybe he missed it. Maybe he had programmed the trajectory wrong. Right when Mac had decided to cut his losses and make a run for it, the *Kilkenny* did its job. Mac had programmed it to slam into the ground. The fireball was bigger than he expected. Its state of the art engines required more fuel than the average ship so the explosion was massive. Everyone noticed, which was exactly what Mac wanted. An explosion led people to think there might be another attack. Officers shouted orders. Everyone was running back to their ships. The soldiers that were with Mac were telling him to hurry, but then someone else called out to them and they looked away.

Mac made his break. He ran for the tanker shuttle. The airfield was too crowded with people running back to their ships for the other soldiers to see where he went. He got to the tanker ship and got inside. There was already someone in there.

"Hey, what are you doing?" the man asked.

The tanker shuttle was already running so Mac pulled the man out and tossed him to the ground.

"General Zinger has personally requested the use of your shuttle. Any questions should be directed to his office. Thank you for your cooperation," said Mac.

That poor pilot would have no idea how to get a hold of Zinger. That would buy Mac enough time to get to Passage and then ditch the tanker ship.

Mac thought briefly about going to retrieve his family's bodies from where he left them in Northgate, but he knew now wasn't the time. He felt jaded for thinking it, but he knew that they weren't going to go anywhere and he wanted to have time to do it right. Staying in Northgate for very long wasn't the plan. The next stop was Passage.

Chapter 8
Passage

There was no airfield in Passage. If any of the villagers needed to travel they would take a hover car to Northgate and use public transportation. That didn't come up much. One of the goals of Passage was to be completely self-sufficient. Everyone there had a job that helped out the other people in the village. Teacher, farmer, doctor, laborer, whatever was needed and whatever they were capable of doing. Luddites were a diverse group so there weren't issues of crossovers or having too much of one skill set.

With no point in wasting time, Mac put the tanker shuttle down in his own backyard. It meant the military might be able to find him more easily but that didn't matter. He was going to grab the only man in Passage with an Imp and Sneed and get out of there. The Narrad's backyard wasn't very big so landing there meant crushing a bit of shrubbery, but that could always be replanted. The sun was setting. None of the lights were on in his old home. He landed the shuttle and quickly exited. The only man in Passage with an Imp lived down the street. Mac ran at a full sprint past the mail box that read *Mr. Smith*. That's what everyone called him but Mac suspected that wasn't his real name.

There were lights on in the house and silhouettes on the curtains. He didn't bother to knock and went straight inside. The living room was full of familiar faces and a couple strangers. None of them was the mysterious Mr. Smith. None of them was Sneed.

Half of them were his old teachers from high school. The town doctor was there. The preacher. Even a couple of the older children were there. One of the guys was someone Mac's age. They had gone to school together. His name was Darren Gable. He sat with his arm around a good-looking girl. She wasn't from Passage. *Good for Darren for being able to find a girl who would date a Luddite.* He didn't look happy about seeing Mac, probably because Mac had been a colossal jerk to Darren in high school. Unfortunately, Mac had gone through a bully phase and Darren, being the smallest in the class, had been the easy target. Was it too late to apologize? In all there were twelve people in the room. They all gave Mac puzzled looks.

"Relax guys. I don't have an Imp anymore," said Mac.

"Mac!" He was a stranger but he acted unusually excited to see Mac. He had a book in one hand and was standing in the middle of the room while everyone around him was seated. There was something familiar about him but his identity remained elusive.

"Do I know you?" asked Mac.

"I'm going to take that as a compliment, but please don't take what I'm about to say as an insult. You look like death. You need to see a doctor."

It was the way the man walked that triggered the memory for Mac. It was Sneed and he had undergone the most amazing transformation. He was wearing clean clothes. His hair was clean and cut. His cheeks weren't hollow with malnutrition. His voice wasn't groggy. His body wasn't shaking. He was a whole new person.

"Sneed?" asked Mac.

"Yes, but call me Quentin Lenoch. That's my real name. Sneed was my disconnected identity." Quentin turned to the other people in the room, "Book club is over. Everyone get back to your houses."

The people that Mac grew up with left Mr. Smith's house. Some of them looked at him sympathetically, others with condemnation. If anything went down they were going to blame him. Quentin motioned to the couch for Mac to rest. Only one other person stayed. Mac didn't recognize the small man.

Mac said, "I don't need a doctor. Right now we need to get out of here. Where is Mr. Smith? And who is that guy over there?"

The other stranger spoke, "I'm Scott Ryder. Shouldn't Lynn be with you?"

Scott was not what Mac was expecting. The guy was already going gray and he had a bit of a pot belly. His eyes were sunk into his head and his mouth was bigger than the average person's. How did he and Lynn end up together? She was much better looking than he was. They must have connected on an intellectual level.

More than that, Scott was not supposed to be there.

"You're Scott Ryder?' asked Mac.

"Yes."

"Husband to Lynn Ryder?"

"That's right. Where is she?"

"How did you get here?"

"Where is Lynn?"

"She's on Ronos."

"What's a Ronos?" asked Scott.

"It's a planet. Don't worry she's...okay." said Mac. He hesitated saying okay because he wasn't 100% sure that was the truth, but right now it was more important that they got out of there so they could go rescue her.

Scott didn't look reassured.

"How did you get here?" asked Mac again.

"Your friend Jace Michaels rescued me. He broke me out of prison and brought me here. Told me you would be here with Lynn, didn't say anything about her being on some other planet."

"Jace Michaels? Tall lanky redhead with big ears?"

"Yeah."

"When's the last time you saw him?"

"He was here a few minutes ago. Not sure where he is now."

Mac looked around him. If Jace was in swarm form then he could be in the room right now without any of them knowing it. They needed to get out of there as fast as they could.

"Let's go. I'm taking you back to Lynn right now," said Mac. He ushered them to the door.

They ran back down the street but they weren't going to make it in time. Four HAAS3's were starting to circle the village. The loud bass of a larger ship indicated a soldier transport was approaching. The truth was he felt exhausted and depleted. There was no way he could show the same firepower and energy he had on the front line. Besides, it was more useful against aliens than humans. He could still get shot by a laser and die.

"These your friends?" asked Quentin.

"Once upon a time. They don't like me too much anymore though," said Mac.

"Where's your ship?" asked Scott.

Mac pointed to his old house right as one of the HAAS3's let loose a volley of destruction. The house and the tanker shuttle exploded under the barrage of laser fire. It was such a trial to get that ship — Mac had almost died — and now it was gone. The explosion threw the cache of water he had stolen into the air. For a couple seconds it felt like it was raining. The clothing of the three men was now wet and sticking to them.

"Did you have a backup plan?" asked Scott.

"Do you still have an Imp?" asked Mac.

"Yes, but Quentin told me to get rid of it. I haven't decided whether it's a good idea or not."

"Who told you to get rid of it?"

"Sneed."

"Oh, right. I only wanted to try and talk to these guys before they start killing innocents."

The Imp wasn't needed. An authoritative voice bellowed out of a loud speaker from one of the shuttles.

"Mac Narrad. Turn yourself in immediately and there will be no more destruction."

Mac wasn't going to do that. He needed to get to Lynn. He needed to get people like Quentin, Scott, and Mr. Smith to Ronos. That wouldn't be possible if he was in military custody.

"Mac Narrad. Turn yourself in immediately and there will be no more destruction," the voice said again.

Mac started running. It must have looked like he was running away because the HAAS3 destroyed the house next to the Narrads. The streets were filling with the people of Passage. They heard the shuttles and the explosions and they were coming out of their houses to see what was going on. They were now being bathed in the light of two burning houses. Ashes and debris were falling from the sky.

Normal people would have gone back inside to hide in the basement or ran away from the explosion, but the people of Passage were distracted by one more thing that kept them planted: young Mac Narrad was back in town and he was running like a mad man.

Mac ran to the house two doors down from his now nonexistent house. It was a jump he shouldn't have been able to make but he had to try. Hopefully he had enough left in him to make it worth it. If not he was going to land in the flames. After what he did to avoid getting burned by the gas it would be an ironic ending. Despite his depleted power he was still able to jump over the fence and from there jump up on the roof. The HAAS3 was hovering above the burning wreckage of his neighbor's house and — suspecting something was up — started to pull away from the roof Mac was on. Without slowing down he propelled himself as far as he could through the air.

As the shuttle pulled away Mac's Ronos powers allowed him to jump far enough to latch onto the outside of the ship — what should have been an impossible feat. He hit the side of the shuttle and slid down before he was able to dig his fingers in to stop himself.

If it hadn't been a heavy armored assault shuttle he might have been able to punch and tear his way into it. Instead he went to the front of the shuttle where the window was and started beating on it. The three soldiers inside were shocked to see him. Each punch landed solidly. The flesh on Mac's hand was starting to tear but there was no blood and he felt no pain yet. A crack started forming on the window screen.

The pilot snapped out of it and pointed the shuttle up into the sky. Mac wasn't prepared for it and flipped over the ship and skipped across the roof. He clung onto a ridge to keep from falling to the ground. A new plan to take down the shuttle was needed. He scooted to the engine as carefully as he could and started kicking the housing around it.

A cover fell off exposing some wires. He had no idea what they did but he started pulling at them. The engines started flickering but the shuttle stayed level. Mac started kicking again. After a particularly powerful thrust and a severe dent the shuttle started spinning. The engines were clicking on and off sporadically.

He looked out at where they were falling. The shuttle had gained some height while Mac was assaulting it, but not much. The spin was taking it out over the village. Now the people were scrambling to get out of the way of the crash site. The shuttle hit a light pole. He decided to make his exit and jumped, landed on the street and rolled several times.

The shuttle hit a group of three trees and then the ground. The engine was still somewhat operational so the impact wouldn't have hurt anyone inside. They were still a threat. Mac got to his feet and made for the shuttle.

The door opened and Mac jumped at the first person coming out before he could do anything. He knocked the man inside. The force of the jump incapacitated him. The other two didn't have time to react. Mac already had the gun from the first man pointed at them and was motioning for them to get out of the ship.

They put their hands up and marched out into the night lit by fires. A crowd had cautiously gathered. A couple hundred people were there — half of Passage. As news about what Mac did spread, the other half would soon show up.

Mac pointed to two men. One was his old math teacher, a thick man who dressed like a farmer, not someone who liked to crunch numbers.

"There's another soldier inside. Go get him and bring him here with the others," said Mac.

He led the other two, a gray-haired man and a young woman, to the middle of the street.

"Sneed! Scott!"

The two men emerged from the crowd. Mac handed the gun to Quentin and apologized.

"I mean Quentil," said Mac.

"Quentin."

"Right. Point this gun at them and shoot them if they try anything."

Quentin looked worried about the prospect of killing someone. Mac did what he needed to do quickly. He searched the two and took their weapons. Each had a small blaster. He gave one blaster to Scott and kept the other. The older man also had an immobilizer. Mac kept that in his pocket. By the time the math teacher and the other man had brought the last soldier the rest of the town had gathered and everyone was talking about what had happened.

"He took out a military shuttle all by himself."

"Did you see how far he jumped?"

"Or how fast he got on the roof?"

"Falling off the shuttle should have killed him, but he's not even limping."

"He looks a bit like death, but it's not slowing him down at all."

If only they had seen him on Ronos. That might have been more than they could process. He looked at the people he grew up with and they all looked at him like he was inhuman. They had no idea who he was anymore. The tall lanky boy that grew up in Passage had become a super soldier and they didn't know how to react.

The mayor pushed his way to the front of the crowd. It wasn't the same person as when Mac lived here, but Mac still knew who he was. His name was Valtteri Happonen, a dark-skinned man who also ran a local construction and reno company. Passage was self-reliant enough that the job of being Mayor wasn't extremely time-consuming, so the mayor could keep his full-time job. Anyone in the village that wanted to run for mayor could. Valtteri was shorter than Mac but his gaze had an intensity that made up for his height. Mac didn't ask, but looking at Valtteri's bright blue eyes and how they contrasted with his dark skin, he guessed that the mayor had done the expensive Imp surgery to become a Luddite and ended up with new eyes. He was wearing a t-shirt and jeans. Today must have been a construction day, not a politics day.

"What happened?" he asked.

"The military attacked us. They destroyed my parents' house and the neighbors. Not sure who lives there now," said Mac.

"Parents? Sorry, Mac, I didn't recognize you. You look like you have a story to tell."

"Yes, but I came back to pick up some friends..."

"Those guys hanging out with Mr. Smith. I knew there was something going on."

The math teacher who dressed like a farmer, John Somerset, spoke up.

"Mac didn't do anything wrong. He saved us. He took out that shuttle all by himself."

The skies were clear now. The destruction of one of the shuttles must have been enough for the military to rethink its strategy. Darren and the girl he had been with in Mr. Smith's house broke through the crowd. They were holding hands. *Who is that girl?* Mac wondered.

"They were here to arrest Mac. I've been watching feeds and Clarissa found out that Mac is a terrorist and a traitor. They're going to send more men in here after him," said Darren.

Mac looked at the girl who was with Darren.

"You're Clarissa?" he asked.

"Yes," she said.

"And you have an Imp?"

"Yes. But I'm getting it removed before the wedding. I only have to find a doctor willing to do the surgery."

She had an Imp and fell in love with a Luddite. Mac wondered how that happened. He was glad that something was going right for Darren now. She was an attractive girl and if she was willing to do what she thought was extremely invasive surgery to get rid of her Imp, all for Darren's sake, then she was really in love with the former outcast from high school. Not for the last time Mac wished he made better choices when he was younger.

"Quitin, do you still have the glasses?" asked Mac.

"Back at the house."

"Could you bring them to me?"

Quentin nodded and took off.

"What's going on here?" asked Valtteri. "Is Darren right about the charges against you?"

"There are charges against me but I'm no terrorist. They made that all up because I know something they don't want everyone else to know," said Mac.

"What's that?"

"That the military is responsible for the deaths of my family and millions of others in the destruction of Northgate.

There were murmurs coming from the crowd. No one was sure if that could be true or not. They had seen the video of the 'alien' ship. They had heard all the analysts. The two conscious soldiers loudly called Mac a liar. They were innocent. They were too far down the ladder to know the truth.

"Do you have any proof?" asked Valtteri.

"No."

The female soldier spoke up, "Zinger wants to speak to you. Face to face and alone."

She was the only military officer who was still conscious and was the only way Zinger could get to Mac without going through one of the other people there with an Imp. What did Zinger expect to accomplish with all this talk? There was no way he was going to talk Mac into anything from a distance.

"I'll take it in the shuttle," Mac gave his gun to the mayor and then went in the shuttle.

The console beeped and an image of Zinger popped up.

"You cause me grief everywhere you go," said Zinger. "Why can't you get things done smoothly? Move with the grain for once."

"Leave these people alone," said Mac.

Zinger waved him off, "I have no idea what you're talking about and it doesn't matter. I need your help."

Mac laughed, "You murdered my family."

"I'm asking for your help to defeat a common foe. Our ships can't get past the gas. We need to know how you got your powers. We need you to come here and help us transform our soldiers."

"You're on Ronos."

"Of course. This is where you learned to destroy those alien swarms. Why wouldn't we come here?"

"Talking to you is such a waste of time."

Mac disconnected and then got up to leave. There was someone else in the room. It was Jace Michaels.

"You left me behind and had no intention of taking me to Ronos," said Jace.

"I don't understand why you think I'm going to take you to Ronos. You're one of the aliens trying to kill all of us. Helping you is like putting a knife in everyone's back," said Mac.

"Don't generalize or assume that we are all of one big hive mind. I don't assume you are all mass murderers and liars because of what Zinger did."

"You're telling me you're not a spy? You're a *good* bad guy?"

"I'm telling you I don't care about you humans or what you do. I exist so I can get to Ronos. If you help me get there then we're allies. If you try to stop me then we're enemies."

"I need to know what happens when you get there."

"It's our home and you know as well as anyone that it has healing powers. None of us want to be swarms anymore. When we get to Ronos I won't have to emulate this human body."

"We?"

"Me and you. Our people don't care about being popular. We don't have status. We don't seek wealth. All of us are focused on only one thing. Reaching home. Reaching Ronos. That's all. Our whole culture is centered on that. We've been traveling for thousands of years. For as long as I can remember."

"When your ships break down then you abduct whole civilizations and use their ships to travel and use their bodies as emulators."

"It's how we survive. It's the only way," said Jace.

"It won't end when you get to Ronos."

"But until we know what happens next it doesn't do any good to plan ahead."

"Why should I take you there?" asked Mac.

"I'll help you save these people. I'll help you take them to Ronos and change them. These are people you trust, right? It's better to change these people than Zinger's soldiers."

"You realize that's helping us try to win the war."

"Then that should help you realize how important this is and how desperate I am to get to that planet," said Jace.

Mac thought about it. He wasn't even sure exactly how to get back to Ronos. When it was quiet outside, in his mind he could feel the faint pull but it wasn't a specific direction. It was nothing but a pull to move from where he was. The *Terwillegar*'s crew said that they felt the pull while in the Nelson Nebula. That would be on the star charts. Mac could go there and then follow the pull. Once they arrived they would have to deal with Zinger. How many ships did Zinger have with him?

Mac walked to the door. None of it mattered if Jace got to Ronos and used its power against them.

"You've been lying to me this whole time. How can I trust you?" said Mac.

Jace started to fade into a cloud but didn't move to attack.

There is a familiar face out there that you haven't noticed yet. She is one of us. She is the one that cannot be trusted. She has two of our soldiers with her and they are here to find a way to kill you for what you did to our ships. Hopefully you learn to trust me before they complete their mission, the alien said in Mac's mind.

Young Narrad looked out at the people who had been a part of his life. These were his friends, teachers, employers, babysitters, teammates, classmates. They were some of the best people he knew. They deserved more than being target practice for the military trying to cover up its own sins.

But which of them wanted him dead?

Chapter 9
Too Many To Count

A day later Phillip had a new awareness of his own stamina. At first he would shift his weight and lean out of habit. Then he stood absolutely still to see how long he could do it. It turned out he could do it for hours and hours on end. His body was in no need of a new supply of energy. He wasn't hungry or tired. It was so strange to stay so still while having a conversation with Ryan and Jazlyn to figure out what was going on.

What kind of ship are we waiting for? asked Ryan.

I'm not sure exactly, said Jazlyn.

What do you mean?

Have you thought about how weird it is that the aliens speak the same language as us?

Ryan was embarrassed that he hadn't thought about it. Phillip had.

I figured mind speaking worked as a translator. We hear the message in the language that we understand the best, said Phillip.

That's what I figured. What I'm trying to say is that they told me what kind of ship was coming but there was no direct translation. There was the hint of sleeping or hibernation or preservation or something. It was weird. Like getting a bunch of words all at once. My brain couldn't get it quite right and kept changing my mind on what the word meant.

At the end of the day a message came to them from an unknown source. It was a female voice, or at least a voice that was more feminine than the rest they had heard so far. Did the aliens have men and women? How did swarm clouds reproduce?

The ship has arrived. Begin the preservation process.

The three humans were worried now. The general was still in the mix and he still knew that they weren't aliens.

What does preservation process mean? asked Ryan.

Does it mean they are being turned into emulators? asked Jazlyn.

I don't know, said Phillip. *But we need more time. We need to make sure the general isn't emulated.*

The three aliens looked up at the ceiling so Phillip, Ryan, and Jazlyn did the same. There had to be some mental commands going on but they didn't know what they were. Phillip made sure to watch what was supposed to happen so that it wouldn't look suspicious if he couldn't tell machines what to do through mind speak. Despite the ominous sound of *preservation process* he needed to do it to keep his cover.

The ceiling started to ripple and turn to liquid. Instead of many little drips one long one formed. When it had lengthened enough to almost reach the ground the liquid look vanished and the drip became solid metal. It was a long metal arm with three joints and a pointed end, similar to the arms used to collect and separate the prisoners, except it didn't have the metal claws on the end. The needle point was unnerving. None of the soldiers were sitting now. They knew something bad was about to happen.

There were four arms fully formed and more on the way. None of them had been conjured by Phillip. He concentrated on the ceiling and tried to call one down. What was he supposed to do? Think really hard about it? He didn't even know what they were called. He looked over at Jazlyn. She was glaring at the ceiling. It must have been hard to concentrate with all the noises in her head. Ryan didn't look like he was doing any better either. Phillip closed his eyes. None of the real aliens were doing that but he needed to concentrate on what he was doing. He didn't know how to call them so he tried picturing it in his mind.

Holy! said Ryan.

Phillip snapped out of it and saw that the number of arms now hovering over the frightened prisoners had doubled.

Is that because of me? he asked.

It happened after you closed your eyes. Were you praying or something? said Ryan.

No.

Well, whatever it was it worked.

Now they were about to find out what they had done. The needle arms started sticking into the prisoners. They cried out when the needle points stuck inside them. The sites were random — arm, leg, stomach, and one guy even got it in the head. He started screaming and his skin turned a horrible green color. Were they being injected with something or was something being sucked out of them? The guy who got it in the head stopped screaming but his eyes remained wide open. His head was enlarged especially where the needle went in. They had to be getting injected with something.

This didn't look good. The general hadn't been injected yet but it was only a matter of time. There were still aliens in the room but Phillip needed to do something to get the general out of there. He left where he was standing and started walking through the crowd of captive soldiers.

Wait! said one of the purple aliens.

Phillip stopped but didn't say anything.

What are you doing?

Transporting the prisoners to the emulators, said Phillip, hoping that was an appropriate answer.

Have you not been a part of this process before?

Not for a long time.

We must preserve them before we can use their flesh for anchoring purposes. They will be emulated once we return with the fleet. Back to your position.

It sounded like the general's secrets were safe for now. Phillip went back to where he was standing. The conversation between him and the alien had been private. Jazlyn and Ryan wanted to know what happened.

They aren't being emulated now. But I think we should still stay with the general. He will lead us right where we need to go. Stick to the plan, said Phillip.

The general was one of the last to be stuck. He didn't struggle. He knew there was no point; if he tried anything he was as good as dead. While the needle pushed the mystery substance into him and his skin turned a sickening green he did not look away from Phillip and the others. If this was his last waking moment then he was going down with a lot of questions. He wasn't saying any of the questions out loud so he must have trusted that they knew what they were doing.

Once the needle arms were done, they all retracted into the ceiling. The prisoners were on the ground. The aliens started walking to the other side of the room and through another hidden door.

Phillip cut through the crowd and made sure to walk right past the general. Quickly, he crouched down and checked for a pulse. It was there. It was weak but it was still there. Plus, he could see the general's chest moving up and down. He was still alive. Hopefully whatever happened to these people would stop them from dying of starvation or dehydration. They had already gone at least one day with no food.

Jazlyn and Ryan were waiting for him back in the hall. It was more crowded than it was before and crowded with more than human emulators. There was a guy with a head growing out of his head, the first head had the mouth and the second head had the eyes. It also had black leathery skin and yellow teeth. Two heads was walking with a giant dog that had a tongue that would hang to the floor for a moment and then retract back into its mouth. It also had feathers on the back half of it. Was that thing intelligent life? Phillip wanted to ask it a question but he wasn't sure what was appropriate. There was one freaky alien after another. There was one brawny, scaly, Cyclops-looking monster that was so tall when he walked the hallway had to grow around him. This ship was made for the awkwardly proportioned.

No one has told us to do anything else and those purple aliens took off. What should we do? asked Ryan.

Let's open another door and wait in a room until something happens, said Jazlyn. She had her eye closed still. A headache. Phillip wondered if he had done something horrible by asking her to come with them. She stood by the wall and was probably trying to make a door appear but nothing was happening. Phillip stepped in and conjured a door almost immediately. It was easy because he knew what a door was and what it was called unlike the needle arms in the other room.

They went inside and waited. Phillip thought up some chairs for them to sit on.

What are we waiting for? asked Ryan.

I don't really know, said Phillip.

Jazlyn spoke up. It was better for her to be out of the crowd. She didn't look as flustered anymore.

I can still hear the others, but it's easier to not be around them. I keep hearing the same word over and over again. Returning. We are going to join the rest of the fleet. It's where they turn people into emulators, said Jazlyn.

Then we wait, said Phillip.

Something is happening, said Jazlyn.

The rest of them kept still letting her have the silence she needed to hear better. By now they knew to do what she wanted because for some reason the new blood affected her differently. Differently, not better. Because she could hear everything that was being said around her but she couldn't filter it to tune into only one conversation at a time. It was a jumble of noise if the group around her was too big and if everyone talked at once.

The look on her face was strained. Her hands moved to her ears but that wasn't going to keep the mind speak out of her head. None of the guys knew what to do. Phillip broke the silence first.

What's happening? Are you okay?

A bit of a dumb question because she obviously wasn't okay. But she did manage to squeak out a few more mind spoken words.

There's...so...many...

They needed to find out what was going on. Phillip left Ryan with the pained Jazlyn and left the room. There were a lot of people in the hallway but that's not what was causing her problem. All the aliens in the hallway were looking at the wall opposite the door he had walked out of. The wall had turned transparent. Phillip didn't know that was possible but apparently someone looked at the wall, thought window and it appeared. Outside the window he could see the collector ship had joined with the rest of the alien fleet.

There were more ships in one place than he had ever seen. If he were to take all the ships he had ever seen in his entire life until now and put them in one place they would still fall short of the number he was looking at now. No wonder Jazlyn was going crazy now. She was in range of millions or more likely billions of conversations all at once.

But he wasn't worried about her right then. Looking out the window there were so many ships it was hard to tell where one ended and another began. He couldn't even see space or stars between the vessels. It was dizzying.

The aliens could trounce the humans anytime they wanted. It was as easy as overwhelming them with numbers or even simply parking the fleet between earth and the sun. No light would get through. This wasn't about them going to war. They were after something else.

Phillip did his best to act like those around him but what he was seeing made him want to vomit. Inside he hoped that he would at least survive long enough to find what he came for and get out of there.

It was a long shot.

Billions of aliens against four humans.

Phillip called for the others to come out and see what they were up against. Jazlyn was able to keep it together enough to not look suspicious but it wouldn't have mattered much anyway because the aliens were busy watching out the window.

Are those all ships? asked Ryan.

Yeah, it's the fleet, said Phillip.

How many are there? They must outnumber us a thousand to one if each ship has the same population density as this one. Why are they fighting us? They could take us out at any point.

I figure they must be looking for something.

Yeah, didn't Mac say something about them wanting to go to Ronos.

I've never heard of it.

Me either. I don't know why they want to go there or what happens when they get there but Mac was very interested in making sure that didn't happen.

Hmm, Phillip thought it through. *It doesn't really make sense that they can't find that planet. It's like they aren't even trying. With how many ships they have here they could have sent a thousand ships in every direction to find it. What are they waiting for? Why are they teasing us with war?*

What do we do now? asked Ryan.

Same as always. We need to stay with the general and the others and follow them to the other emulators, said Phillip.

Do you think they all go to the same place?

We'll find out soon either way.

They all stood there for a while. Phillip wanted to see what the aliens would do next. The collector ship was still moving around the fringe of the fleet. Soon other collector ships could be seen. It was easier to spot them. They had a smooth dome without even a seam or rivet. They stuck out from all the others. Phillip noticed that other like ships grouped together. The whole fleet was a hodgepodge of weird looking vessel designs. Right beside the collector ships were several red metal ships that didn't look like any kind of aesthetic planning had been used to construct them. Metal was welded together randomly until a ship was formed. Each one was different, made from whatever parts were available. The only thing that made them similar was the red metal used to create them. What alien species had been wiped out to get these ugly ships?

The collector ship they were on wasn't stopping to join the other collector ships, which numbered in the hundreds. It was moving somewhere else in the fleet.

After they passed the collector ships the aliens around Phillip started to move. They became less fascinated with what they were doing and more interested in being prepared for where they were going. No one was standing still anymore except for the three of them. The wall stopped being a window and all they could see was the familiar gray that was everywhere on this ship.

Let's get back to the general, said Phillip. *We don't want to lose him.*

Before they could do anything all three of them got a message from the fourth member of their party.

Follow me, said Nelson. His voice was quiet and distant. Where was he? How far of a reach did mind speak have? He had to still be on the ship somewhere.

Nelson? Where are you? asked Phillip.

There was no vocal answer but Phillip thought that he could see something in his mind. The image reminded him of the collector ship in that it was completely smooth and devoid of imperfections, but it didn't look at all like a ship to Phillip. It looked more like a silver metal ball. For all he knew it was the size of a baseball because there was nothing else to compare its size to.

What on Earth was that? asked Ryan.

You saw it too? asked Phillip.

Yes, but I don't know what it was. Did it come from Nelson?

I think it's a ship. I think he wants us to go there, said Jazlyn.

Why would he want us to go there? We have to find the emulators with the general, said Phillip.

Maybe he did already. Maybe that's why he wants us to go there, said Ryan.

Phillip tried calling out to his nephew to confirm Ryan's suspicion but there was no response. What was stopping him from talking back to them? After Phillip tried again there was another picture message: the same silver smooth ball. For some reason Nelson couldn't talk but he could send pictures.

Can we trust Nelson? Is this ball thing important enough to ditch the general? asked Jazlyn.

There has to be a reason Nelson wants us to come there. He knows our mission and I don't think he would call us there for sightseeing, said Ryan.

I agree. My nephew is immature but he's not dumb enough to waste our time. I think we should try and find him now, said Phillip.

Then let's do it, said Ryan.

But we can't leave General Roy.

Then let's not do it.

One of us should stay behind. Stay with the general and keep us updated on where he is and where he's going, said Phillip.

I thought you said we needed to stick together, said Jazlyn.

It doesn't matter. It's more important that we do what we can to keep the general's secret. The best way to do that is keep our cover right up until he gets taken to be emulated. To do that we need someone with him at all times.

Then it should be me, said Ryan. *I'm less likely to draw attention to myself than Jazlyn, and as the leader of this mission it shouldn't be you, Phillip.*

You sure? said Phillip.

Yeah. I'm not looking forward to being all alone, but we will still be able to communicate through mind speech, right?

Right. Then Jazlyn and I will go find Nelson and come back here.

Once they had made the choice they all wanted to see the picture that Nelson had sent. Phillip found out that they didn't have to wait for Nelson to send it again. If they concentrated they could conjure the exact image back into their mind's eye. It was a lot like having an Imp. It creeped Phillip out but also helped him realize they hadn't found the true potential of their new bodies and abilities. Yet.

When Nelson had first sent the message it had felt so foreign and confusing that Phillip's mind had dismissed it before he could get a really good look at it. But now that he was willingly studying it, more details were springing up and certain things were so obvious now that he couldn't believe he didn't notice them before.

For starters the ball was in space. There were stars in the black background. He hadn't seen them before because he was so distracted by the ball. Obviously if there were stars then the object wasn't a ball for some cosmic alien sport. It was a space ship, probably made from the same technology as the collector ships because there were no imperfections.

I think it runs on mind speak like the collector ships, said Phillip.

Let's talk in privacy, said Jazlyn. *Somewhere where I can act like a human again.*

The strain of hearing everything was getting to her. Her mind speak voice was choppy and she had to force each word out. Her volume was high, like she was talking over all the voices in her head.

Phillip called a door and found an empty room for the three of them. When they were inside, Jazlyn curled up on the floor in the fetal position with her hands on her ears. There's no way that helped but maybe it made her feel better.

What are we going to do about her? asked Ryan.

I don't know, said Phillip.

She was only outside for a few minutes and she could barely hold it together. How is she supposed to help you? Maybe we should leave her here with me.

Let's think about this first. We need to figure out where Nelson is. What do you see? asked Phillip.

I see a ship out in space.

That's our first clue. It's out in space. Not surrounded by any ships.

It can't be with the fleet, said Ryan.

That's right. We're going to need a ship to get to it.

Ryan shook his head. Phillip knew what he was thinking. Now they had to steal a ship and start running off to wherever Nelson was. It had to be because he had found the emulator generators.

Don't worry about the ship, Ryan, I have an idea.

Okay, but what's your idea about her?

Jazlyn spoke up from the floor. I'll be fine. *If you can get me on a ship then we'll be fine as long as we are getting away from the fleet — from the voices.*

Are you ready to go now? asked Phillip.

No, I need more time.

Ryan, stay here with her, I'll be right back.

Where are you going? asked Ryan.

To get a ship, said Phillip.

He had a fantastic idea in his mind about how this would work, but there was a good chance he was living a pipe dream. The first problem was finding the room where the general and the others were.

Phillip was wandering the adaptive hallways of the collector ship. It was impossible to retrace his steps because everything was always changing. The big hallway he remembered from before was only big because there was a ton of people in it.

He also kept getting distracted by the people he passed. There was one guy who walked on five legs and who wasn't taller than Phillip's waist. The creature's head wasn't human. Its head and torso looked like the same thing. He wasn't sure how it worked. Instead of looking for the room with the general he was looking at all the different aliens walking around him.

It felt like he had been walking for an hour. He had already opened a few different doors that didn't lead anywhere productive. Half the rooms were empty. The other half had aliens in them doing alien things that he didn't understand.

The last door he opened had a purple alien, although there was no way to know if it was the same purple alien from before, and a guy that looked like a shaggy bear walking on two legs. They were using a computer console. Phillip wasn't interested but he noticed something before he closed the door. The two creatures stepped away from the console and it melted back into the wall. When the two aliens walked past Phillip out of the room, he stepped inside and studied the wall where the computer console had been before.

At a casual glance it looked like any other wall, but he knew that wasn't right. There was something else there. He had been trying to get to the room with General Roy and the other prisoners in it. Not because he wanted to try and save them but because he wanted access to the liquid-like ceiling in that room. Now he was seeing that same liquid consistency in the wall he was standing in front of, but there wasn't enough there for him to do what he wanted. The wall only had a square that was a couple feet across.

He was going to use it for something else. He looked at the patch and thought a word in his head over and over.

Map. Map. Map.

It only took three times for a console to show up again. The display was an outline of the ship — a map — precisely what he asked for. He could see the hallways and rooms shrinking and moving throughout the ship. Most of the rooms were moving. There were some like the collecting and sorting rooms at the bottom of the ship that had to stay in one place, but for the most part the rooms shifted freely around the ship.

There were more hallways surrounding the outside of the ship where the ship wasn't as flexible. Getting to a room was easy. If it already existed, all he had to do was use mind speech to bring it to him. A door would open and the room would be there. When he thought up empty rooms he wasn't opening random doors he was creating new rooms.

There was something else that set the rooms apart from each other. Certain rooms had more potential. The one he was in right now could only conjure computer terminals or other small things. Rooms like the one the general was in could do much more. When Phillip first got on the ship it looked like anyone could create a door anywhere but that wasn't true. There were assigned spots where the metal was malleable. Phillip could see it more easily now that he knew what he was looking for. The changes were subtle and hard to describe, but it was impossible for him not to notice them anymore.

He put the computer console back in the wall and walked to the wall where he could create a door.

I want to go to the prisoners.

The door opened and the crew of the *Bears Paw* was there. There were no aliens so he was able to get a closer look at what had happened to them. He was worried at first because they looked greener than they had before. The whites of their eyes were even an unsettling green. Luckily, not all of them had their eyes open.

Phillip found the general. He still had a pulse but he wasn't breathing. That shouldn't have been possible. When he touched the general's skin it felt incredibly warm and sticky.

He felt like he could risk using his voice.

"General?" he whispered in the man's ear.

There was no response so he tried yelling at him in mind speak.

General Roy! Can you hear me!

Nothing. Probably because Ryan was the only one who could mind speak to the human prisoners. Phillip left the general alone and looked up at the ceiling. Like Jazlyn had a gift of overhearing and Nelson had a gift for sending pictures — something none of the others could do — Phillip had the gift of being able to easily communicate with the ship to get what he wanted. Closing his eyes, like he'd done with the needle arms, he pictured what he wanted and repeated the name over and over again in his mind. When he opened his eyes he smiled. It had worked.

Floating above him was a HAAS3. Normally they didn't have interplanetary drives but he pictured one that did so he hoped that translated in the new creation. The room was three times as big now to accommodate the ship. There was no way that he was going to fly this thing down the hallway. He could easily bring the room with Ryan and Jazlyn to him but that wasn't going to get the shuttle out of there.

He kept his eyes open this time. Over and over in his mind he thought the same thing.

Smaller.

He had no idea how concentrated the liquid metal could get, but every time he thought the word, the ship got smaller until it was so small it could fit in the palm of his hand. How could he not be impressed with himself? Now they had a ship that was made out of the same living metal that controlled the collector ship. Once they were flying in it they could use their mind speaking abilities to make it do things a real HAAS3 would never be able to do.

Getting off the ship was easy. Phillip and Jazlyn said goodbye to Ryan and then went back to the collecting and sorting room. It was empty. Phillip put the miniature ship out where all the people had been floating before and ordered it to grow back to normal size. Then the two of them got inside and they thought one last command at the collector ship to turn off the field keeping them from falling out into space.

And then they were gone.

Since it was just the two of them, they decided it was easier to talk instead of mind speak. For Jazlyn, it helped to block out aliens' thoughts if she could hear an actual human voice.

"This looks like the real thing," said Jazlyn.

"I know. I wasn't sure it would work," said Phillip.

"Are you thinking about it right now? Like if you stop thinking about it is this going to turn into a gooey ball of liquid metal again?"

"I guess not, because I stopped thinking about it. Maybe once it hits a solid state it doesn't have to be controlled by me anymore."

"Is it still malleable?"

"Let's try after we clear the fleet," said Phillip.

That was going to be a while. The fleet covered a lot of space. Phillip thought they were on the edge of it but it kept going and going. More than once he thought they were going in circles. Jazlyn occupied her time by looking out the window at all the different ships but even that got repetitive after a while. There were so many and they were so different that the inconsistency got to be overwhelming.

When they broke free of the fleet, Phillip used his mind speaking powers again and called up a map again. He thought 'star chart' and 'Nelson.' A screen popped up showing them and the fleet behind them, but there was no Nelson indicated.

"Try thinking about the ball ship," said Jazlyn.

He did and the ball ship appeared on the screen. It was close.

"Interesting," said Jazlyn.

"What?" asked Phillip.

"It kind of looks like it's far enough away from the fleet to not pick up any extra noise. Not real noise of course but thinking noise.

"Do you hear anything about what's going on in there?" Phillip asked Jazlyn.

"No. No mind speaking at all," said Jazlyn.

"Why would there be no talking? Do you think it has to do with the emulators?"

"I don't know, but I don't have a good feeling about things. This looks like the same technology as the collector ships, so it should run on mind talk."

"Maybe we should try communicating with them," said Phillip.

That would be the easiest way to get to the bottom of things, but there was still something unsettling about it all. Why would Nelson tell them to go there? In the end that was what had convinced Phillip. His nephew was young, immature, recklessly adventurous, but he wouldn't call them all there for nothing. The emulator generators had to be there. If it all worked out then Ryan and the general would get here eventually.

Open docking bay doors, Phillip said to the ship.

Doors opened immediately and then two beams of light enveloped the ship and pulled it towards its destination. The docking bay was small and there were no other ships inside. There were, however, several human looking aliens standing outside the HAA3 when they got out. The aliens looked mad. Exaggeratedly mad. Aliens didn't normally show any emotion so it was very weird to see them looking angry.

"They have guns that look like ours," said Phillip.

There was no point in delaying it any longer. The two of them opened the door of the fake HAAS3 and Phillip led the way out.

There was a man in a uniform that Phillip didn't recognize, but he was clearly the leader of the aliens gathered because he stepped forward while the soldiers on either side of him held guns pointed at the newcomers.

"Which ones of you makes the noises?" he asked. He was short and pudgy. Each 's' had the tip of his tongue poking out from between his teeth.

Phillip and Jazlyn looked at each other. What was he talking about? Mind speak? Why was this ship deliberately isolating itself from any noise? This was also the first time that he had ever heard an alien talk out loud. It was awkward. The aliens words were a little off and his voice had a slight buzzing sound to it.

Phillip wasn't going to let Jazlyn take the fall for him. He put his hand up.

"That was me. No one told me I wasn't allowed to make noise."

"Comes with us," said the alien.

The two guards with guns stood on either side of Phillip and prodded him along. Jazlyn was left behind.

This was the most alien enemy ship Phillip had been on, only because it was the most normal. Even though he was sure it was all run on mind speak, all the doors had knobs and hinges, all the aliens talked to each other with their mouths and broken Earth Common language, and instead of using swarm attacks as weapons the guards escorting him to wherever he was going had guns. He had never seen an alien with a gun before.

Everything about this was unusual. Especially the way they were walking. They were all moving at different paces. Some were even running. None of the movements looked natural. One guy swung his arms so high he almost hit himself in the back of the head. Another guy looked down at his feet and made sure they moved when he wanted them to. It was like he was practicing walking.

Maybe these aliens were getting used to new emulators. That would explain some of it but something still felt off to Phillip. Why were all the emulators human, and why was it against the rules to use mind speak but not to talk out loud?

The hallway they were in curved around ever so slightly that he could tell they were near the outside of the ship. They walked for so long it felt like they were on the verge of completing a lap. They came to some stairs and moved to another hallway and started moving back around the curve the other way.

"So, where are we going?" said Phillip.

"To keeps you quiet," said one of the guards.

He was a stocky Asian fellow in a Spacer uniform. There was no name tag, which was too bad because Phillip felt like he knew the man. As a doctor on the *Bears Paw* a lot of injured soldiers had come and gone. It was very likely Phillip had treated the young man before he was captured.

Unfortunately, that was the one thing he didn't see as they walked. There were no emulators or green skinned prisoners like the general and the thousands of others who had been taken. They stopped walking. One of the guards opened a door and pushed Phillip inside. They closed the door leaving him there.

"Let me guess," said a familiar voice. "You were noisy when you shouldn't have been."

"Nelson!"

The room wasn't very big and only had two uncomfortable metal chairs in it. There was a single light in the ceiling illuminating the bland gray walls. Nelson was lying on the floor with his fingers interlocked behind his head. He looked comfortable and satisfied with his position, not injured in the slightest.

"If you called us here to rescue you, then I'm going to club you," said Phillip.

"Nice to see you too, Uncle."

"Is this where the emulator generators are?"

"No."

"Then why did you call us?"

"We need to blow up this ship," said Nelson.

Chapter 10
There is a Plan

Mac exited the shuttle after talking with Jace. Quentin was standing with the surgical glasses next to the soldier. Scott and the mayor were standing nearby as well with their weapons ready. Mr. Smith was still missing but probably somewhere in the crowd. The crowd had spread out a little but everyone was still there. They were talking in small groups about what was going on. Darren and Clarissa were nearby. Mac walked over to them. Was Darren the one who wanted to kill Mac? They hadn't ever really gotten along and that was mostly Mac's fault. It would be normal for Darren to have ill feelings towards him.

But Jace had said she. Whoever was out to cause Mac harm was a woman. Could it be Clarissa? Could he even trust Jace's warning?

"I know you don't have any reason to trust me or even like me, and it may sound hollow right now for me to say that I'm sorry for being a jerk when I should have been your friend," said Mac.

"You're right. It is hollow," said Darren.

"I have something to offer you. Clarissa, you want to get rid of your Imp, right? And you think the surgery is going to be risky and invasive?"

"It is, isn't it?" said Clarissa.

"Come with me. I'll show you a better way."

Mac led Darren and Clarissa over to Quentin. He showed them the glasses.

"It's actually very easy. I got mine removed in about five minutes. This burns it out of your eyes so that it can't work anymore."

"Did you say burn?" asked Clarissa.

"It's harmless. Quentil got it done as well."

"Whose Quentil?"

"He means me. Quentin."

"Why haven't we heard of this before?" asked Darren.

"Because the Imp companies don't want fence sitters to know how easy it is to get rid of their Imps. The more Imps that are online the more information and control the government has," Mac said.

"There is no way she is going to put those on. What if she goes blind?" said Darren.

Mac was prepared for this argument. He had Quentin and the math teacher hold the gray-haired soldier and then put the glasses on him. There was a lot of struggling at first because the soldier had no idea what was going on. As the process moved along he struggled less. Clarissa made a yucky face at the smell of burning that was in the air, but after the glasses came off it was obvious that the man was okay except for not having an Imp. She was starting to seriously think about putting the glasses on.

"Why are you helping me?" asked Clarissa.

"It's the right thing to do. And after how I treated Darren, it's the least I can do."

Clarissa cautiously put on the glasses to burn her Imp out. Darren was by her side the entire time and demanded to know what was going on. She told him about the spray, the tiny arms, the heads-up-display, and eventually about counting the bunnies to test her vision.

She blinked several times after the glasses came off. He couldn't be sure but to Mac it also looked like she was trying to access her Imp. She couldn't of course. Not anymore. The smile she gave the man she was engaged to was worth it all, but Mac had to try one more thing.

"Darren, do you want to come with me?" asked Mac.

"Come with you where?" asked Darren.

"Back to the planet that made me like this. I was able to take out that shuttle because I underwent a transformation."

Darren rolled his eyes, "Do you hear what you sound like?"

"Zinger destroyed Northgate because in his crazy mind that was somehow going to galvanize the people into supporting the war effort. While I was investigating that, me and another person, his wife —" Mac pointed at Scott "— found a way to change ourselves to be immune to the alien attacks."

"Are you recruiting me to fight in the war?"

"Yes. Both of you."

"Have you lost your mind?"

"Zinger wants to give this power to his own people. The people who are responsible for destroying Northgate. The only way we are going to win this war without losing ourselves is if good people like you and Clarissa are the ones who get the power."

"It sounds like you are looking for an army. Who else are you wanting to join your cause?" asked Darren.

"To start I was thinking of every willing person here."

"Well, try to come up with a better pitch than secret planets."

"Will you come with me?"

"We'll think about it."

The two left to go talk it over. Their conversation wasn't private. Quentin, Scott, Valtteri, and the three soldiers were all there listening. After Darren and Clarissa moved on they all looked to Mac for an explanation. There was still a crowd behind them. Mac looked for any signs of a threat. There were plenty of reasons for everyone there to be angry at him. Before tonight Passage had been a relatively peaceful place. Now the military was attacking them and it was all Mac's fault. They were all angry with him, but who wanted to kill him? He couldn't make eye contact with everyone. Whoever it was could be standing in the back out of sight, waiting to make her move.

"It's the only way we are going to win the war. We need as many people as we can get," Mac said to his audience.

"How is jumping really high going to win the war?" asked Scott.

"Me and Lynn went through the same changes. We don't need to breathe anymore. We can survive the cold of space. We don't need to eat. We have super speed and strength. When I was on the planet that made us this way I could even heal myself. There is a gas in the atmosphere that gives me my powers. What you saw tonight wasn't anywhere close to my potential. I'm a bit depleted now. We also have the ability to talk to each other with our minds."

"You can talk to Lynn? Right now, with your mind?"

"Yes…Well, no. She's not answering right now. But I have done it before and it's how the aliens talk and operate their ships. Having mind speech, she and I can fight them more effectively."

"Does that mean she's dead?"

"No. All it means is that she can't answer right now."

"And you want to recruit us to fight in your war?" asked Valtteri.

"It's not my war. It's our war. I came from the front. Without more people like me we are going to lose. Without us it's only a matter of time before they make it to Earth. At the very least, even if you don't want to fight, you should come with me for your own protection."

"We aren't warriors."

"I know. But we have to try. Can you talk to these people? Try and get them to agree to come with us?"

Valtteri shook his head, "I'm just the mayor. I can't ask them to enlist."

The mayor left without saying anything else.

"What about you two? Will you be coming with me?" Mac asked Quentin and Scott.

"Absolutely. Adventure is becoming my new drug of choice," said Quentin.

"I'm going to wherever Lynn is," said Scott.

"Good. Then it's us and hopefully Mr. Smith whenever he shows up."

"What about Jace?"

"He's not coming."

As word of the secret planet and the transformation spread around the crowd, the distance between Mac and the crowd got bigger and bigger. They looked more angry than frightened. Had he lost their trust?

Everyone was so focused on Mac and the crazy stories he was telling that no one noticed people were going missing. The time was moving on to midnight. Some people had gone home to bed. There weren't any more children around. However those weren't the people who had gone missing.

Mr. And Mrs. Parkington had walked off into the dark to talk about what they had heard. Initially they dismissed it as ramblings from a bad drug trip from a kid who had given into the world and gotten an Imp. But there was something encouraging about what Mac was saying. What did he have to gain personally? All he was asking for was for them to help themselves, really. He acted like he genuinely wanted to make things better for them.

The two elderly people didn't think for a second that they were going to fight a war, but they wanted to talk about whether they should support Mac's ideas even if they couldn't physically fight the aliens.

They never got a chance to say a word to each other. Before they even got to their destination they were drugged and dragged into the dark without a sound.

The street was still full of people. In the center of the crowd, in the cul-de-sac with the trees and broken HAAS3 shuttle, were Mac, his friends, and the prisoners.

The soldier in the middle, the one who had his Imp taken away, looked bored out of his mind. He kept trying to start a conversation with people around him but no one was listening. Mac and the others were busy waiting to see what the rest of the people were going to decide about coming to Ronos. The news was traveling quickly. Some people looked at Mac like he was crazy. Others took a couple steps closer to him.

"Zinger keeps trying to contact you," the woman soldier said. "He says you need to come to Ronos."

"Yeah, I know."

"He's saying some pretty outrageous things."

"He always does."

"Stuff about Northgate, you and Lynn, and the war. He keeps going through me because you don't have an Imp."

"So are you saying you want me to get rid of your Imp for you?"

"Yes, but only after you or your friends are done listening to it."

Mac wasn't going to listen to Zinger anymore, the asinine ranting of a man who was bent on saving humanity by killing innocent people. Then Mac realized what the woman was trying to tell him.

"What's your name?" asked Mac.

"Tayma Alon."

"No rank?"

"Not anymore."

It was easy to sync up Tayma's feed to the shuttle's loud speaker. Quentin had also lived in the world of the Imps long enough to know how to broadcast it while the person who was sending it, Zinger, still thought that it was a private message. Mac, Tayma, and Quentin were inside the shuttle. Mac made an announcement over the loud speaker before showing them what the General was saying.

"By now most of you have heard about what I'm proposing. That I'm going to Ronos and I'm willing and wanting to take as many of you as want to go. When we get there, there will be a transformation that will make you like me. You get power that you never thought possible. You will become weapons in a war.

"This is my plan. Using this power to save us all. But there is another plan. General Zinger wants to give the power to his men. The men who destroyed Northgate. Murderers. He is the one who sent soldiers to Passage to stop me. He thinks that the only way to survive is to make his soldiers powerful like me, but I know he is wrong. There aren't very many of us right now but it doesn't take many. Once we are all changed by the power of Ronos we will be unstoppable and we will be able to find others. We will be the first in an army able to stop the invaders and then stop Zinger."

Even in the shuttle Mac could hear some chortling outside the shuttle. Mac knew how crazy it sounded to form an army out of old people, kids, families, and people who had never even fired a weapon before.

"If you want to know what I'm talking about when I say Zinger needs to be stopped, have a listen to this feed," said Mac.

In the shuttle Mac responded to Zinger and made it seem like they were the only two people in the conversation. As soon as the general had him on the line he opened up. Mac switched channels so that Zinger was blaring over the speakers for everyone to hear.

"You are making a fool out of yourself. The longer you delay the more people will get hurt. Dozens of people here are already burned because you are keeping your secret power to yourself. How many more people are you going to sacrifice? Your choice is very simple. You either help me win this war or the consequences are going to be more extreme than what happened to Northgate. I will figure out how to get through the gas without getting burned and I will win this war. With or without you. I will get it done. If you aren't dead by then I'll punish you and everyone who ever knew you. Every Luddite will be killed. Everyone will be forced to have Imps or they will be killed. You've shown me that giving people a choice is a bad thing. I'll decide what is best for us. Do you understand what I'm saying?"

Mac turned off the feed and left the shuttle. He didn't know what the people on the outside were going to say about what Zinger threatened. Was that going to convince them to join Mac or was it going to convince them that they needed to run and hide or, at the very least, go off and get Imps?

Everyone was looking at him. It was dark outside, but the street lights and the remaining fire from the burning houses cast enough illumination so that everyone's face could be seen.

Valtteri stepped forward.

"I knew your parents. I helped build your house. I know that they didn't deserve to die and neither do we. If there is anything I can do to help preserve what is good in this world then I'll help. But we need to know you have a plan, that you're not sending us off to die."

"I'm not going to send you off anywhere. I'm going to lead you."

Several more people stepped forward. Not everyone did, of course. Some citizens still thought Mac was a crazy person and were even angry at him for bringing such danger to their village. There were enough people that wanted to help that plans were made. Everyone was told only to bring essentials and advised they might not ever come back. They would leave as soon as they had transportation. Mac knew that the military was still out there. They wouldn't be giving up after one attack shuttle was taken down. Their next attack would happen at any moment.

Tayma asked for her Imp to be removed and then asked to come with them. Mac was more than happy to oblige. Recruiting as many real soldiers as they could would be the best. The other two soldiers weren't as cooperative. The one without the Imp was named Steve. The one who Mac had knocked unconscious was named Mikhale.

Steve was being loud and belligerent. They found some rope and kept him tied to the tree outside. No one wanted to listen to him. Mikhale was being quiet but he wasn't about to switch sides either. He couldn't be trusted. They burned out his Imp and tied him to another tree. It was warm outside. They would be fine there overnight.

While they walked back to the house, Mr. Smith showed up.

"Solid job rallying the troops like that, Mac. Too bad you couldn't get everyone," he said.

"Where have you been?"

"Getting things ready."

"Jace is an alien."

"I know."

"What?"

"I found out soon after he got here. I found his emulator generator, kind of by accident. It sucks up a lot of energy and I was trying to see where the energy was all going."

"Where is it?"

"We shouldn't turn it off."

"I don't know how to turn it off. I was going to destroy it," said Mac.

"I think we can trust him," said Mr. Smith.

"But he's one of them."

"He hasn't done anything to earn the label of enemy."

"I'm not taking him to Ronos."

"Do you know what will happen when he gets there?"

"No."

"I think with or without you he is going to make his way to Ronos. If we go there with him then at least we'll know what happens to the aliens when they get to where they are going. Maybe we can find a way to control the situation."

"If we can believe Jace, then even they don't know," said Mac.

"Exactly. Right now it's one guy. We can handle one guy better than millions of people," said the only man from Passage with an Imp.

"So what do you think will happen when Jace gets to Ronos?"

"I think we'll find out where his loyalties really lie. Right now he seems okay with helping the enemy, but we'll see what happens after he gets what he wants."

Mr. Smith kept walking to his house but Mac stopped and grabbed him by the arm. "I know you're talking like the decision has already been made, but it's not your decision to make. We cannot let Jace get to Ronos."

"Are you sure that's what you want?"

"I don't think it's a good idea."

"Hope you're making the right call."

They started walking again to Mr. Smith's house. There was someone sitting on the front steps. A young girl with long blond hair. She had a smile on her face and her eyes were verging on tears when she saw Mac, like he was a canteen full of cold water in the middle of the desert. He was everything she needed.

Mac forced a smile. The mystery of who wanted to kill him was over. That was not Janelle Stewart. There was a swarm inside her.

"When did she get here?" Mac whispered to Mr. Smith. They both stopped walking.

"Not long after Jace. He's not with her. So he claims," said Mr. Smith.

"What is she doing here?"

"If you are the most powerful weapon against the aliens then they are probably here to kill you."

"They?"

"Two others came with her but we haven't seen much of them."

Mac figured they were in swarm form, probably listening to that very conversation. They were probably buzzing around Mac as soon as he got back to Passage.

Janelle got up from where she was sitting and started walking towards them. She was still smiling. Did she really think that Mac was going to fall for this? If she was real then why had it taken her so long to find him? Where was she when he first got there?

"You might want to get out of here," Mac said to Mr. Smith.

"I'll stay. I have some fight in me. You'd be surprised," said Mr. Smith.

Once Janelle was close enough Mac called out to her. "I know what you really are and what you're here to do."

Janelle stopped walking. The loving look was replaced by a surly glare.

"I heard your speech to these pathetic people," said Janelle. "You think you can use them to defeat us? You have no hope. These people aren't warriors and we can't be killed so easily."

"Neither can I," said Mac.

"We'll see about that."

It wasn't Janelle who attacked. There was a rush as an alien in swarm form enveloped Mac and lifted him off the ground. He thrashed and yelled but there was nothing he could do to stop them. He was carried high above Passage and then let go. They were trying to kill him, alright. He landed on the ground and didn't get back up right away. That had taken a lot out of him. He flashed back to the base near Northgate when he had accidentally done the same thing and then thought he had died.

Janelle walked towards him. He had landed near the shuttle where he had given his speech for people to join him.

"It's going to be easier to kill you than I thought," she said. Hearing Janelle say that was so unsettling. It was her voice but he had never heard her so angry and violent. "My people on the front greatly embellished your power."

Mac stood up as the only man in Passage with an Imp attacked. He had pulled out the mailbox from his front yard and charged swinging it. The metal box slammed into Janelle's head with such amazing force that she was forced down onto one knee. The box had crumpled but Mr. Smith was still determined to use it as a weapon.

Janelle reached up and grabbed the post with the mail box connected. She tore it from Mr. Smith's grasp and then used it like a bat to hit him out of the way. The old man flew across the street. Mac didn't want to think about what damage had been done to his friend.

Janelle was walking towards Mac. Two more aliens appeared behind her. Mac recognized them both. He didn't know their names but one was the massive dark-skinned man and the other was a pale middle-aged woman. He had seen both of them on the first collector ship he had been on. On that ship they hadn't been wearing uniforms. The emulators kept the clothes that the people being emulated wore. That meant these were people who had been abducted at the beginning of the war.

Mac remembered one of the last conversations he had with his father who said he had found Janelle. That was possible. But he hadn't found the real girl, only someone pretending to be her. Before the attack on Northgate more than one abductee had returned. That's what his father said. Now Mac knew that they were all swarm spies. All he had to do was find their emulator generators and destroy them.

"You are dangerous to our cause," said Janelle.

"You're going to kill me?" asked Mac.

"You are trying to stop us from reaching our goal."

"I'm one of the few people who know where you're going. I've been there."

"Then you will be killed for disgracing our home with your presence."

Mac looked over at where Mr. Smith had landed in the grass across the street. Was he still alive?

There was no time to waste. Mac got up and ran to his friend. The aliens who had been standing over him looked confused. Why would he run? There was nowhere he could go that they wouldn't find him.

Mac knelt by his Mr. Smith.

"Can you hear me?" he asked.

Mr. Smith opened his eyes, "That was quite the hit, but it didn't do me in."

"We need to find their emulator generators. You did that for Jace, right?"

"You got it."

Mr. Smith sprang up like nothing had happened to him. It was the most amazing thing Mac had seen all day and he had seen some incredible events within the last twenty-four hours. Old men weren't supposed to be that spry after getting a vicious beat down.

The three aliens let the old man go. They didn't know what he was trying to do and didn't consider him to be a threat. They were all in swarm form now. Mac thought that they might be trying to pick him up but he didn't leave the ground. Instead they were forcing themselves into his body. The particles making up the swarm were so small they could penetrate his skin. They were trying to take control of his body and they were succeeding. No matter how much he thrashed around in an effort to swat them away it was completely futile. They were inside him and the buzzing in his ear was almost deafening.

151

They forced him to his feet. There was a ton of buzzing around his feet as the swarms forced his feet to move. He fought against them but with three of them inside there was nothing he could do. He felt so weak. They were leading him to the HAAS3. Mac tried to force his legs to obey him. The steps slowed slightly but it wasn't significant. Mr. Smith might need more time.

Mac tried to fall over. The aliens were focusing on moving his legs so he was able to toss his own body over on the ground but that didn't stop his feet from moving forwards. Now he looked like he was possessed. His feet were dragging his own body across the ground. One of the aliens left Mac and went to the shuttle. The other two kept dragging him.

Janelle was the swarm in the shuttle. She took human form again as she exited the shuttle. She had a gun in her hand. There wasn't going to be anymore talking. Without wasting any time she pulled the trigger and a laser burned into Mac's chest.

He couldn't believe how much pain he was in. The black man and the pale middle aged woman took form on either side of Janelle. Mac wasn't going to be able to go anywhere. Looking down at his chest he could see his shirt was burned but his chest only looked like it was bruised. He had survived one laser blast. Would he survive the next?

Janelle shot again and again. Each time the laser hit him squarely in the chest. Now he was too weak to even hold himself up. His chest looked like it was going to be permanently bruised after this. It was scarring again. If he had been normal then there would have been blood everywhere. Instead there was torn, exposed, and singed flesh. Mac waited for the next laser to strike. He was on his back looking up at the stars; looking up at where the real Janelle was somewhere.

But the next blast never came. He rolled to look at the aliens but no one was there. The gun was on the ground. Mr. Smith had found the emulators' generators.

Chapter 11
Plunge

At first the pull machine was dark and foreboding. After Lynn had moved away from where Raymond was pounding on the door, she tried to turn on some lights.

Lights.

Nothing.

Turn on the lights.

She tried screaming it in her mind like she had when she was trying to reason with Raymond and had accidentally opened the door to the pull machine, but still the only light came from her.

She walked slowly through the ship. It was evident pretty early on that whatever this structure was, its purpose as a ship was secondary. There were few hallways — not nearly enough for a ship this size. There were no rooms suited to storing and eating food. No sleeping quarters. The few rooms she did find were full of wires and tubes. There were monitors but they weren't powered up. Lynn tried turning them on but couldn't, physically or with her mind. The more she explored the more it was obvious that this was a large, complex machine meant for an unknown purpose.

Even the material it was made out of was unique. Her footsteps weren't echoing or clanking like she was walking on metal. The noise was muted. As she walked she used the light coming off of her body to light up the corridor. The walls were a dark color, maybe black. It was hard to tell in her purple light. The color wasn't the thing that caught her attention. To her the walls felt porous, less like metal and more like rock. She flicked it with her finger.

"Yep. That feels like a rock."

Was this thing made out of rock from Ronos? That made sense. If it were made out of foreign material then it would have burned up in the gas. Even the wire and tubes didn't feel like the plastic or rubber on Earth. This was something else. The workmanship made her more curious than anything.

Something else tugged at the back of her mind. Something about this place felt familiar, but she couldn't quite place it. Whenever she felt anything mysterious yet familiar she always went back to her childhood and what her parents told her about Grenor. They never did go back to Grenor and she never had any siblings, which was fine with her. The only real family distractions she ever had growing up, besides when her best friend died and when her dad got in a hover car accident when she was in university, were the occasional awkward conversations about Grenor and the power that her family was responsible for.

The stories of her past occupied the back of her mind as she wandered to where the wires and tubes led. So far she had seen no evidence of power to the ship, but she knew that couldn't be right. Without power the pull wouldn't work and the light wouldn't be pulsing. It was hard for her to be sure, but she felt like she was now heading in the right direction. Maybe she was still feeling the subtle pull. She picked up speed, tired of being so careful and worried about stumbling in the dark.

Eventually she came to another door, her first one without a handle on it since she had fallen into the ship. Trying mind speak to open it, she commanded 'open.' Three doors opened: the one right in front of her, which was at the end of the hallway, and then a door on either side of her. The two doors she hadn't even suspected of being there caught her so off guard that she looked at them first. The one to her right was another room with monitors and wires spreading out from the monitors, like it was a fly caught in a spider web. She had seen rooms like this already; the only difference was that these monitors were on.

There were foreign characters on the screens. No pictures, only symbols that looked like the ones carved on the cave walls the beacon occupied. The symbols on the monitor changed every few seconds. It could have been a countdown for all she knew.

She turned and checked the room on the other side of the hallway. Even from the doorway she could tell that this room was different from all the other ones she had looked at so far. It wasn't very big but there were actual lights inside. All along the walls from ceiling to floor were shelves that lit up, illuminating the small blue vials resting there. There were thousands of vials. Connected to each of them was a small tube that led away from it to another part of the ship. There was a single monitor in the middle of the room on a pedestal. The screen was blank. Whatever went on in this room had not been activated yet.

The strangest thing about this room is that she didn't feel alone when she was inside of it. It was like the vials of blue liquid were alive and looking at the stranger that had walked in.

Lynn stepped out and shook her head. She was starting to lose it. Too much time in the dark. She needed to focus again.

She turned to the last room, the door she had been trying to open in the first place. Here she found the most promising room yet. It might even have been the command deck for the entire beacon. There a dozen monitors spread out and each one of them had power. Similar to the first monitor, these were full of hieroglyphics like in the cave. Some of them stayed the same, others changed every few seconds.

There weren't as many wires in this room or at least they were hidden. The clutter had been cut down and the terminals were organized instead of randomly sitting in the middle of the room and against the wall. In the center of the room was the only chair. All the monitors could be moved to be used from the chair.

Lynn got closer to the seat and realized it was not meant for a normal-sized person. If she sat in it she would look like a small child sitting in an adult's chair. She sat in it anyway. Even after all these years — the chair, like everything else, was covered in dust — it was still remarkably comfortable. The simple act of sitting made her sigh in relief. There was nothing like resting in a giant comfy chair after being almost killed by a deranged madman.

There was definitely power in this part of the beacon. She needed to see if she could somehow turn the pull off, or see if she could unlock anymore secrets. At the very least she could turn the lights on. The only light in the room came from her and the monitors.

Lights, she thought in her mind.

The lights flickered on, and the room was fully illuminated. Not being in the dark anymore felt almost as good as sitting in the big comfy chair, even though the lights were generating a strange smell from the dust on the bulbs heating up. It was much better than what she had before.

"That's more like it."

There was a beep and then a garbled message in an alien language. It startled Lynn and she sat up to look around and see if there was anyone else in the room. She noticed that all the monitors were changing…they were changing so that she could read them.

The voice returned, but this time she knew what it was saying.

"Language preference recognized. Switching display and communications to Earth: Common. Welcome back Ryder."

For a long time Lynn didn't do anything. She didn't look at what the monitors said, she didn't try to talk back to the voice, she didn't do anything but sit on the edge of the only seat in the room with her eyes wide open in disbelief while she processed what had been revealed.

Was it really possible? Had she heard correctly? This machine not only knew her language but it knew who she was. That meant one of two things; either the machine could read minds — and that was possible, as far she could tell it was at least partly organic — or she was back on Grenor.

It called her Ryder. Lynn had no maiden name. When she and Scott had gotten married he had taken her name. Not that Scott minded too much. His original name had a silent 'V' and two silent 'L's. Using the last name Ryder made life much easier for Scott. Maybe the beacon thought she was the first Ryder because they shared similar DNA. That could also explain why it knew her language. Maybe the first Ryder, who if the stories are to be believed, was trapped on the planet for so long he was able to program his own language so that future generations could use the machine if they needed to.

Lynn could hardly even form the thoughts in her mind she was so beside herself at the possibility. Ronos was Grenor.

She didn't know where either name came from, but it made sense that they could be the same place and have two different names. Once the first Ryder found out the truth of the beacon and that it had the potential to control time, he would not use the name Grenor anymore. He would make sure that the planet stayed hidden and erased from the star charts. That didn't work of course, and whoever discovered it next named it Ronos. Luckily it was the military and they wanted to keep it a secret like the first Ryder did, but for different reasons.

There were still holes in Lynn's theory about Ronos being Grenor. If it were true, how did the first Ryder get in the pull machine to begin with? Did he change himself like Lynn did? If he did, would that mean that her kids would be born normal humans? Do the powers given by the Lynn Rock not pass on to the next generation? Was there no gas back when the first Ryder got there? How did he find the pull machine? What was he doing exploring caves on an alien world? If this was Grenor, did that mean she really was born here?

There were so many things that Lynn didn't know the answer to. She could have stayed in that chair for years and puzzled over the possibilities. Instead she got up to look at what was on the monitors. It felt weird walking. This was her long lost home. She looked at everything with new eyes. Maybe as a baby she had been in this very room.

Wouldn't her mom or dad remember this? If she had been born here then they had to have been here before, right? She added the questions to her list.

The first monitor she went to was still cryptic about what was being displayed. The first Ryder must have been doing some guesswork when he reprogrammed the language settings. The sentences were not complete and there were words missing. As far as she could tell, this monitor controlled some kind of regenerating system.

Regeneration possible in ashryknd.
Sknde with mechanism responsible for foung.
Pull activated.

Specimen status:
1-20 reasonable condition.

21-30 good condition
31-40 failure
**specimen 33–vren–failed preservation.
**33 is a splead specialist with traits of humor, intelligence, and kavorka.
**use specimen 47 as a replacement sans humor.
41-50 optimal
51-60 needs increased nourishment. Use monitor klev.
61-70 contaminated. Do not regenerate.

The list continued scrolling. There was a video option in the top corner of the monitor which she selected. The monitor changed to show the room she had been inside a moment before. The vials sat on shelves and each vial had an accompanying image.

121-130 progressing. Need more nourishment. Do not regenerate until rect values are higher than the olped levels.

Lynn looked on the video and saw that not all the vials were blue. Vials 121-130 were a dark pink color. There were extra tubes leading to them with a small amount of blue liquid being added to the vials. She had no idea what was going on. How could the vials remain the same volume when more liquid was being added to them?

More importantly, what was being regenerated? The way specimen 33 was being described it was being given human characteristics – at least the ones that she could understand. Were these sentient beings waiting to be brought back to life? She didn't know, but she did know that whatever this machine was it did much more than pull things to Ronos.

Another monitor read **Power maintenance**.

Passive Attraction (Green)
Active Attraction (Green)

Reach (Red)

Regeneration Chambers (Green)

Specimen Chambers (Green)
Specimen Maintenance (Red)
Specimen preservation (Green)
Specimen Nurturing (Green)

Glak Generation (Red)
Terraforming (Red)

Blistic Energy (Red)
Blistic Power (Green)
Blistic Generators (Green)
Blistic containment (Red)

She had a good idea of what this monitor was trying to tell her. Besides the list, each item was lit up by either a red light or a green one. This was a read out for what was and wasn't working on the ship. If that were true then this ship had a lot of things wrong with it. As far as she could tell, whatever those specimens were they weren't going to last long because their maintenance was down. The pull itself must have been the Passive and Active Attraction because they were both green. The Reach was red. She wondered if that had anything to do with the pull.

Messing with the pull machine's power wasn't something she wanted to do quite yet. Yes, it would be nice to turn the pull off, but she had to wait until Mac got back. Unless he memorized the planet's coordinates he was going to need the pull to find Ronos again.

Something else in the room caught her eye. On the third monitor she came to she found that the wires had been pulled out of the base and a small electronic device had been attached to one of the many wires. The device had some kind of electronics spliced in. The writing on the device was in the Earth Common language.

It was the name of a familiar electronics company. This wasn't part of the pull machine. It was something her distant relatives had added. But why?

She looked at what the monitor displayed. They were familiar words.

Passive and Active Attraction

This is where the pull was controlled from. The display showed a map of the plant. The entire map was covered in unfamiliar characters but that didn't matter. She could tell what was going on. There was only one red part on the map. That must be the corridor that allowed ships to leave Ronos. That wasn't part of the original design. The first Ryder had added that so he — or she — could leave the planet.

There was a legend beside the map with some familiar words on it. She touched the one that said **Reach**. A star chart came up, showing how far the pull reached into space. Lynn suspected that something had gone wrong with the ship because the reach went off the map that was provided. Luckily the first Ryder had crudely programmed in his own map adding some familiar labels. The closest one to her was the Nelson Nebula. But if she pulled out farther she could see Earth and its solar system. Luckily the pull didn't go past the Nebula.

An alarm went off. The message accompanying the alarm wasn't in the common language so she had no idea what was going on. She looked at the different monitors but couldn't see any immediate changes. Had she pushed a wrong button?

The lights switched from a sallow hue to red as the alarms continued. Lynn thought that she could hear something making noise nearby. It was Raymond. It had to be. But it didn't sound like a person. It sounded more like rushing water. Why would that set off alarms?

Then she saw a change in the room. On the ceiling there was a wet spot forming, as if she were in an apartment building and her upstairs neighbor left the water on to soak through. Whatever the pull machine was made out of it was ultra absorbent. The liquid spread quickly and dripped onto the floor and monitors.

It was liquid rock. Every drop stained and spread. When it hit the monitors they started to flicker and make a whining noise. The drip was right over top of the monitor for the pull. The display turned all red and more sirens rang out. There was a hum of energy like the beacon was gearing up to enter a new level of energy output.

Lynn ran to the monitor and tried to see if she could turn the pull off, but it wasn't responding to her touch anymore. There was nothing she could do.

The same changes that came over humans when they interacted with the liquid rock was happening to the pull machine. Lynn didn't know what the results were going to be. Was the pull turned off or magnified? Were Mac and Scott still going to be able to find their way back to Ronos?

The first question she needed to answer was where the liquid rock was coming from, although she already had a guess. She ran back out the way she came. Looking for a hatch or a door leading out, she thought *open* and found herself on top of the pull machine near the pulsating red light.

The light wasn't acting like it normally did. Instead of pulsating on and off it was staying on, starting dim and then getting brighter and brighter until it couldn't get any brighter and then it went dim again. There were sounds accompanying this new light characteristic. The brighter the light the louder the strain in the machine became. Something was happening to the pull, but she couldn't tell what it was from down in the cave.

She could hear something else. A grunting noise. She walked toward it and found Raymond.

The pull machine had several cracks and crevices throughout. When Lynn and Mac had first seen it they thought it was a crashed space ship. Raymond was in a crevice full of tubes and wires. He was trying to find a way into the ship but couldn't find a walkway or hallway. Using a hollowed out rock — something that was easy for people like him and Lynn to create — he hauled liquid rock to the pull machine and dumped it in. He had discovered that soaking the beacon made it easier to punch through, and now he was digging his way into the machine while contaminating and permanently changing it.

Lynn had to stop him. She didn't know if what he was doing would help or prevent Mac and her from getting out of there. Although now that she knew Ronos was Grenor, she wasn't sure that she wanted to leave without learning more about her family and their secrets. That didn't mean she needed to let Raymond have his way contaminating everything he came in contact with.

"Raymond! Stop! You don't know what you're doing," she yelled.

Raymond did stop what he was doing. Then Lynn remembered that he was probably only trying to get into the beacon so that he could kill her. He threw his makeshift bucket at Lynn before she had time to react. It hit the side of her face and forced her back. She tried to shake it off and, while doing so, accidentally stepped off the top of the beacon and down into the broken part of the ship where Raymond was.

Falling past him, she landed on the ground. The gas was super concentrated there. She was only a few feet away from the fissure in the ground that the Mac Gas was seeping out of. She instantly healed from the fall.

That's also why when Raymond jumped down and landed feet first on her stomach it didn't squeeze the life out of her. She punched at his leg to get him off of her. He stumbled and she was able to free herself to run away, but she didn't get far. Raymond struck her as she fled and forced her to the ground again. What did he hope to accomplish now? Whatever damage he was going to do would be healed instantly.

That didn't stop him from trying. He bashed her face against the edge of the fissure, each time tearing tissue, but she healed herself completely between each bash. All he was doing was chipping away the edge of rock making the crack bigger.

Screaming in frustration, he whipped Lynn around like a rag doll. She didn't know what to do. This was the best spot for her to be if he was going to try and kill her, but she couldn't stay and wait for Raymond to get bored and leave.

Then she realized it didn't matter because she was about to be thrown somewhere altogether new. The fissure — from Raymond using Lynn as a human hammer — was now big enough for her to fit through. He threw her down the crevasse and farther into Ronos than she had ever been before. Not content with that, he jumped down after her.

She hadn't really thought about what was under the pull machine. As it turned out, there wasn't much of anything under there. At first she was bouncing off rocky walls but she was falling so fast that she couldn't reach out to stop herself in time. Soon there was nothing to latch on to. There were two sources of light. The dim purple light that came from her and the far away red light from the pull machine, but neither of them were bright enough for her to see what was around her as she fell. It was like she was falling into another giant cavern. Luckily the gas was thick there, otherwise the fall would kill her.

Not being able to see meant hitting the ground was a surprise. She wasn't prepared to slam into the ground so suddenly. Extra surprising was that she didn't smash into the rocky bottom of the cave; she sank deep into a mud-like substance. Her body sank a foot into it and she had to pull herself out. The black mud she was surrounded by tried to suck her in, but she pulled herself free. It wasn't like the cold mud she had experienced on Earth. This mud was unsettlingly warm. She hadn't felt temperature since her change, so the fact that she could feel heat coming from the mud told her it was much hotter than she thought it was.

While she looked down at her completely black body and clothes she heard a splash in the distance – the sound echoed off the walls indicating the cavern's size. Lynn guessed the cavern was only a little smaller than the beacon cavern. But she didn't think about it for too long. That splashing noise was troubling.

If it had been a rock then it would have splashed and sunk into whatever body of water was out there, but the splashing persisted. Raymond had fallen behind her. Had he fallen or followed? She didn't know, but she knew she needed to get away from that single-minded murderous fiend. He was laughing now. The laughter made her sick. What joy was he finding in their situation?

Do you know where we are?

"Leave me alone," she didn't want to talk to him anymore. It never amounted to anything good, and she was tired of her life being constantly threatened. It was getting old.

It's a lake full of everything I need to scrub you right out of existence.

Now Lynn knew why the mud was warm and where the splashing came from. There was an entire lake of liquid Lynn Rock out there. Under this lake was a heat source that melted the Lynn Rock. Where she was on the muddy shore was far enough away from the heat that the rock didn't completely turn liquid, but it did lose its rocky qualities.

There was as much Lynn Rock as there was Mac Gas in this new cavern. She and Raymond were going to be trapped, forever locked in battle, if she stayed in that room.

She could see only one way out of there. Because the cavern was so dark it was easy to see where they fell through. It was high above her head and looked like a crooked red smile. That was her goal, unless she wanted to dig her way out — and she didn't.

She couldn't see Raymond, but she could hear his splashing getting closer. Any moment now she knew she could expect another attack. Her departure wasn't any quieter than Raymond's splashing. Each step was accompanied by a loud sucking noise as she pulled her feet clear of the mud.

The farther she got from the lake the more solid her footing became and she was able to pick up speed. Soon she was at the rocky wall. Raymond's splashing had turned into mud sucking. He was catching up to her.

The crooked red smile exit from the cavern was far above her head. She would have to climb up and then over horizontally to reach it. That would have been impossible before, but now she felt up to the task and started punching and kicking hand holds and foot holds.

The rock she was climbing wasn't soft Lynn Rock. That was probably why the lake was here and not any bigger. It was surrounded by rock that wasn't susceptible to the heat. Lynn kept climbing. She had no idea how high she was or how much farther she needed to go. The crooked red smile wasn't getting any bigger. Her goal was to go as fast as she could, but the walls of the cavern were jagged and the light coming from her wasn't bright enough to see very far ahead. More than once she reached out to climb up higher but there was nothing there and she almost fell.

Raymond had reached the bottom of the cliff wall but it didn't sound like he was climbing up after her. Knowing his penchant for throwing boulders, Lynn didn't have to think too long about what was happening down there. He was carving out the wall so he would have ammunition.

The first rock struck immediately above Lynn. Little bits got in her face before the large rock fell into her shoulder and almost knocked her down. She held on by one arm. What was she going to do? She was a glow-in-the-dark target in a big black room. There was no hiding.

Raymond had a cache of throwing boulders and he launched them one after another. The first one was thrown with such force that it clipped her leg and broke it. The gas healed her, but as she healed she glowed brighter. That helped him see her more clearly.

She tried to climb but the attacks came too frequently. She was forced to dig into the side of the cliff and wait for him to run out of ammo so she could climb again. But was that what she wanted to do? Eventually Raymond was going to be able to knock her down. She was barely hanging on while being assaulted by the boulders.

The Mac Gas was making her glow brighter as she constantly needed to be healed. The assault stopped. Then she noticed a large crack in the side of the cliff wall directly to her left. While Raymond attempted to make more boulders — every time he smashed into the wall down below to accomplish this task she could feel a reverberation — she climbed over to the crag. It went deep. It was a possible hiding place. The crack didn't go down to the bottom or up to the top. She scooted her way in and went as deep as she could. How far did her glow extend? Would Raymond be able to see where she was hiding?

Ha. Clever. But you can't hide forever, Lynn. I can feel you, remember. I know you're close.

This wasn't a real plan but Lynn now knew that climbing back up to where the pull machine was would be impossible with Raymond down there. That meant she had to resort to her only other plan which was to dig her way out. She started punching at the rock in front of her.

It doesn't matter how far you run. You and I both know there is no way off this planet. We'll follow each other till you give in and let me do what I have the right to do.

Lynn couldn't believe that Raymond thought he had the right to kill her. He really was crazy. Apparently he didn't want to squander the boulders he had made and started throwing them near where he had last seen her in an effort to flush her out. None of them were close to where she was; that meant he couldn't see her glow.

But he was throwing with such force that the rock walls around where she was digging were shuddering with each strike. How much of the rock wall bellow her had he chipped away?

You won't get out of this cavern. I have all the power here.

Raymond must have known what she was doing. She could hear him tear into the rock wall. He was going to try and collapse the section of the cliff wall that she was hiding in. She needed to do something while he was distracted.

She stopped digging and went to the edge of the crack she had been hiding in. Raymond had dug deep into the wall and now was pulling out as much of the wall as he could and throwing it into the lake. He had dug far enough in that he had gotten through to a new layer of Lynn Rock.

Lynn got an idea about a new place to hide. There was no time to second guess herself. Any second Raymond could look up and see her. She didn't need to breathe, and if the liquid rock covered her glow then she could hide at the bottom of the lake and attack Raymond from behind.

She jumped out of the crack, pushing away from the rock wall as hard as she could. It wouldn't do any good to land in the mud again. She made it to the water. Her splashy entrance was covered up by all the other rocks landing around her as Raymond continued to discard boulders.

She was about to go under the surface when she heard a thunderous crack. A massive slab of rock was separating from the wall. Raymond's plan of collapsing the wall was working. Lynn realized she was treading too close to shore. The slab was falling right towards her.

As she frantically swam away the rock hit the lake causing a huge wave. She had to make sure that she stayed under where she wouldn't be seen.

But even under the surface she could tell that the lake was getting more tumultuous. The wave must have knocked more of the rock wall off, or maybe Raymond was still digging and opened up to a river system. She went back up to get a look. It was hard to tell in the dim light, but it looked like Raymond had dug all the way into an underground river and a torrent of black liquid was pouring into the lake. The muddy shore was disappearing. Raymond was gone, possibly swept away.

This was good for her. Maybe there would be enough liquid rock to fill the cavern and then she could more easily climb out. It had been so long since she had seen sunlight, or anything else besides rocks, Raymond, and the beacon.

While she waited under the surface in the warm liquid she noticed another change. It felt like there was a current forming. The extra liquid was finding new places to flow. She didn't want to get out of there bad enough to ride an underwater river. There was no way to tell where it led. What if it went farther into Ronos?

The current was getting stronger. She started swimming to the other side of the cavern. If Raymond went with the river then she did not want to get sucked in there as well. The water level was rising faster and she was being pulled into the current. There was nothing she could do.

As she got closer to leaving the large cavern where the lake used to be, she made one last-ditch effort to stop what was happening. When she was about to be sucked into the underground river, she reached out for the rocky wall. Her hands latched on, but the current was strong. Using all her muscle to pull herself out of the undertow, she struggled to make progress. She couldn't understand why it felt like the current was getting stronger.

Lynn was sick of being underground. She didn't want to be here anymore. If she got sucked into that river then she wouldn't have a choice. She would be forced to go wherever it went.

One of her arms gave out and flopped into the flowing rock river. There was no way she was going to pull herself out, but she wasn't going to surrender to the river. If it wanted to take her then it would have to suck all the energy she had in her and force her off the wall. She could have held on longer, but the rocky wall she had been white knuckling crumbled in her grip forcing her to succumb to the will of the dark river.

The river churned and moved swiftly through the rocks, twisting and turning trying to find the most direct route to wherever it was going. Lynn was along for the ride. As the river carried her along she crashed into the sides of the walls. She tried swimming, but most of the time it was useless. When the river was calm enough for her to swim she swam straight up to see if she could see anything, but there was no surface and all she accomplished was banging her head on the cave roof.

More than once the river passed through several thin cracks that Lynn could not fit through. She had to break the rock in her way or risk being broken in half by the force of the river. Every time she did this the speed of the river picked up. She was fine with that. It meant she would get to wherever she was going faster.

But she wasn't sure where she was going. It was hard to think at the same time as being tossed around a raging underground river, but somewhere in the back of her mind she guessed that she was being taken to the ocean.

She was right. The river burst out of a cliff wall twenty feet above the rocky coast of the horseshoe continent. The pressure of the river was enough to shoot her out into the ocean to avoid most of the rocks and into water deep enough to allow her to land without breaking her legs. Lynn had no energy left but somehow managed to get to shore where she flopped down and passed out.

She woke up to a completely new world. The contamination of the ocean was the next big change to happen to Ronos. It used to be a safe refuge from the Mac Gas which didn't mix with the water, but that wasn't the case anymore. She didn't know how long she had been out, but when she woke up there was black water as far as she could see. A little liquid rock went a long way.

Before there had been a thin band of less concentrated gas right above the ocean, but now with the rock contamination that band was gone. This was going to dramatically change the water cycle. The water and the rock were mixing together to become something new. It was going to rain this stuff. As long as the rock kept melting and kept coming out of that cave, before long all the lakes and rivers would be made up of liquid rock.

The flow was still going as strong as ever. From where she was now she couldn't see much of anything other than the ocean and the cliffs behind her. There was no point staying there. She turned and started to climb the cliff. Maybe the most amazing thing of the day was that she could still tell her body to do impossible things like climb cliffs and it wouldn't protest or declare a mutiny.

The top of the cliff revealed that she was near the foothills. She had no idea if these were the same foothills where the secret military base was. As she started walking it didn't take her long to realize that something had changed. The farther she got from the sound of the waves crashing on the rocks the more she started to hear other noises, noises that weren't there before. She hadn't seen any animals yet, but now she was hearing bird noises. Looking up, she saw several birds cutting through the air, periodically swooping down to feast on some small, unsuspecting animal. Where were these birds before? Had they been here all along and she hadn't noticed them?

She was so busy looking up that she tripped on a dip in the ground. Only it wasn't a dip. It was a foot print. Bigger than any foot print she had seen before. She measured it with her feet. It was three of her feet long. No toes. It was an oval shape that was thicker at one end than the other, kind of like a stretched out egg.

The hills were silent around her. The kind of silence that makes minutes feel like hours. What had made these prints? She scanned the slopes. For an instant every tree took the shape of the monster who left the track before she realized it was only a tree. Whatever it was she needed to be careful. Something that big could only be trouble.

Chapter 12
Pull

Mr. Smith had destroyed the emulator generators of the attacking swarms, but Mac wondered if Jace was still out there.

"How many generators did you destroy?" asked Mac.

"Three."

"You think we should trust Jace?"

"That's right."

Mac didn't say anything. There wasn't time to worry about it. The military would be moving in any time and that was more worrisome to Mac. He needed to protect the people of Passage.

They made it to the house. Mr. Smith got Mac a new shirt to replace the one with the laser burns in it. Everyone started getting their stuff together. Everyone except Mac. He didn't really have anything to get ready. Neither did Tayma. She got something to eat while Mac waited in the living room and looked out the window. He had never been so drained of energy in his life.

"Do you want something to eat?" she asked.

"No," said Mac.

He still wasn't hungry. That meant Lynn wasn't hungry. She wasn't starving to death.

Out the window he had a view of the two soldiers they left behind tied to trees. Then Mac spotted a shadow moving. There were people out there sneaking around. The emulators were gone, so the shadows had to be humans. The soldiers were making their move into the village.

"Hey, Tayma," said Mac. "Where did the other shuttles go?"

"To a rallying point outside of the village," Tayma said.

"What were your orders?"

"To take you in however we could."

"Mr. Smith!" Mac yelled.

The only man in Passage with an Imp came into the living room. When they heard Mac yelling everyone else came as well.

"There are soldiers in town. We need to gather everyone up. Head for the sports field by the school. That's the only place in town that's big enough for a transport. Everyone needs to get there now."

"What transport?" asked Mr. Smith.

"I'm going to find one and get out of here with anyone else who will come with me."

Mr. Smith went over to his computer terminal. The entire town was looped into a network. It was the next best thing to everyone having an Imp. Mr. Smith sent out the message.

"Hand me a gun," said Mac.

"Where are you going?" asked Mr. Smith.

"I'm going to buy us some time."

"Then I'm coming with you."

Quentin, Scott, and Tayma were ushered out the door. They left with the lights off so that it looked like no one was home. Mac and Mr. Smith waited in the shadows while the other three moved quickly down the street to the other side of town. The sports field was at the school. The group kept to the streets and moved at a quick pace. Scott was out of shape and struggling to not fall behind.

"I never got a chance to thank you for helping me get out of Zinger's space yacht," said Mac.

"No problem. That was actually more fun than work," said Mr. Smith.

'What do you think of Sneed?"

"You mean Quentin? He's a got a mischievous mind. It's a good thing he's on our side."

With the house dark and their eyes adjusted, it was easier to see into the shadows outside. Mac could see at least five men. They were moving from house to house. Or at least to each house with lights on. They would go in and carry people out — unconscious. At least Mac hoped they were only unconscious.

"Let's go see where they are taking them," said Mr. Smith.

He led the way out the back door, careful to not make noise. During the day when he was around the other people in Passage, Mr. Smith would hobble a bit and always walked slowly. Everyone thought of him as an old man.

Now he was running with stealth and control over his body, not stumbling even once and not breathing heavily. Mac was having trouble keeping up to the old man's caliber of sneaking around.

They were moving down the back alley. The street with the Narrad's and Mr. Smith's house was on the very edge of the village. The back alley bordered a canal and beyond that was a field. In the middle of the field was a large grove of trees. It was a popular place for teenagers to hang out. It was out of town, and in the middle of the grove you couldn't be seen by the outside world. It was the only place for miles where anyone could hide.

Mac and Mr. Smith got to the canal. The water was low enough that they were able to simply step over it. Then they lay down on the bank and peered over the edge towards the grove. That was where the kidnapped people of Passage were being taken. Obviously they were intended to be used as bargaining chips, hostages meant for Mac to turn himself in.

"How many?" whispered Mac.

"I see a couple dozen soldiers," said Mr. Smith. "You think you can take care of them?"

Mac was confident he could take out every one of them. But he was not confident he could do it without losing a hostage. Mr. Smith sensed his hesitation.

"You have the element of surprise. Be as quick and as silent as you can and you should be okay. Get to the hostages and protect them," said Mr. Smith.

"You aren't going to help me?"

"I'll wait here and stop the ones coming and going. I'll be loud about it to cause a distraction."

"They might have some ships over there we can use to evacuate people."

"I'll meet you there."

It was as good a plan as any. Mac tucked his gun into the back of his pants and took off across the field. The laser would reveal his location so he would use his hands until the surprise was gone.

Passage was in the middle of the prairies, a very flat place. People used to joke that the land around Passage was built with a level, but that wasn't completely true. There was a slight dip in the land beyond the village boundaries. It was so subtle that most people didn't notice, but Mac knew it was there because Janelle took him there the night she was taken. The dip in the landscape was enough to hide the lights of Passage and the nearby highway. She told him it was like time-traveling to before people existed. The soldiers had landed their ships there in an attempt to keep them hidden. Mac could still see the tops of three HAAS3's and a HATS (Heavy Armored Transport Ship).

Mac ran close to the grove, dropped down into the tall grass, and inched himself closer. He looked at who had been taken. Mr. And Mrs. Parkington were there. There was a family he didn't recognize with a bunch of kids being told that if they didn't stop crying there would be repercussions. The mother was trying to calm down the children while the father tried to calm down the soldiers. One of the soldiers had his hand on his weapon. Was he really going to shoot a kid?

A soldier on patrol walked past Mac who soundlessly subdued him. Mac moved closer to the grove. There were a bunch of guys standing around waiting to be told to do something. They looked eager. Mac purposely made a lot of rustling noises and the three men wandered out into the prairie to investigate. The speed with which Mac attacked prevented any of them from calling out or pulling and firing their guns. The key was to strike the throat. Once that collapsed they would be too busy trying to breathe to worry about him.

The closer he got to the trees the harder it was going to be. There were lights set up and at least one soldier for every hostage. From what Mac could see there were eleven villagers there. A lot of soldiers were coming and going. Mac decided to wait for Mr. Smith's distraction.

He didn't have to wait long. There was yelling and laser fire coming from the village. All the soldiers noticed. Many left their hostages to go to the edge of the grove to get a better look. The Parkington's were unguarded and Mac was able to sneak right up to them.

"Mac, where did you come from?" asked Mrs. Parkington. She looked excited to see him. This was the same woman who constantly complained to Mac's mom that her feral child kept eating the apples off her tree. He had been grounded for a week. The grounding didn't take. The apples dripped with too much deliciousness not to be eaten.

"I'm here to get you guys out of here," said Mac in a whisper.

"And take us to a secret planet and turn us into super heroes?" asked Mr. Parkington.

"If you want to come with us we'll be glad to have you. If not, at the very least I should get you out of here."

The soldiers started mobilizing. Orders were yelled. Half the soldiers ran for the village, the others ran for the hostages and the HAAS3's. They were going to attack.

Mr. Smith's distraction was working, but it was also causing more trouble than they wanted. No doubt the soldiers suspected that Mac was behind the attack and were moving to take him out. Two of the HAAS3's took to the air leaving one behind with the HATS.

In the chaos no one noticed that there was an extra hostage in the grove. Mac needed to get to one of the ships. Clotheslining a passing soldier and then knocking him unconscious, he grabbed the gun and, after making sure it was on its lowest setting, gave it to Mr. Parkington.

"Let's get the others," said Mac.

He dialed down the settings on the gun so that no one would get killed and then took aim at the soldiers guarding the family he didn't know. Mr. Parkington took aim at random soldiers running past. He didn't get the concept of what they were trying to do.

"We need to free the hostages," said Mac.

Mr. Parkington got the message. The father of the family knew what was going on as well and grabbed a gun. Now the soldiers were wise to what was happening and some had stopped running. Mac and the others took cover behind the trees. They had gotten attention from some of the soldiers but there were still enough to fly the last HAAS3 into the village.

"Stay here. I'm going to go get a ship," said Mac.

"You want me to help you?" asked Mr. Parkington.

"Keep the soldiers off my back as much as you can."

Mac ran from tree to tree, looking around the bark and then shooting anyone who got in his way. He needed to be quick. When the soldiers got to the village they weren't going to find what they were looking for. Either they would start shooting until Mac showed himself or they would come back realizing he was the one freeing the hostages.

As Mac ran he had to snipe at the men running for the ships. The soldiers who were about to get in the last HAAS3 stopped and turned their attention to the attacker. Mac didn't even hesitate. His ability to aim a hand gun while running had been incredible before his transformation and now, even as depleted as he was, he still was better than anyone there by a long shot. The first few soldiers went down without him even working hard. The last four put their hands up. What they saw Mac do was supposed to be impossible; no one could aim that well. It wasn't so much that they surrendered as they were only capable of standing there in amazement. Had there been children there, they would have asked for autographs. Mac never lowered his gun.

"I can't have you following me. It's on the lowest setting," said Mac.

As if wanting to test his skills the last four men started running all in different directions. They were easily taken care of.

There was a rush of people coming from the grove. It was the hostages being led by Mr. Smith. Darren and Clarissa were there. Scott and Quentin as well. They must have been caught and then rescued by Mr. Smith. The HAAS3 only had three seats but it could hold all of them uncomfortably. Most of them would have to stand.

"Everyone get on, hurry!" said Mac.

Mac stopped Quentin from getting on. "Can you pilot?"

"Not a hawthree. I'm not that good. I'll take the transport ship."

"You know what we are doing with it?"

"We are going to save the people from Passage before more reinforcements show up."

"You can handle that?"

"You keep the skies clear and I should be able to handle it."

Mac waited for them all to get onboard. Everyone was keener on getting on the HAAS3 than the HATS. The HATS was a large, slow, defenseless, target flown by a former Imp addict. Being squished on the smaller shuttle was more appealing. Mac didn't have any doubt about Quentin's abilities. The HATS had already taken off and was heading for the sports field where everyone was supposed to gather. The only man in Passage with an Imp was last to move. He was waiting away from the shuttle, so Mac ushered him onboard.

"I'm not going with you, Mac," Mr. Smith said.

"What? Why?"

"I have no reason to go with you. I can't change myself on Ronos."

Mr. Smith held out his arm and then peeled back his skin and some flesh. There was machinery underneath, circuits that Mac didn't think were possible. It was the most advanced human technology he had ever seen.

"What are you?" asked Mac.

"I am what's left of a man named Mr. Smith. But only in mind. His body has been dead for many years. He worked in robotics."

"You mean you. You worked in robotics."

"Yes, I did. I also helped invent the Imps. The legislation about prolonged life using robotic carriers of our memories and personalities was used to outline the laws around Imp research. I kept it a secret because people aren't allowed to exist after they die. I found a way around it and a place to hide where no one would ask too many questions."

"We could still use your help. You should come with us."

"I'll stay. I'll help prepare other people to come to you. I'll look for the good in people. We can save humanity while we try to win this war."

Mac wasn't sure what to say. What was the social protocol governing what to do when you found out a friend and ally was a robot? Mr. Smith reached around to the back of his neck and lifted up the hair at the base of his skull. After exerting a little effort he pulled out a small card, no bigger than a thumb nail, and handed it to Mac. It was all black with one red stripe down the middle on one side and a silver dot on the other.

"What's this?" asked Mac.

"It's the reason advancements like me are scary to people who like to be in control. I'm not the only one like me. You've run into Zinger's body guard, right?"

"The guy with the widow's peak?"

"Yes. He's like me. If you want to stop him then you have to use this chip. And you're never going to get to Zinger unless you can get through his body guard."

"I thought it was weird how that guy never blinked."

There was an explosion from inside the village. Something was going wrong.

"Get out of here," said the only man in Passage with an Imp.

"Thank you. For everything."

"We'll see each other again. Don't worry."

Mac boarded the ship, worked his way through the crowd to the pilot's seat, and opened a channel to Quentin's transport ship.

"What's going on?" asked Mac.

"We are being shot at! Where are you?" asked Quentin.

"On my way."

"No time. We're leaving."

"Did you get everybody?"

"Only the ones who want out of Passage."

Mac took off at the same time the boxy transport ship at the sports field did. One HAAS3 followed. It was giving glancing blows to the ship trying to force it to the ground. How much longer would that last?

Mac flew to intercept but that's when the other HAAS3s showed up. Mac's shuttle started shaking as the armor took hit after hit. He wouldn't be able to save Quentin if he ended up exploding.

"What's going on?" asked a muffled voice behind Mac.

"We're under attack. Hold on to something. It's going to get wild for a bit."

He couldn't help but grimace as he did up his own safety restraint. There was no way anyone else would be able to do that. The two other seats were occupied by more than one person. Everyone else was standing.

The attacking shuttle was right behind him. He dodged to the right and then turned tightly to the left and ducked down into the village. Laser fire flew wide of Mac's shuttle.

Mac kept low to the ground. His maneuver wouldn't fool an experienced pilot. True enough the shuttle was on them in seconds and gaining speed. But that was because Mac slowed down a bit. Once he got to the end of the street he punched it back up to full speed and pulled the nose straight into the night sky.

The following shuttle didn't see it coming and ran into the brick building at the end of the street. It would have been enough to ground a normal ship but this one was heavily armored. It was only enough to slow it down so that Mac could flip the ship around and bare down on his opponent with all the fury his shuttle could muster. Lasers cut through the sky to meet their target.

The explosion was more than satisfying. Mac knew the right places to hit. It didn't matter how heavily armored the ship was, it still had weaknesses. Everyone started jumping around and cheering. Someone accidentally hit one of the controls and cut out the engines. The shuttle sunk and everyone hit the ceiling before Mac was able to turn them back on. The cheering was replaced by groaning.

"Careful about what you touch," said Mac.

"Yeah, thanks," said some sarcastic guy in the back.

"Quentir, where are you?" asked Mac over the radio.

"Finally out of the atmosphere. The military's hawthree let off now that we have security from the ESP trying to stop us. I need to go to hyperspace sooner rather than later," said Quentin.

"I'm in a shuttle. I can't follow you."

"Then you better get close enough to get pulled along with us. Where are we headed?"

"The Nelson Nebula. If we get separated we go to the Nelson Nebula. When you're there you'll feel the pull to Ronos, but you need to hold off 'til I get there because Zinger is already at Ronos and we need to come up with a plan to deal with him first."

"Sounds good."

Shuttles didn't have the engine power to jump into hyperspace, but that didn't mean they were incapable of being in hyperspace. Quentin's Transport ship had a hyper drive engine and if Mac got close enough, within a few feet of Quentin, then he could piggyback on their engines.

The sky around them got darker as Mac cleared the atmosphere. It wasn't hard to find where they needed to go. Dozens of ships were swarming around the large boxy ship. Some were firing shots to remind them how serious things were getting. Others were swarming around trying to stop him from making the jump. If Quentin went into hyperspace with an attack shuttle right in front of him then they would both end up as fireballs.

Mac caught up to him and used his HAAS3's weapons to clear a path. The security ships stopped trying to block their exit vector. Mac kept his shuttle as close as he could to Quentin's transport ship and held his breath. The space warped around them and the HAAS3 was pulled along with the rest of the citizens of Passage into hyperspace.

The crowd on the HAAS3 cheered again, more conservatively this time because no one wanted to be responsible for accidentally pushing something that dropped them out of hyperspace.

Once the jump had been made the distance between the two ships didn't need to be so extreme. Mac let the shuttle drift a bit but he still had to make sure he didn't wander too far. The real danger in piggy backing like this was dropping out of hyperspace and being stranded. They didn't have an interplanetary drive so they would be stranded there until someone came to look for them. Mac was done spending time trapped on a shuttle with nowhere to go.

"Something strange is happening over here," said Quentin a few hours after they left Earth.

"What's up?" said Mac.

"We keep losing power. I noticed when I first started up the shuttle that it wasn't running at full power, but I thought maybe it was warming up. It's been a few hours now so I'm starting to think there might be something sucking the power out of the ship."

Mac knew what it was immediately. Jace's generator was somewhere on the shuttle. If only Mac knew what it looked like. He had traveled with Jace at the Northgate Recovery Base and through the ruins of Northgate itself and had never seen it. It couldn't have been the same thing that he had seen on the collector ships, the bodies floating over a blue glowing platform — that would have been obvious. It had to be something smaller and easier to move around.

"Who's all there with you? Is Jace Michaels there?" asked Mac.

"Yeah. I didn't think he was, but he kind of showed up out of nowhere."

I told you. You can't stop me, said Jace in Mac's head.

We'll find your generator.

Hopefully you find it in time. Or you could focus your energies on our common enemy. I can help you get rid of Zinger.

First you said you could help us save the people from Passage, now you want to help us take out Zinger. You should realize by now that I don't believe you.

After everything we've been through and all the times I could have hurt you and those you care about, you still don't trust me. I warned you about the other swarms in Passage, didn't I?

What happens when you get to Ronos?

We'll find out soon enough.

"See if you can find the source of whatever is sucking up your power and turn it off," said Mac. He also wanted to warn him about the alien on his ship but there were a lot of scared and nervous people over there already. Jace wasn't going to hurt any of them unless he had a reason to. No need to start a panic.

They waited. The HAAS3 and the HATS got closer and closer to the Nelson Nebula.

Mac closed his eyes and tried to block out the people around him. He knew that if he concentrated that he would be able to feel the mysterious call of Ronos. They had only been traveling for five days. It took barely over a week to get to Ronos. They wouldn't be able to feel the pull yet. Last time they traveled for much longer before they noticed anything. He waited a few more minutes and then it happened.

It wouldn't have mattered if Mac had his eyes closed and was concentrating. The pull was much more powerful now. Both ships were jerked out of their straight and narrow path. Everyone on the assault shuttle felt the pull.

"What was that?" asked Mrs. Parkington.

Mac didn't know how to answer. It was like the pull he felt before but way more powerful. Before it was a constant force that started out subtly. Now it was freakishly strong and came intermittently.

The next time it happened it was so strong it pulled both of them out of hyperspace. It lasted for three minutes and was pulling them at incredible speeds.

"Mac? What was that?" asked Quentin over the com.

"I'm not sure exactly."

"It's coming at intervals of ten minutes and twenty-two seconds."

Scott took a seat beside Mac and started studying the console in front of him. He was punching in numbers and doing calculations.

"You know what you're doing there, Scott?" asked Mac.

"I didn't only make munitions for these ships. I know what I'm doing," said Scott.

"And what are you doing?"

"Finding out where that pull came from."

"Don't waste your time. I already know. I've been there before. It's where your wife is."

"Really?" said Scott. He looked up briefly from the console screen to see if Mac was yanking his leg or not.

The pull came again. They were more prepared this time, but everyone still tensed up and held their breath waiting for the unnatural pull to be over. They were being pulled faster than hyperspace. The ship rattled under the strain. Mac did his best to relieve the stress by pointing the ship in the direction it was being forced. The real problem was that the ship was built to be pushed from behind and not pulled from the front. Before he could flip the ship around to test if being pulled backwards would help at all the pull ended.

"The pull lasts for three minutes and pulls us farther than we could travel in the ten minute break between the pulls. We are trapped no matter what we do. Even piggybacking through hyperspace won't get us out of this," said Scott.

"And it'll probably tear this ship apart in the process," said Mac.

"Sounds like we might as well get this over with," said Darren. He was bracing himself against the far wall and had his arms wrapped protectively around Clarissa. Her eyes were wide and kept darting around at all the computer monitors, trying to soak in as much information as possible. It was probably some kind of Imp withdrawal. When in distress or facing the unknown she was used to seeking comfort and knowledge from the invisible lines of code that ran through her brain. She wasn't used to being natural.

Darren was right though, and Mac was already thinking the same thing. He maneuvered to stay close to Quentin. They were going to get to Ronos sooner than they planned. That meant confronting Zinger before Mac had any idea how to deal with him. That meant trying to find a way through the corrosive gas to rescue Lynn. That meant they needed to find a way to turn off the pull so they weren't trapped there.

One problem at a time.

Chapter 13
Searchers

Phillip couldn't believe what he was hearing.

"We need to blow up this ship and I can't do it from here. I needed your help," said Nelson.

Phillip shook his head. It wasn't a good idea to be yelling these things at each other from across the room. What if someone was listening? He walked over to where his nephew was and sat on the floor beside him with his back leaning against the wall.

"Maybe we should keep those kinds of things a little quieter, eh?" said Phillip.

"No one's listening. I've checked. You want to know what's going on here?"

"Sure. Tell me what you thought was more important than winning the war."

"There was no way for Mac to know what was going on here. He gave us the only mission he could. It would be short-sighted on our part if we assumed that the mission was beyond adaptation to a better idea."

"Fine, fine. What's your better idea?"

"This is a training ship. One of several, but it looks like it's the last place for training before they send human emulators to the other side. They have aliens doing to us what you, me, Ryan, and Jazlyn are doing to them."

"This is where aliens learn to be human."

"Right. They've always had access to the memories of the people they emulate, but here they put what they know to the test and try to live like humans. There are speech classes, eating classes, and even a bizarre kind of alien potty training.

It would have been funnier if I didn't know they were doing this to get close enough to bring us down faster."

"Potty training?"

"People would get suspicious if they didn't know how to flush a toilet. They need to be able to completely take over the lives of the people they are emulating."

"So you want to blow this ship up because of that?" said Phillip.

Nelson continued, "That's only the first reason. And that's not even the big one. There is a reason they do all that training here. There is no mind speaking here. Before me and you I don't think anyone even would have considered breaking this rule."

"Why's that?"

Nelson closed his eyes and projected an image into Phillip's mind. Phillip dismissed it immediately.

"You aren't supposed to do that," said Phillip. "We're in enough trouble already."

"Relax. Pictures aren't noise. This was the picture I was going to send you guys to begin with but it's hard to project over great distances and I wasn't sure you would understand what you were looking at anyway."

Nelson sent the image to Phillip's brain again. The doctor accepted it this time. There was a certain amount of subconscious information going on with the image. Phillip could also see what Nelson was thinking when he first saw it. The room he was looking at was at the center of the ship. As Jazlyn had suspected this ship was out of range of the thoughts of the main fleet.

The room was dark and as big as a gymnasium, but the space was not being used by very many people. There were twelve bodies sitting on the floor. Like the rest of the decor guided by the aliens, the room was big and gray.

The twelve people sitting on the floor were not human but they had all the same extremities and features. The major difference was that none of them were over three feet tall, their skin was dark blue, and their bald heads were as big as their torsos.

"What kind of emulated people are these?" asked Phillip.

"They aren't being emulated. The swarms only turn people into emulators so that more than one alien can use a single body. The aliens can also turn into a swarm and take over your body and that's what happened to these blue guys. Being an emulator diminishes their power so they have to be constantly inhabited by a swarm."

"What powers?"

"They are called searchers, or at least that's what the swarms call them. They act as the compass for the rest of the fleet. They stay in this room with their eyes closed, remain as still as possible and constantly have their inner eye looking outward. When you combine the blue dudes' abilities to see things that no one else can and the aliens' natural ability to be drawn to one place they become like a radar, honing in on exactly where they need to go."

"These guys are looking for Ronos, right?" said Phillip.

"Yes. While I've been waiting for you guys to show up I've been trying something myself. When I imitate the searchers and remain absolutely still and close my eyes and quiet my mind I feel a pull. I don't know where it comes from or where it wants me to go, but I feel it and it makes me want to move. I bet it's the same feeling that all the swarms feel, this constant pull to get to Ronos, except that they don't know exactly where it is so they have the searchers."

"They must know they are close," said Phillip.

"I think so. That's why they are biding their time. You saw the fleet, right? They could wipe us out anytime they want but they are waiting until they find what they are looking for."

"We don't have a chance of stopping the fleet," said Phillip.

"And they aren't ones for diplomacy," said Nelson.

"Why are they so obsessed with getting to that planet? What happens when they get there?"

"I haven't been able to figure that out yet, but do you get what I'm saying? If we can blow this ship up then we have a chance of stopping them. Or at least delaying them while we find the generators."

Nelson was right. So far the only damage the human fleet had managed was blowing up a collector ship while sacrificing one of their own. That wasn't going to win any wars. Striking this blow was a solid chance to make a difference.

"We left Ryan with the General. It's the three of us now. If our cover's been blown then he might be in trouble too," said Phillip.

"Our cover isn't blown. They think we're aliens that have broken the rules. They keep us here until the new recruits get sent out to infiltrate the enemy," said Nelson.

"Do you know how long that will be?"

"No."

"Then we better start making a plan now."

All their plans went out the window when back on Ronos the beacon was assaulted and transformed as Raymond doused the control room with liquid rock and the pull became more powerful than it ever had before. Both Phillip and Nelson felt the change. They were both lying on the floor with their eyes closed and their minds empty because they were tired and trying to rest before their scheme to blow the ship up was implemented.

They could both feel the amplified pull towards Ronos now and both knew exactly where it was. That could only mean that every swarm alien knew the same thing. The pull tugged at them for about sixty seconds before a thought was broadcast to everyone in the fleet in an authoritative voice. The leader of their entire civilization was speaking.

The next vector point has been established. The final stage of our pilgrimage has been initiated. All ships form up around the Searchers Sphere.

"What's going on?" said Phillip.

"How would I know? I'm right here beside you."

The ban on mind speaking has been lifted. They aren't worried about sending anyone else behind enemy lines anymore, said Jazlyn.

I take it the fleet is on their way here.

Yes, Phillip, that's what it sounded like. We should stay on this ship for as long as we can until we find where we need to go. If the fleet is coming here then I want an excuse to act a little like a human.

Good idea.

Phillip went over to where he could tell there was a section of malleable metal to call something out of the wall. He asked for a sensor display and it was granted to him. There was no embargo on thought speech, so there was nothing keeping them prisoner anymore. Through the sensor display he could see that the ball ship was back to rooms that adjusted their sizes depending on the occupants, like a collector ship. No one was worried about the two rule breakers. Through the map and sensors he was able to find where Jazlyn was and moved his room closer to her, and then opened the door when she were right in front of it.

"Have you guys been on the other side of this wall the whole time?" asked Jazlyn.

I'll explain it to you later. I think we should go back to mind speaking to avoid suspicion, said Phillip.

Right.

They all left the room Phillip and Nelson had been held captive in. They didn't want to be labeled as criminals or anything. Instead they wandered up and down the halls. Nelson didn't say much. Phillip figured maybe he could reach Ryan and they were talking to each other. Jazlyn confirmed his suspicions.

Ryan and Nelson are talking about you behind your back, said Jazlyn.

All they're doing is showing their immaturity. That's why we needed you on this mission, said Phillip.

Why?

We needed more maturity.

Is that a polite way of calling me old?

We're both old, and there was no way I was going to do this with a couple young adventurers with only one brain between the two of them, said Phillip.

So why did Nelson bring us here? asked Jazlyn.

To destroy this ship. It's the one looking for Ronos, but now it doesn't matter cause the secret's out and soon all the swarm aliens are going to be converging on that planet.

I hope Mac knows what he's doing.

What are the chances he's changed enough people to be like us to fight a war? asked Phillip. *Even if he's changed a million people, and there's no way he has, he still won't be able to stop these guys from getting to Ronos.*

We don't even know what happens when the aliens get to Ronos.

We know it can't be good. They've extinguished entire civilizations to get there, and I doubt they will have a moral revelation about murder and genocide once they arrive. I can't imagine they will leave us alone.

What if getting to Ronos makes them even more powerful than they are right now? asked Jazlyn.

We need to make sure we never find that out. We still need to find the prisoners being emulated, said Phillip.

Is there any way to talk to Mac? It would be nice to know what's happening on his end.

I haven't tried yet. I didn't have high hopes. Who knows how far away he is.

The pain returned to Jazlyn's eyes. Phillip thought he had said something wrong but then he looked at the sensors. The rest of the fleet was arriving. She was overhearing a million conversations again.

He thought about using the liquid metal technology to create some kind of helmet that would block out all the voices, but he wasn't sure if it was possible to create things that didn't exist. Otherwise he could easily imagine an off button that when pushed would destroy all the aliens. The best he could do was leave her alone and remind Ryan and Nelson not to mind speak more than necessary.

He turned his attention back to the sensor screen he was looking at. The space around the Searchers Sphere was rapidly filling up with the rest of the fleet. It looked like they were mobilizing so that the sphere was at the center. Was that important? Why would the searchers still be protected? They weren't needed anymore now that Ronos had been found.

There was no way to tell one ship from another so he tried narrowing it down. He felt bad about mind speaking and adding to Jazlyn's misery, but it was the only way to try to get information.

Show me where the emulators are kept.

Blue dots popped up on every single ship in the fleet and they were moving around. How was that possible? Why were the general and the others being taken to a central location if there were emulators on every ship. But then Phillip realized his mistake. He was being shown all the emulators and he wasn't looking for the emulators. He was looking for the people being emulated.

He tried searching for *the emulated* but nothing came up so he tried *prisoners*. That didn't work either. It showed him where the general was; Ryan was still with them making sure the general didn't reveal his secrets. What did the aliens call the people they emulated? He tried humans. That didn't work. He tried aliens. That didn't do anything either. How was it this difficult?

What are you doing? asked Nelson.

Trying to find where the people being emulated are kept. It's not really working out, said Phillip.

Ryan and I had an idea.

Is it better than your idea to bring us here?

"What's your problem?" demanded Nelson. His voice was a little too loud.

Keep it down, said Phillip. There were still aliens around but they didn't do more than glance at where the noise was coming from. This was a place where they practiced being human. Learning to control the volume of your voice was part of that.

I brought you here to try and win the war. How was I supposed to know that something was going to happen to negate my plan? There was nothing I could have done, said Nelson.

That's fine. But now we need to get back to Ryan and the general.

Don't you want to hear my plan?
Do you know how to get to the general? asked Phillip.
We don't all need to go to the general, said Nelson.
What?
Ryan's there. Why do we all need to go back?

Phillip shook his head. He was done following the leadership of his kid nephew.

Nelson took a step closer to the doctor. The frustration showed on his face. His fists opened and closed as he tried to control his actions. *I'm not asking. I'm telling. I'll go back to Ryan and help protect the general. You and Jazlyn do whatever you can to slow down the fleet.*

Slow them down how? asked Phillip.

Guerilla warfare.

That's crazy.

A door opened in the wall behind them. Phillip hadn't called for it. Nelson didn't look fazed by it. Maybe he was the one who thought it into existence. Regardless, Phillip went inside so that they could talk without causing suspicious gazes. Jazlyn followed behind them.

There were only three people in the room yet it didn't adjust to their size. It was much larger than it should have been.

"You aren't the leader here," said Nelson once they were all inside.

"I know, but what you are saying is crazy. If we separate we will never see each other again. We'll all end up dead and the mission will be a failure," said Phillip.

"Don't be arrogant. This is a good plan. You target specific ships. Take them down. The swarms will be so busy looking for you that I will have easy access to get back to the general."

Phillip shook his head. "You can't even make a room that is the proper size for four people. How are you supposed to get back to the general?"

"You made this room. Not me."

"No," Phillip looked to Jazlyn but she was too busy trying to force out the voices in her head.

They were all quiet now. Someone else had made this room. They looked around but couldn't see anyone. There could have easily been an alien in swarm form in the room. They wouldn't be able see it. If that were true then Nelson's plan was known to them now.

"Who's there? Show yourself," said Phillip.

There was an immediate change to the feel of the room. Nothing visual changed, at least right away, but there was a new energy. It felt like there was an air current. Like the room was alive now and trying to communicate with them.

Then they started to see particles swoop from all corners to form several beings in the middle of the room. Phillip counted at least nine, but they were still cloudy and forming themselves into their human shapes so there might have been a few more.

"Well, it was good knowing you," said Nelson. "These guys heard everything we were saying."

"Be quiet. I'll do the talking," said Phillip.

The crowd of human-looking aliens shuffled and an old woman stepped forward. She had dark skin and wiry hair. She was a foot shorter than Phillip and about a foot wider. Of the entire group she was probably the least intimidating, yet there wasn't a human alive, besides the ones who were changed on Ronos, that she couldn't easily kill.

You are one of us? the woman asked.

Yes, Phillip lied.

There was a pause. The aliens must have been talking to each other before she continued. Another person stepped forward, a skinny pale kid in a military uniform who didn't look old enough to enlist. The kid spoke.

We know what you are. You are one of them. You are human.

Phillip wasn't sure what to say. He didn't want to answer the question so he posed another one. *What do you want from us?*

The old woman spoke, *If you are here to stop the progression of our people then we are here to stop you. If you are here to save the human race then we are here to help you.*

How are those two different things? Nelson said only to Phillip.

We need to return to our home. But there is no need to kill anymore. We have no more need for emulators. It is only the vanities of our people that demand new bodies despite the fact that we will soon be at our new home. We need to return home. We do not need to destroy anyone else. Why are you here? said the old woman.

What's your name? asked Phillip.

Aleeva.

My name is Phillip. I'm from Earth. I'm here to save our people.

That's what we thought. We have revealed ourselves to you so that we can help you, said Aleeva.

You're going to have to explain yourself a little, said Phillip.

We are here in the Searchers Sphere to learn to be human. We were going to sneak to Earth and help with the fight. Help defend it. But now no one else is being sent. The fleet is positioning to sweep through the rest of your people and move straight to our home. Since we can't go to Earth and help anymore, we want to help you complete your mission.

So all the swarms that were sent to Earth are on your side? Double agents trying to win the war for the humans? asked Phillip.

No. Only some — most can't be trusted. We are few.

How many.

There are few of us.

Right, said Phillip.

He looked back at his companions, who looked unsure. It didn't look like they were about to randomly trust a bunch of aliens because they said they were on the same side.

We need some sign of trust, said Phillip.

This war is about to end, one way or another. There is a plan in place. We will include you in the plan, said Aleeva

What's the plan? asked Phillip.

Chapter 14
Collide

Mac let himself relax a bit. Someone on the HAAS3 had to. The Passage people were still tense. The pull made them uncomfortable in their own skin, all except for Darren and Mrs. Parkington. Darren had the wild look of excitement in his eyes. Mac knew how he felt. Being in Passage all your life meant that you didn't have the chance to do anything really cool. Without an Imp he didn't even have the chance to have simulated adventures. Darren was smiling, but only when Clarissa wasn't looking.

Mrs. Parkington didn't look excited by the developments but she did look ticked off in a way that only ladies over sixty can. She had the angry grandmother look perfected. Mac felt guilty looking at her, but he also knew that she couldn't be angry with him, could she? He hoped not and immediately vowed to not get on her bad side. How would the Lynn Rock affect the older people? Would they improve their current physical potential or would they recover the physical prowess they had when they were in their twenties and thirties?

Scott was paying more attention to the console screens than Mac was.

"I found your secret planet," said Scott.

"Already?" asked Mac.

"Yeah."

The ships were able to stay in hyperspace while they hurtled toward Ronos. Every ten minutes and twenty two seconds the hyperspace would get hyper active and the ship lurched forward at an uncomfortable speed.

Mac felt the small computer chip in his pocket with the tips of his fingers. That was all Mac had left of the only man in Passage with an Imp. And it turned out that the man was actually an android preserving the memory of someone who had long been dead. That was illegal, but Mac couldn't remember why. What was wrong with androids? Human potential had been retarded by power-hungry politicians and controlling military leaders.

"When will we get there?" asked Mac. Everyone else on the shuttle leaned in to hear the answer.

"Within the hour I would guess," said Scott.

There were a few more minutes of silence before Darren spoke up.

"What are we going to do once we get there?" he asked Mac.

"We are going to find a way to get down to the surface."

"What do you mean? Can't we take this ship down there?"

"No, the planet's atmosphere is made up of extremely dangerous gas. If you fly a ship down there it's not going to be able to fly back out and you're going to get burned in the process."

"Why do we have to go down there?"

"Because down there is the means to change you to be like me. Once you are like me the atmosphere will change from deadly to life giving."

"But how do we get around the killing part?" asked Darren.

"I'm not sure yet."

Scott interrupted the conversation, "I thought you said this was a secret planet."

"More of a secret military planet. Why do you ask?" asked Mac.

"There is a lot of chatter out there. I'm trying to lock in on a conversation to see what everyone is all up in arms about, but I can't get it done."

"How many ships are out there?"

"I'm guessing there are over a dozen or so."

Mac sat up in his seat. He was not expecting that many ships to be there. Zinger was good at keeping secrets. Were these his ships or were they other ships that got caught in the pull?

"What can you tell me about them?"

"Not much. Transport ships as far as I can tell. Not much out here for tourists. The ships are traveling to and from the front. There is a luxury cruise ship out there but who knows why. For sure there's one capital ship — that must be the general's — but we'll know more in about twelve minutes when we get there.

Mac looked out the front window. Space was still mostly black with the exception of distant blinking stars. Typical. Nothing alarming. Except that Ronos was minutes away instead of hours.

When the pull came for the last time, Mac squeezed the armrests of his chair. What was waiting for them when they stopped? The HAAS3 still hovered mere yards above Quentin's transport ship.

"Drop us out of hyperspace," said Mac over the comlink to Quentin.

Hyperspace ended and Ronos took up their full view. They were being pulled to the same orbital point that the *Terwillegar* had been pulled to. The trouble was that so were all the other ships that were already there.

The space around Ronos was a mess of metal. The biggest ship and the one that Mac recognized first, was Zinger's capital ship. It was long with attractive bumps coming out of the ship at random points. Random in looks, but Mac knew what each one was. One was the command deck, one was the infirmary and so on. While other military ships were a standard gray that all metal seemed to come in, Zinger's ship was pearly white. But it must have gone through some recent trauma because black scorch marks were scrawled along the side of it. Had someone attacked Zinger?

It would take only a few more seconds to learn the danger of the new pull. The HAAS3 was in the pull for only a minute when it got to Ronos, but unlike the *Terwilligar*'s experience, the pull didn't stop once they had reached the planet. The beacon was pulling them to a lodestar — a focal point in space right outside the atmosphere — and as long as the pull was still going, for three minutes every ten minutes and twenty two seconds, they were going to be held at that point. And not only them, but everyone else who was in range. The point they were being pulled to was not big enough for all of them to fit.

The ships in front of Mac and Quentin were colliding into each other as everyone was forced into the same space. The engines on Zinger's ship were going in full reverse to avoid ramming into everyone and destroying them, but all that did was delay the inevitable. There was a heavy duty long haul ship at the middle of it all. That ship was a schematic relative of the transport ship Quentin was on. It was tough and built to withstand harsh conditions. Even with all the ships crowding in around, it was still holding up better than any of its neighbors.

One of those neighbors was a small military ship. It would only be able to hold a dozen or so people. It was similar to the HAAS3 except that it had an intersystem drive. It was thin and streamlined. The windows were elongated and the colors could be customized. Right now the ship was dark red.

It was trapped between the heavy duty long haul ship and General Zinger's capital ship. There was nothing that could be done. They were all being pulled to the same place. The little engines on the small red ship shone bright in an effort to move, but the pull was stronger the closer they were to Ronos and this was as close as they got without going down to planet.

The small red ship exploded, killing everyone inside and adding a new black scorch mark on Zinger's pretty white ship.

Mac and the other people on the HAAS3 had no time to mourn. They were being pulled into the same situation. They were in danger of hitting against a stronger ship and tearing a chunk out of the hull and venting their atmosphere.

"How much time 'til the pull is over?" asked Mac.

"Thirty seconds." said Scott.

"Full reverse!"

"It's not going to do anything."

'We have to do something!"

Scott threw the ship into reverse and put as much power to it as possible. If it made a difference Mac couldn't tell. He watched with wide eyes as the HAAS3 smashed into a sharp angled luxury cruise ship. It had a triangular shape to it and a lot of points and sharp edges. It was an odd looking ship that was impractical for atmospheric travel because it was nowhere near streamlined. Ships like this were usually owned by luxury travel companies.

The pull held them captive so that they couldn't even maneuver around the sharp edges of the triangle ship. The HAAS3 collided and scraped along the outside of the other ship. Mac was convinced that the only thing that saved them was armor they had on their hull. Hopefully Quentin and the others were doing okay.

The pull ended before any more damage could happen.

"You guys okay over there?" asked Mac.

"Yes, but barely. Our outer hull was getting close to being compromised," said Quentin.

Not a problem for you and me, Mac, but these friends of yours will not mix well with the vacuum waiting for them outside, said Jace in mind speak.

Mac thought for a moment. *What about your emulator generator?*

It can survive in a vacuum, but I don't think it could survive being sucked out of the ship through a hole smaller than itself.

That would be too bad, Mac said sarcastically while he wondered if aliens knew what sarcasm was.

I'm going to ask for your help again. Only part of me has to get down to the surface. Remember that there's more to me than what's on this ship. There are parts of me still back on the front. If one particle of my being gets to Ronos the rest will follow. All I need you to do is get any little bit of me down there. Can you do that?

Mac was still hesitant to help Jace. Right now there was only one thing Mac could think to do. Scott had started a countdown to the next pull. There was only nine minutes to go. The ships that were still able to move were frantically jockeying to get on the outside of the group, where they were only going to be crushed on one side.

It was chaos. There was as much crashing and bumping into each other now as when the pull was happening. No one was organizing or thinking about anyone but themselves, except for the armored long haul ship. It didn't move from the focal point of the pull as if it realized that it was indeed the focal point. Besides the scarred capital ship, the long haul was the strongest ship and the one most likely to survive the dog pile of ships that came every ten minutes and twenty two seconds.

More people were going to die needlessly because everyone was too busy panicking to think about the best way to survive without screwing everyone else.

Mac opened a comlink to the capital ship.

"Go tell General Zinger that Mac Narrad needs to talk to him," he said to the communications officer.

There was a pause and then an antagonistic voice erupted from the other end.

"What did you do!" demanded Zinger.

"What?"

"There was a way to escape before, but now the corridor is gone and the pull is supercharged. What did you do?"

"I didn't do that," said Mac.

"Then who did? We were the only ones here before and we didn't do anything that could have caused this."

"It must have been down on the surface."

"The surface?" Zinger thought about it for a moment. He realized why Mac was there now. "Lynn's down there, isn't she?"

"I'll give you the whole story, but I want to give it to you in person. Let us dock. Your ship isn't in danger of being crushed by anything bigger than it. Let us onboard and anyone else who will fit and I'll tell you everything I know."

"Don't play hero. Not everyone will fit. Especially not their ships."

"The people will fit. We don't need a bed for everyone. All we need is a place to keep them safe. If their ships won't fit then we can ferry them over with a shuttle."

"There's no way that will happen in the next six and a half minutes."

"You're not even trying. Start loading people up. No one else has to die!"

Mac surveyed the ships trying to survive the pull. The sharp triangle cruiser was adopting the same strategy as the armored transport. It could survive being pummeled — or it was more likely to anyway — so it was positioning itself to take the punishment from someone else. Everyone else was rocketing away as fast as they could. The farther away they got the less time they would have to spend in the scrum. Some of the ships were far enough away so that they couldn't be seen. That would only buy them a few seconds. Other ships were so damaged already that they best they could do was limp away. There were two small personal military ships left, precursors to the *Kilkenny* — which would have been a good ship to have in this situation — and they were following close behind Mac as he circled Zinger's capital ship. They wanted to dock like Mac did. They knew if anyone was going to explode it was going to be them. How many times had they asked to dock before and been denied?

The seconds were ticking by. Soon it wouldn't matter what Zinger's response was, there wasn't going to be enough time to dock.

"If I die out here then you have nothing," said Mac.

"What do I get if I let you on my ship?" asked Zinger.

"The only person out here who can survive the gas."

No doubt Zinger was still reluctant to trust him like Mac was reluctant to rely on the man who murdered his family. But Mac knew that the general knew Mac was worth more alive than dead. For now.

"We are opening the doors to the docking bay," said General Zinger. "You better hurry if you want to make it in time."

Mac looked at the clock. There was only two minutes left. Hardly enough time, especially for what he wanted to do. He could see the docking bay doors open and he opened a communication channel with the other two ships trying to seek shelter.

"I got permission to dock, but I want you two to go in ahead of me," said Mac.

"There's not enough time for all of us!" said a nervous woman on one of the ships. The other small ship had moved past them and was almost inside the pearly capital ship.

"Just do it!" said Scott interrupting what Mac was going to say.

The woman's ship started moving into position and Mac followed dangerously close behind her but there was no other choice. He kept one eye on his piloting and the other eye on Scott's clock. They were down to the last thirty seconds and he still hadn't got into the docking bay. Why was that chick going so slow?

Ten seconds. The nose of the HAAS3 breached the docking bay, but before the doors closed the pull started again. Mac could feel the shuttle being pulled out of the docking bay.

"Get inside so we can close the doors!" shouted Zinger's communication officer.

Scott reached past Mac to punch the shuttle to full speed. The shuttle inched toward the docking bay doors. That would have been impossible out in open space, but because they were already mostly inside the ship the pull wasn't as strong. They were able to get far enough inside so that the docking bay doors closed. Mac had to quickly turn the engines down so that they didn't explode after jetting into a wall because the engines were still at full with no pull.

Mac, Scott, and the others on the shuttle were safe for now. Quentin, Jace, and the rest of Passage were on their own until Mac convinced Zinger to fill his ship with new passengers. Mac landed the shuttle and then led the way off with everyone else following closely behind him. Scott kept to the back of the group hoping to not be noticed. The General was one of the men in charge of concocting the story about Scott being clinically insane for not supplying the army with ammunition in a time of war. Even though the war was real he still felt he was justified in his decision. There was no way to tell whether the lasers would be shot futilely at the aliens, into the backs of the government and military's opposition, or at Northgate's civilians.

The docking bay was huge. It could fit almost half of the ships that were out there right now struggling to keep together. If it had been someone who hadn't ordered the deaths of millions of people, Zinger's cold indifference might have been a shock, but now it was disturbingly typical. The general strode into the docking bay with anger in his eyes that seemed to say that it was somehow someone else's fault that his brow was so furrowed.

Mac was within striking distance of the man who murdered his family. He felt a rage that he didn't feel when he saw the fat man on the vid link. How was the last Narrad supposed to stand there and act like he didn't want to avenge his mom's murder? Was he supposed to forget about his toddler nephew whose last moments in life were spent in a pool of his own blood? His father. His siblings. Mac was alone because of the man standing across from him.

Several scenarios ran through Mac's mind. His first thought was to charge the general right now and take him off guard. With his fury and adrenaline rush, Mac was sure to get in several face shots before anyone could do anything about it. He might even be able to break a few bones. Making Zinger's remaining life uncomfortable, and hopefully painful, was much more appealing than straight out killing him. Although Mac left his gun in the shuttle it would be a simple matter to go back and get it or simply take one of the other soldier's guns and shoot Zinger in the leg to give him a permanent limp. After everything that Mac had been through he was justified in causing Zinger a little pain. The general couldn't get mad at him for that, because at least Mac was showing restraint.

Mac, you still alive? asked Jace.

Yes. I'm with Zinger trying to figure a way to get the Passage people to dock here, said Mac.

And a way to get down to the planet, right?

Mac didn't acknowledge the question. He was still going to do what he could to keep Jace from getting down to the surface. There would be time for revenge and pain inflicting later. There were too many people depending on Mac right now. His family would want him to put serving others before getting revenge.

The stress of the situation was taking a toll on Zinger. Where once Mac thought the general carried himself well and was a strong and forceful leader, he now saw an overweight old man who was tired of people not listening to him when he clearly, at least in his own mind, knew better than everyone. More than once on his walk he wiped his head with a cloth to clear it of perspiration.

With the general, like always, was the man with the widow's peak who Mac now knew was an android meant to protect Zinger. That's why it seemed like he never blinked. He never needed to. It also explained how he was the only one that Zinger could trust with his life. Anyone with a soul would eventually figure out that Zinger wasn't worth taking a bullet for.

Instinctively Mac felt around in his pocket for the chip the only man in Passage with an Imp gave him. It was the only weapon Mac had against the android but he had no idea how he was going to use it without Widow's Peak knowing. That was a problem for another time. The android wouldn't be an issue until Mac needed to get to Zinger which was on the latter half of his to do list right now.

The other refugees were getting out of their shuttles as Zinger and his man approached. The first one had two male soldiers in it. The second had the one nervous woman, also in fatigues. The three of them looked surprised that there were so many people in the HAAS3.

"I need you to make my soldiers like you," said General Zinger once he had reached Mac.

"Then I need to go down to the surface," said Mac.

"How did you make it down there before?"

"Use your brain. The gas didn't cover the whole planet before."

Zinger got an even angrier look on his face. He pulled out the laser pistol holstered at his side. He said, "You are going to cooperate or you will be made to cooperate."

"The only way to make others like me is to either go to the surface yourself or to let me go down and bring back what I need," said Mac.

"What will you be bringing back?" asked Zinger.

"I can't get into specifics," said Mac. If he told Zinger he needed to bring back some special rocks it might tip the general into a murderous frenzy that none of them could escape from. For sure Zinger would think Mac was telling lies.

"How are you planning on getting there?" asked Zinger.

"I still have to think of something, but I'm sure I can do it."

"Why?"

"Because I don't have a choice. I'm the only one who can," said Mac.

"And because you know that having enhanced soldiers like yourself is the only way we are going to win the war," said Zinger with a smile.

"I won't do anything for you until you allow as many people to dock with your ship as you can fit. You can save lives. We can change those people to be like me. Start our army now," said Mac.

"Don't be ridiculous. I can't have random people out there who have this power. I will be giving it to my men on this ship first."

"I have friends out there. I can't leave them to die."

Zinger shook his head and grabbed a portable console pad from one the men standing next to him. He started punching in some numbers and then he waved Mac over to show him what he was doing. On the screen was what the capital ship, the *Rundle*, had found on long range sensors. Mac wasn't sure what the general was getting at so he waited for an explanation.

"We were out here all by ourselves when the pull shifted into something much more powerful. It's not a big deal when you're by yourself, but when new ships started to turn up things got complicated. With each pull the reach and strength increased and more ships were brought here with each wave. We started plotting it so that it could be predicted. Right now, twenty ships have been pulled here. Whether they survived or not I don't care, 'cause it's only going to get more congested out there. In a day there will be a hundred ships pulled here."

"Send out a warning. Tell everyone to avoid coming here," said Mac.

"The pull blocked transmissions even before it changed into this new nightmare. Didn't you know that? After two days, the pull will reach the space station *Lendrum*." Zinger pointed it out on the pad. It was ten systems away. Mac couldn't believe the pull could reach that far. "We don't know if the new pull is strong enough to bring that thing here, but if it is, then it doesn't matter who we save. That thing is a quarter the size of our moon back on Earth. It will crush any ship that is still here. Do you understand why we need people down on the surface? It's not to win the war. We need to turn the pull off so that we don't all die."

Zinger looked at his pad again to check on the timing. "Now, you have seven minutes and eighteen seconds until the next pull. Maybe your friends will survive and maybe they won't, but we are all going to die if you don't do as I ask. So figure out a way to get down there or you will kill us all. You have the ship at your disposal, but don't do anything stupid with it."

Everyone in the docking bay was quiet except for Zinger and his men who were now walking away. Five stayed behind to make sure Mac did as he was told. No one spoke until the waddling general left the oversized room.

First things first.

"Everyone get out of the docking bay. We're going to open the doors," said Mac.

"No, you're not," said the remaining soldier with highest rank. He had a square jaw and squinty eyes.

"You heard Zinger —"

"General Zinger," said Square Squinty.

"He said I had the whole ship at my disposal. Right now I have need of it," said Mac.

"Why?"

This was annoying. Mac decided to lie to move things along. "There is someone out there who knows how to get to the surface and we need to get him inside here. Do you have a problem with that?"

The man thought about it for a moment before he responded. He decided it wasn't worth arguing about and ordered everyone out of the docking bay. Mac didn't follow. They must have heard about his new abilities because none of the soldiers tried to stop him or bring him with them.

Jace, I'm going to open the bay doors on the capital ship. I need you to fly in here as fast as you can, said Mac. He wasn't close enough to a computer to talk to Quentin so he went through Jace.

I'll do my best but we took on a lot of damage that last time. We got pinned between the luxury liner and a racing ship. I think our engine was damaged and part of our hull was breached. I got everyone into the container section and sealed them in the in the middle of the ship. If worse comes to worst they'll last the longest in there.

Racing ships were not the sexy streamlined things that racing cars were on Earth. Going fast meant that you would be creating amazing amounts of heat, which meant you needed a buffer zone between you and the engine. The bigger the engine, the bigger the gap between it and the pilot needed to be. Running into one of those was almost worse than running into a heavily armored ship. It was bad news for everyone out in the scrum except for the pilot of the racing ship. He was now wrapped in a protective sanctuary.

Until the space station *Lendrum* got there.

The doors are open! Get here as fast as you can! said Mac.

Mac was glad that other people saw what was happening. Most of them must have noticed the three small ships docking with Zinger's *Rundle* and were now eager to do the same. That was part of the plan: to accidentally save as many people as he could.

We are really limping here, said Jace.

Mac moved to the doors of the docking bay as ships flew overhead and boarded. The crew and passengers waited for the doors to close so they could disembark. Four ships had boarded. None of them were Jace's. It wouldn't be long now before the pull came. None of the remaining ships wanted to be anywhere near the capital ship when the pull came, so now they were all moving away. The only one still inching itself forward was Jace's.

His ship looked tattered. One side of it had a huge gash and the other side was completely caved in. There was a smaller room on the inside of the ship that everyone was hiding in and it looked like it was still intact, but how long would that last? The engine was flickering on and off, which was pretty good considering it looked like it had collapsed in on itself.

They weren't going to make it. As the countdown reached zero and the pull started again the bay doors closed and everyone got out of their ships. The guards came back inside.

"Where are the others?" asked Darren.

"They couldn't get here in time. We'll have to wait three minutes and then try again," said Mac.

We'll get you next time. Try to stay out of trouble for a couple more minutes, said Mac.

No good. We lost all propulsion, said Jace.

Then we'll come to you.

You already are. We are going to get pinned between Zinger's ship and the luxury liner. Look, the guys in the cargo compartment will be safe for now. The hull has to take an enormous beating before that compartment fails. If anything they will die from lack of oxygen before the ship comes apart.

I'm going down to the surface. I'll make sure they're the first ones I change when I come back.

No answer.

Jace?

Nothing.

The ship didn't explode, but wherever he kept his emulator generator it was gone now. That was going to make it a lot easier for Mac not to take Jace down to the surface with him.

Chapter 15
Indigenous

"What happened? Where are they?" asked Clarissa when the docking bay doors closed without the transport ship carrying the Passage people.

"We'll get them in next time, don't worry," said Darren.

"No. The ship is too damaged. We'll have to go for them. After I go down to the surface," said Mac.

"I want to go with you," said Darren.

"I don't think so," Mac and Clarissa said at the same time.

Darren immediately deflated.

"The only way you could help me Darren is if you're a pilot," said Mac.

"And you're not, so you are staying with me," said Clarissa. She clung a little tighter to her security blanket of a boyfriend.

Mac looked around. He couldn't find what he was looking for, so he went to the soldier with the square jaw and squinty eyes.

"How many Hawthrees do you have onboard?" asked Mac.

"What do you need Hawthrees for?" asked Square Squinty. He was going to be unnecessarily antagonistic.

"I'm going down to the surface. You heard Zinger-"

"General Zinger."

"What's your name?"

"Spacer Quake."

"You don't trust me do you, Spacer Quake?"

"No."

"Well, I don't trust your general, but I'm still going to do what he asks and go down to the surface. I don't care if you trust me, but I need to know if you're going to help me. There is no way I'm going to make it down to the surface unless you tell me what shuttles you have on this ship. Can you help me with that?"

Officer Quake looked disgusted that he was being asked in a reasonable and logical way to help someone he disliked. How dare he be talked to like there wasn't animosity between them. His only options were to increase his hostility or to cool off and help out. He turned to one of the other officers.

"Take everyone to deck eight," then to Mac he said, "follow me."

Mac waved Scott over.

"He's not coming," said Spacer Quake.

"I need his help," said Mac.

"For what?"

"I don't have time to lay it all out for you right now. Let's get to the ships and I'll explain everything there."

While they walked to the other side of the *Rundle*, Mac quickly devised a plan. It was sloppy but would probably work. It would mean sacrificing a few ships, but it would get some Lynn Rock off the planet. He only brought Scott because he didn't want to lose him again when they were so close to getting Lynn back.

There was so much about mind speak that Mac didn't know. Maybe it was because he was thinking about Lynn, maybe because he hadn't tried to contact her in a while, or maybe because Lynn had fixed the problem on her end. Whatever the reason, Lynn's voice suddenly popped into his head.

Mac! Can you hear me? she asked.

Yes. No need to yell. It was all Mac could do to not jump out of his skin at the sound of her yelling in his head.

Where are you? You need to come back for me. You need to get me out of here.

What's wrong? Are you okay?

I can't escape him. I've been lost in the caves for who knows how long. This is the first time I've been to the surface since we lost communication.

Maybe that interferes with it. You need to stay above ground. I have Scott with me now.

Scott's there!

Yes, Mac turned to Scott. "Lynn's talking to me in mind speak."

"Mind speak?"

"We can talk to each other in our minds."

Tell him I love him, said Lynn.

"Tell her I love her," said Scott almost at the same time.

Mac passed the messages along. There wasn't much more time for anything else. Lynn sounded nervous and anxious. Something was going wrong down there.

I can't stay on the surface, said Lynn. *Things have changed here. Everything is evolving. It's more dangerous to stay up here than to be down there with Raymond.*

Something more dangerous than Raymond? That didn't sound good.

I'm coming to the surface to get some rock, said Mac. *I won't be able to stay longer than a few seconds. I'm not even landing; I'm skimming the surface. Get up to the mountains. That's where I'm going. I'll try to pick you up at the same time.*

I don't know if I can do that.

You have to try. This is the only way until I find a ship that can survive the gas. Go to the mountains closest to the where the base was. When I get closer I will look for your glow.

Okay, I'll try, said Lynn.

Just make sure it's a mountain with plenty of Lynn Rock. If I don't bring some of that back then people will die.

Okay. Mac, what's going on up there? I see ships and explosions.

You might know better than me. When's the last time you were at the pull machine, 'cause it's ridiculously stronger than it was before.

There was a pause while Lynn thought it over.

That might have been my fault, but I can't talk about it right now.

Is there any way for you to reverse it? asked Mac.

There was no answer. Was she ignoring him or did she go back underground? Mac knew better now than to assume something was wrong. Lynn was too strong. Nothing would stop her from getting back to Scott now.

Mac needed to remember to contact her every so often to make sure that she was able to meet him if he could stumble his way to the surface. It was a big if. The plan was only partially formed.

One shuttle wouldn't survive in the gas long enough to get down to the surface. In his mind he solved it with using more than one ship but that didn't really work either. He needed to do it like Russian nesting dolls. A small ship inside a slightly bigger ship and so on and so forth.

The HAAS3 was the smallest armored shuttle on this side of the front line. There wasn't really a smooth transition into the next nesting doll. The next smallest armored shuttle or ship was the much larger HATS. Even if there was one on the *Rundle* that only got them down to the planet. How were they supposed to get back to space? Any vehicle they used to get to the planet would be burned so thoroughly that it wouldn't be able to make the return journey.

This was turning into a plan with way too much winging it. It might be a one way trip for Mac reuniting with Lynn and becoming trapped on the surface with her. If that happened then everyone left up here would be doomed until and he and Lynn figured out a way to make a spaceship out of raw materials on Ronos. The people from Passage didn't have that much time.

Mac laid out his plan for Scott and Quake.

"You're an idiot," Quake said at several points throughout the explanation and at the end.

"There are so many holes in your plan there is no way it can work," said Scott.

"It has to work. This is the first step to getting Lynn back," said Mac.

"Then there has to be a better way. This one relies too heavily on dumb luck and chance."

"You don't have to take the risk. I do."

"Not to mention the ships you want to destroy in the process," said Quake.

"Do you know how long it's going to take for the ships to get eaten to the point of uselessness by the gas?" asked Scott.

Mac didn't know. It all depended on the concentration of the gas where the ships were going. When he, Lynn, and Raymond were trapped in the cave it took a while for the small amount of gas in the cave to destroy the shuttle but when that finally did happen the explosion released a ton of concentrated gas into the atmosphere that destroyed the military base in only a few minutes. If the gas was still that concentrated then Mac didn't have a hope of getting off the planet. When he looked down on the planet it didn't look overpoweringly purple with gas. However, that could have been his wishful thinking.

Mac was surprised that Scott was so opposed to his plan. This was a do or die kind of thing. They didn't have time to sit down and come up with a plan that was foolproof. Quake was done trying to tell Mac he was being an imbecile and went off to get someone to do something about it. Mac pulled Scott aside.

"What's up, Scott? Don't you realize that there is no other way?"

"Of course I do. But when you get back they are going to use whatever you are bringing back to make as many enhanced soldiers as they can. General Zinger's men are the ones that are going to get to be like you. If those guys get that kind of power then we are all going to be on the wrong side of the war. First he'll take out the aliens and then he'll take out anyone that doesn't follow orders from him."

Mac had already thought of a contingency plan for this. He filled Scott in. Scott smiled but he still looked worried.

"We can't let Zinger get this power," said Scott.

"The people of Passage get it first. Then we move on from there to people we trust," said Mac.

"Passage first," agreed Scott. "By the way. This thing with Quake is all an act. It's Zinger trying to get you to think he cares more about something other than what's down on that planet."

"Good. Then I'm leaving."

Mac got in the HATS and headed for Ronos.

Lynn you still there? He called out.

I'm here. I'm on my way to the meeting point.

Good. Me too. I hope.

Just be careful. There are these giant gargoyle looking creatures that are trying to get me. I assume they'll try and get you as well.

Gargoyles?

You'll see when you get here. Don't leave me behind this time, okay?

Considering I'm going to wherever you are on the surface, I think it's a safe bet to say you'll be making it back.

The docking bay doors opened but Mac waited until it was clear to go. There was another pull going on right then. He looked out at the chaos to see if the HATS the Passage people were on was still intact. He couldn't see it. Despite all the ships that had been destroyed and all the ships that found refuge in the *Rundle* there were still noticeably more ships out there than the last time Mac had looked.

It was frightening. How strong was the pull now? How far was it reaching? All the ships out there were still small transport or personal ships. There used to be mostly military ships but now the pull reached far enough to get civilian ships. While waiting for the pull to be over Mac cued the com and called out to Quake.

"Can you send me the *Lendrum* timeline," Mac asked.

"To your Imp?"

"I don't have an Imp. Send it to the ship."

The information came through. The scanners on the *Rundle* could only reach so far, so some of the data was speculation, but it was speculation based on measurements of the pull's velocity — where they could measure it — and by the locations of where the new ships being pulled in were coming from. According to the countdown clock the pull would get to the *Lendrum* in a day and a half. Mac could have sworn it would be at least two days. Things were happening faster than anyone anticipated. They needed more people than just Mac and Lynn to be able to go to the surface before anything could be done to turn the pull off. There wasn't a lot of time, but they still needed to take it one challenge at a time.

The pull ended and Mac engaged the engine. Some of the new ships were trying to do what he was doing, go to the surface. They would never make it. The pull point was far enough away from Ronos that no one was going to get burned, but it was close enough that it was only a matter of time before space got too crowded and someone got pushed into the deadly gas.

In an effort to stop the others who were trying to get to the planet from killing themselves, Mac pulled ahead of all of them. It was difficult because he had to weave between wreckage and bodies. It was a dump up there now and impossible to miss everything, so he had to choose to hit only the little things and the things that wouldn't splatter.

When he entered the atmosphere the hissing started. So familiar. There was a rush of dread and helplessness from what they had gone through when they were first trapped on Ronos. He thought it might be the last thing he would ever hear and it almost was.

He checked the readout on his console telling him the armor was being eaten away by the gas. Red lights were going off faster than Mac had anticipated. This was already turning into a bad idea. All he could do was push the engines as fast as they would go.

The location wasn't exact for Mac and he was banking on being able to see Lynn glowing in the gas from far away. He figured she would be somewhere on the horseshoe continent but he was having trouble remembering where the base had been. Things looked different down there. There were more trees and rivers than there were before. The prairies were shrinking. The ocean was also different. The color was off. Now it was much darker. Then Mac remembered how he was able to avoid the gas by going under water.

Lynn! Meet me at the cliffs by the ocean near where Zinger's base was. I can protect myself with the water. I'll be able to last longer.

No, you won't. The water is susceptible to gas now. That was kind of my fault.

Lynn had said something about things evolving down there. Is this what she meant? Contaminating the oceans would dramatically change everything on the planet. Maybe it was speeding up the evolution of the planet. He pointed the ship at the strange, unnaturally straight line separating the foothills from the prairie. He could still see it even though it now looked like it was covered in dense foliage.

The gas had eaten through the armor and the hissing was louder than ever. The power to the HATS was flickering on and off. This was all expected but Mac hadn't expected it quite so soon. He unbuckled his safety harness and moved to the cargo room where the HAAS3 was.

The possibility of spinning out had always been there so the HAAS3 was strapped down with lines that could be detonated. All the power went out and the HATS started free falling as Mac got in the assault shuttle. He had planned to fly out of there as soon as the HATS stopped working but now he needed to wait longer so that he was closer to the ground, otherwise the HAAS3 would burn out too early for Mac to move onto the next phase.

The cargo room was a dark shade of purple now as the gas made its way through the walls. Mac looked at the computer in the HAAS3 to make sure he didn't smash into the ground. The gas was already starting to mist into the room. It was time for Mac to leave

The HAAS3 was facing the bay doors but they were still locked. Mac fired the shuttle's weapons and the back of the HATS exploded with shrapnel. At the same time he blew the straps holding him down and barreled his way free of the transport ship.

The transport ship hurtled toward the ground while Mac got his bearings and punched the engines as fast as they would go for the mountains. The speed pinned him to the back of his seat and threw the boxes that represented the next phase of his plan to the back of the cockpit. He hoped they weren't damaged.

Lynn! I'm close but I can't see you.

I'm trying to get to one of the peaks. You'll be able to see me soon I think.

Mac couldn't see her and scanning for life was no good either. There were large creatures all over the place and the computer couldn't tell the native animals from Lynn.

Let me know as soon as you get to the top, said Mac.

The mountain range was expansive with jagged edges that stretched to the sky and valleys that plunged to the depths of Ronos. She wouldn't be very far into the range but she did need to find a peak that had Lynn Rock on it.

I'm up. Can you see me? Said Lynn.

Mac looked.

I don't see you, he said.

I can see you. Fly around and head south.

Mac did as he was told. The day was bright and everything was well lit. That might have added to the problem of trying to find a glowing person. Painfully he slowed down. The gas was still hissing but he didn't want to blow past Lynn. Thankfully the gas was thinner closer to the surface but that only slowed down the inevitable.

Then he saw her. There was a faint purple glow jumping up and down. He sped up again.

I see you!

Lynn didn't respond.

Lynn?

Nothing again, and now the glow was gone. It looked like she had fallen down the far side of the mountain.

Something was wrong. Mac sped up. He got to the mountain Lynn had been on. It wasn't the top of the mountain but a ridge leading to the top. It was sharp and crumbly. There was no way to put the HAAS3 down. He moved the ship to hover on the other side of the mountain to see if he could tell where Lynn went but he couldn't see her glow anywhere. Would her glow go away if she died? Would falling off a mountain be enough to kill her?

Then he saw what Lynn had described as a gargoyle. It was big enough that it could kill Mac with a bear hug. There was no human who was that big. Its skin was gray leather which stretched across its thick arms and torso. It ran on all fours but Mac saw it rear up on its hind legs. As far as he could tell it didn't have any opposable thumbs or digits of any kind. Maybe it had hooves like a cow or horse. But it did have wings, so did anything else really matter? To go with the wings was a long mouth filled with teeth that resembled the mountain range Mac was hovering over. A long thin tongue danced in and out of its mouth and around the teeth. Mac wondered how often that thing bit its tongue. He was happy to see no blood dripping off the long noodle-like tongue so he guessed that Lynn was hiding somewhere. Its eyes were big disks on the sides of its head giving it a full view of everything around it.

Lynn? Are you there?

There was no answer but Mac felt confident that she was okay. He could feel something inside him that said she was still alive. It wasn't her voice but a feeling that she was okay and that she had a good reason for not answering. It probably had something to do with the gargoyle.

The view of the gargoyle was starting to get obscured by the front window getting eaten up by the gas. It was a reminder to stop staring and get back to it. Mac was about to get up and open one of the large packages behind him but then realized he didn't need to do that. The HAAS3 would last a little bit longer.

What he needed now was a boulder of Lynn Rock. He thought about opening fire on the gargoyle and creating some movable boulders at the same time but he wasn't sure that was safe with Lynn down there somewhere.

The window was too obscured now to see through, so Mac had to use the console and scanners to make sure he didn't crash. Those were starting to flicker as well. It was getting close to time to abandon ship.

Lynn! If you can hear me you need to get up here. I can't stay any longer. Get out here!

The ship rocked as something hit it. Was it the creature? No. It was something thrown at the ship. Whatever it was hit and bounced off.

Then it happened again. This time a huge boulder came crashing through the front window of the ship. Mac didn't even see it coming. He was struck by the large rock and thrown aside. At least it was a Lynn Rock.

Was it the gargoyle creature that did that? Gas was filling the cockpit as he looked out the hole the rock had left behind. The creature was looking up curiously at the flying machine above him.

Mac! Are you okay? Lynn finally broke her silence.

The moment she used mind speak the monster of Ronos turned his head and motored down the mountain. He could sense her when she used her mind speak. That's why she hadn't been saying anything.

*I'm okay. But I don't think I can stay much longer. Where are you? We need to get out of here!*The gargoyle stopped its descent and looked back at Mac. It could hear him as well. And Mac was low enough for the monster to easily run and jump into the ship. It was time to leave but he was going to try and help Lynn in the process.

I'm going to lead it away. Find somewhere to hide until I can get back there.

You're leaving me again.

Just for now. I won't leave orbit, trust me.

When will you be back?

I don't know. But the next time Scott will be with me. Now stop talking so that it follows me and not you.

Lynn continued running away down the mountain looking for a cave to escape into. Until she was gone Mac had nothing to do but talk to the monster that had been trying to kill her. The hissing in the shuttle was getting louder. The armor was almost totally gone. He wasn't going to be able to stay much longer.

Hey you ugly monstrosity! Mac yelled towards the creature. *You look like a rhino mixed with an overweight bat. A bino or maybe a Rat. Oh wait, that's a thing already. A rato. Hurry up and jump at me so I can get out of here.*

Something did jump at Mac but it wasn't the monster. It was Raymond. His tattered clothes billowing in the wind, he leaped from the rocky mountain to the shuttle. He landed on the nose of the ship and pulled himself into the cockpit beside Mac who was too stunned to do anything about it.

Mac could barely look at Raymond without wanting to throw up. His face was half burned off. The big gash in his neck made his breathing sound like a cat slowly dying. Mac sat there not sure what to do. This worked to Raymond's advantage and he lifted Mac up and threw him out the broken window with a look of blood lust in his crispy black eyes.

Mac flew through the air away from the shuttle. Everything was moving in slow motion. He was spinning end over end. Each time he caught sight of the shuttle it was moving farther and farther away. When he caught sight of his destination, the mountain and the monster, they both got bigger and bigger, the monster more exponentially than the mountain.

The monster had chosen to pounce at the same time Mac was thrown. They met mid-air but the collision didn't slow the monster down. Mac smacked against the beast's leathery torso and the beast held on to Mac as it flew to attack the shuttle.

The beast landed on the front of the shuttle and Mac was propelled back through the broken window. He hit the large boulder of Lynn Rock. Part of it broke off. Raymond looked too stunned to know what to do.

"Get us out of here!" Mac yelled as he staggered to his feet.

Raymond shook his head and tried the controls again. He pointed the ship straight up but it wasn't responding to controls anymore.

The beast clung to the shuttle with retractable claws from its egg-shaped elephant feet. They stuck out long enough to latch onto the ship. Its wings beat furiously pulling the ship back to the ground. Its teeth tore at the hull trying to kill this new prey. They were never going to get out of there. The ship was already turning a magnificent purple color that may have been considered beautiful under circumstances that didn't involve Mac's exit from mortality.

Mac would have to accelerate his plan. Fortunately Raymond was there to distract the gargoyle. The piece of rock that was broken off was too big for Mac to carry himself. He punched at it to turn it into smaller pieces he could put in his pocket. A gravel pit was forming in the back of the shuttle.

His pockets loaded, Mac opened one of the boxes on the deck and removed a personal jet pack that had been hastily armored. Would it be enough for Mac to escape to space? It would have to be.

He opened the side door and jumped out without even saying goodbye to Raymond. He didn't feel their relationship warranted one anyway. As he left, the hissing of the gas eating away foreign material quieted but never went fully away. Parts of the jet pack were still burning, but not all of it.

When he was encompassed by the gas he glowed purple with power. Anything within that glow was protected, like his clothes and, if he bear hugged the jet pack with his arms and legs, most of the jet pack.

It wasn't fool proof. There was no way for Mac to steer and parts were still being burned, but all he needed it to do was get him back into space. There would be someone there waiting to pick him up.

Scott, I'm on my — Mac started to say but then realized Scott would be unable to hear the message. All he could do was hope Scott would be there to pick him up.

Using thought speech was a bad idea. The shuttle was completely powerless but it was still moving up thanks to the winged beast that had its claws sunk into it. Its wings were massive and could easily pull the shuttle and Raymond up faster than the jet pack could pull Mac closer to space. The shuttle was being pulled from behind. The contents were cascading out of the hole in the main window. Had Raymond already fallen out?

The gargoyle let out a horrible screech that sounded like the agony of a bear being ripped apart. There was nothing Mac could do but hold on. He didn't even have any weapons unless he wanted to throw rocks at it.

It roared again and the sound was so terrifying that Mac was tempted to let go and fall to his death rather than get picked off by the gargoyle, but there was no guarantee the gargoyle wouldn't swoop down and chomp him before he went splat.

The atmosphere was thinning and going darker. The gas was thickest at the top right before he would break into space. The hissing was intensifying but by holding the jet pack backwards he was keeping the important parts like the fuel and the engine close to him so they weren't burning as bad as the other parts. The heat coming off the engine was so intense that no normal human would have been able to do this and survive.

The monster was close enough to start snapping its jaws and extending its neck to try and reach him. The shuttle it was hauling was crispy black now and losing its shape. The monster snapped again and again and then Mac realized it wasn't snapping at him. It was trying to breathe. Its wide eyes were bulging out of its head. Its tongue was flopping in and out of its mouth and its wings were starting to beat irregularly. In one last attempt to take out Mac it used its hind legs to throw what remained of the shuttle.

It hit and knocked the jet pack out of his grasp. He started to fall. There was nothing he could do. The shuttle continued up out of the atmosphere.

The jet pack was nowhere near him but for some reason the hissing was getting louder as Mac started falling. Then there was something underneath him. Another HAAS3. It was Scott! Mac landed on top of the shuttle and held on as it turned up and headed back for space. There was one last ominous screech from the creature.

Chapter 16
Down to the Surface

The ships were drifting apart after a pull cycle ended. Mac wanted to go straight to the others from Passage and give them the injection that would save their lives, but he needed to melt the rock first. The HAAS3 had no air lock in it. Every ship with a hyper drive had one, but only certain shuttles had them. The battle-ready HAAS3 didn't waste space on an airlock.

Ships drifted away from the center of the pull. New ships were flying foolishly towards the *Rundle* thinking it would shelter them, but there was no more room. There were a couple explosions from ships crashing into each other in the frantic attempt to get away. The hollow triangular holiday cruiser had finally started to show signs of struggle. One side of the equilateral triangle had collapsed, its hull breached and beds, chairs and clothes from the luxury suites in the cruiser were spewing out of it. There were also several computers and the kitchen must have been hit as well because the food was all mashed together and being sucked out into space. No bodies though. Either the ship was empty or the passengers had been evacuated to more secure parts of the ship before anything went sideways.

Just as they planned Mac waited for the door to the HAAS3 to open. Scott was in a bulky space suit with a round helmet. His mobility was severely handicapped. The suit was thick and it didn't look like he could even sit down. If that had been the kind of space suit that had been in the shuttle when he, Raymond, and Lynn had first crashed on Ronos, things would have turned out differently.

Raymond. He was on the shuttle the gargoyle had thrown into space. Could Raymond survive space or were they finally rid of him?

Mac closed the door but they had to wait for the life support to charge back up before Scott could take off the helmet.

"You should keep the suit on," said Mac. "In case something goes wrong during the next pull."

"Where's Lynn?" Scott asked.

"She's still down there. But I talked to her. She's okay."

"I thought you were bringing her back."

"I was, but we were attacked. I didn't have any choice but to leave."

"What!"

"She'll be okay. She knows where to hide. She'll be safe."

"Are you going to change me so I can go down there?"

"As soon as I can. How much longer until the next pull?"

Scott stumbled over to the control console. He couldn't sit in the chair but he leaned over the controls to study the readout.

"Just under five minutes," he said.

"Can you fly with that suit on?" asked Mac.

"Yes."

"We won't be able to get to them before that happens. Do you think you can keep us from getting crushed during the pull?"

"Don't really have a choice."

Mac figured there was something more to it and waited for Scott to fill in the blanks.

"Well, they weren't going to give me a shuttle were they? I had to humble Quake a little. He'll wake up taken down a couple more notches by a old fat man like me."

"They didn't send people out after you?"

"Yes, there were ships after me but then we caught sight of you and that monster. I think they went to recover the hawthree you took down there."

"Lucky us."

"For now."

Mac grabbed a weapon and dialed it down to the lowest setting. Then he put the rocks in a container and shot down at them through the lid. The rocks vibrated and scorched and at first Mac thought that he might have grabbed the wrong kind of rock but then they started to lose their structural integrity. They became gloopy and started molding into each other, becoming less and less solid.

"Hold on to something," said Scott. The pull was about to start.

Mac moved to the seat beside him and buckled up as tightly as he could. He held the big glass jar between his legs and continued to liquefy the contents. Shooting a laser so close to his crotch was a bad idea if ever there was one, but Mac was sure the liquid rock he injected in himself was less viscous than the rock in the jar and there was no time to waste waiting for the pull to end. Multi-tasking might result in him becoming a eunuch but it was a risk he had to take.

The first jolt of the pull almost stole Mac's manhood.

"Don't fight the pull!" said Mac.

"Don't fire a laser at yourself like that!" said Scott.

Mac decided he was partly right and kept one eye out to make sure they weren't about to run into anything. All the engines of all the ships that weren't disabled glowed bright as they struggled to stay away from the clustered mess at the center of the pull.

Scott was pulling some fancy moves to avoid the biggest obstacles. It was like running a race uphill with people rolling barrels full of explosives at you. Except that the top of the hill was the most dangerous spot. Going with the pull meant that they would be getting there sooner. Out the window Mac spotted the transport ship with all the Passage people on it. Mac had been there only a few short cycles before, but the pull had already changed it into something more disturbing. If the ship lasted through this one it wouldn't survive the next.

The HATS was nestled with all the other dead and useless ships being squeezed harder than it was designed to withstand. Would the people inside die from a hull breach or from being crushed into each other?

The worse news was that the triangle shaped cruiser had lost its engines and one of its points was now set to pierce the dead ships in the middle of the massive mess of metal. Mac felt hopeless watching. There was no way to stop the pull.

The sharp edge of the luxury ship cut through the first derelict ship like it wasn't even there. It was going to take something with more structural integrity to stop it. The ship was so far into the vortex of crushing metal that it was impossible to see if the people of Passage had avoided it or not. There was no way to tell where one ship ended and another began and it was getting more and more messy as the pull continued.

Then their own HAAS3 crashed into the other ships. Scott's hands flew over the controls to try and free them or at least keep them from getting sandwiched. But it was no use. The shuttle was assaulted again and again. It felt like it was going on forever but Mac knew that it couldn't be more than three minutes.

Alarms sounded as more and more ships plowed into them. The armor couldn't protect them. It was meant to ward off laser damage, not being rammed.

"How much time left?" asked Mac.

"Twenty seconds, but I don't know if we'll make that without a hull breach," said Scott.

"Go put your helmet on then."

They were still a ways away from the fuel getting ignited by accident.

Scott put on his helmet. He had it sealed as the hull above his head buckled and the air started hissing out of the shuttle. The crack was small enough that he was able to get back to his seat and buckle himself in.

Mac was still alive. It was weird how he was still making breathing motions when there was nothing to even fill his lungs right now. It was like his body was going through the motions, like breathing was nothing more than a bad habit he couldn't quit even when there was nothing to breathe.

"Now what?" asked Scott.

Some of the ships were able to drift apart, their HAAS3 was one of them. But others were wedged so close together that big machinery or a strong laser blast would be needed to pull them apart. Their HAAS3 still had some power although it was intermittent and could go at any moment.

The ball of contorted metal that they were part of now had doubled in size. Mac couldn't even see the Passage shuttle let alone get to them and give them the injections. He used the computer to see if he could scan for life forms.

Scott saw what he was doing and asked, "Do you see them?"

"Yes. There," Mac pointed at the screen.

There were warm bodies amongst the pile of what used to be space ships. And most of the people were concentrated in the same area. That had to be the Passage people. The transport ship's integrity had held up.

"How are you going to inject them without letting out their air?" asked Scott.

"What?"

"There's no air lock on those transport ships. I mean, no airlock for the cargo area at least. The rest of the ship is ripped open so the only air they have is in the room with them. As soon as you open it up they'll be dead."

With everything else going on Mac had pushed that problem to the back burner thinking he would deal with it when it came up. Well, it was here and he wasn't sure how to get it done. He looked over at the clock. A minute had already gone by before the next pull would get there. Whatever he was going to do he wasn't going to get it done from a busted up shuttle.

"I don't know how we're going to do it but I'm going over there. You stay here and guide me with the computer so I can find them faster," said Mac.

"How am I going to talk with you?"

Mac looked around and found a comlinker in one of the drawers. It was a small electronic device that fit in the ear. There was one on every military shuttle for emergencies. Otherwise the normal mode of communication was an Imp.

"Did you bring the syringes I asked for?" asked Mac.

"In the first aid kit."

The kit was big enough to fit the jar of liquid rock inside once Mac took out the medical supplies he wouldn't need. It had a long strap so he could wear across his chest. He tightened it to keep it close to his body.

"Does this thing still have engines?" asked Mac.

"Yes. Barely."

"Try to make it back to the *Rundle*. If I take longer than eight minutes then you won't make it through the next pull."

Mac thought about injecting Scott but he wasn't sure it was a good idea yet. There was a very limited supply of the rock and Scott had a space suit that would keep him alive for a bit longer. Scott must have realized this as well because he didn't protest as Mac left the armored shuttle.

Space was supposed to be big and empty but the space around Ronos was crowded and deadly. Even the airspace around Earth's spaceport, where there were often thousands of ships, didn't look like this. Everything was so lifeless, like a man-made asteroid field. Ships bumped into each other and spun off into different directions and there was nothing anyone could do. Mac remembered the life sign readout on the computer. There was no one breathing on any of these derelict ships.

As Mac jumped away from Scott and the shuttle he asked, "Keep me up to speed on the countdown as well okay?"

"Absolutely, you're at eight minutes twenty seven seconds, by the way."

The damaged shuttle started to pull away and head back for the faux safety of Zinger's capital ship.

Mac was out there alone now. There was nothing for him to do but get to it, no time to gawk or mourn. As fast as he could he scrambled over the mess that used to be ships. He had to be careful not to accidentally launch himself into space. He could be floating out there for a long time. Spending an eternity drifting uselessly was a nightmare to Mac. The only solace for him would be the thought of someone finding him. Imagine the look on those people's faces when they pulled a living man without a space suit onto their ship.

But that was only another distraction. Mac also had to pay attention so that he didn't get crushed as the ships started to drift apart. He wasn't sure that it would kill him, but he was sure that it would slow him up enough that he would be trapped outside during the next pull.

"Eight minutes," said Scott.

"Thanks. Am I close?" asked Mac.

"You need to follow the cruise ship. The tip has stabbed in almost right to where you need to go. Follow it like a road and you should be okay."

Mac crawled over to where the ball of space garbage was being stabbed by the luxury liner. It looked like an oversized fancy candle in a really small and unappetizing cupcake. He realized his first problem as soon as he got there. There was no way to penetrate the collection of smashed ships. Was he supposed to dig his way through? He reached out tentatively and tried to remove some of the debris. It was hard to pull and to stay grounded at the same time but he managed to pull off a section of the ship.

He pulled himself inside and moved forward. When he got as far as he could he gripped the walls and tried to tear new holes through the weakest parts. Everything around him was grinding together. The sound of metal being pulled and broken was almost constant. He probably could have waited outside for an opening to appear but he was too impatient.

"Seven minutes."

"Can you tell where I am?" Mac asked Scott.

"Yes, you're close."

"Which way should I go? I'm all turned around in here." Mac was afraid of doubling back on himself.

"Turn to your left."

Mac pulled himself around as Scott instructed.

"Now if you go straight you should be able to get to the remains of the transport ship. I think you'll land right in the control room but it's hard for me to tell. Don't worry. The life form sensors are still warm."

In front of Mac was a solid wall. How was he going to get through this? He looked around for a seam or a window but there was none to be seen. It was going to have to be opened the hard way. In the zero gravity Mac spun around so that his back was pressed against the opposite wall and he started kicking. The first kick caused a small dent. Mac was a little surprised that's all it did. He put everything he had into it. No matter. He kicked again and again. The dent got deeper but what he needed was a hole he could force bigger. What he really needed was an explosion. Maybe there were explosives on the Passage shuttle — it was a military shuttle after all — but he needed them now.

"Six minutes."

"Where are you right now?" asked Mac.

"Approaching the *Rundle*. They are not happy with me but they are letting me dock, probably so they can punish me."

"I'm trapped right now. I need your help. Can you get a lock on my location?"

"What do you mean a lock? Like a weapons lock?"

"Yes."

"Are you crazy?"

"How much time is left?"

"Five minutes thirty seven seconds."

"Well, we could argue about it and run down the clock or you could trust me and do it. I need things shook up down here so I can get free. Fire toward me but not so that you hit me or the transport ship. Make sure it's on a low setting."

"Fine. Get ready."

"I'm ready."

The world around Mac started to rumble and then spin. The ship he was in had been thrown free and was spinning away. As it broke away from the main bulk of ships an entire wall went missing. It must have been snug up against some other ship but now the two were separated. Mac pulled himself along the wall and through the gap. The ship was spinning away from where he wanted to go but he couldn't jump out; he had to jump so that he was propelled back the way he came.

He waited for the ship to rotate one more time and then made his jump.

"Five minutes. It looks like you will drift in the right direction. The transport ship is exposed now. Make sure you inject them before the next pull though, because now that they are exposed like that they are more vulnerable."

Scott was right. Mac needed to hurry but no matter how much he swung his arms and no matter how much he kicked his legs there was no way for him to move fast in the vacuum of space. When he reached garbage floating around he tried to use it to propel himself farther but it wasn't as effective as he wanted it to be. He lost the speed he gained every time he latched onto a new piece of garbage.

"Four minutes, Mac. I'm on the capital ship now. I think it will only be a matter of time before I'll be out of contact with you."

"Thanks. I'll be there soon."

"Hurry."

Four minutes to go. Mac could see the transport ship ahead of him but it was still far away. He would get there in the next four minutes but he knew there would be no way he was going to inject all those people before the next pull started, and he still had no clue how he was going to do that without killing them.

Finally he got to the transport ship. The big bulky ship was still twisted into two other ships. The large boxy shape was beat up and contorted so that it could easily snag onto others. He crawled in one of the openings and found himself inside what used to be the cockpit or control deck as they were called on larger ships. It didn't look anything like it used to. The control panel was completely smashed and at the front the ceiling was almost to the floor. Everything that wasn't bolted down was long gone.

Mac pulled himself along the floor to the back door where the reinforced cargo bay area was. The door was blocked by some twisted wreckage. He would have to move that later.

He hit his fist against the wall repeatedly to get someone's attention inside.

"Is someone out there?" came a muffled voice from inside.

"It's Mac! I'm here to get you out of there," said Mac.

"Did you guys hear something?"

"Get us out of here before we die!"

They couldn't hear him. Before Mac could do anything the pull started again. The ship was jerked to the side and Mac went crashing into the wall. The first aid kit he had on his back slammed first. While he could he spun it around and checked to make sure that what was inside was okay. He wrapped his body around it to protect it. It needed to survive the next three minutes or this was all for nothing.

There was a little bit of a break after the initial pull started but then all the chunks that Scott had blown apart started coming back together. Mac had a terrifically terrifying view of it all. From where he was drifting he could see dead ships being pulled towards him. He had to find cover, but where? There was nothing left on this ship except the cargo bay.

The first sizable chunk of garbage hit and he was thrown against the wall. He had to reach out with one hand to stop himself from getting impaled on a serrated piece of what used to be a wall. Then he caught sight of a dangerous goods compartment. Mac could hide in there.

When he got to it he found that the door was partially blocked by the same piece of jagged metal that had almost stuck through him seconds before. With one hand he twisted the metal away from the door, pushed it open and went inside. It wasn't a perfect dome of protection. He could see stars through a crack above his head, but it was better than nothing.

As he waited for it to all be over he noticed something abnormal. He wasn't sure how to describe it at first. The first word that came into his mind was vibration, but he wasn't sure if that was really what was going on. There was a buzzing in his ear that sounded like a creepy, quieter uncle to the hissing noise of the gas eating through foreign material. Was it the pull?

No. When Mac moved his hand over certain parts of the shuttle there was an undeniable tingling, vibrating sensation there. It felt uncomfortable but Mac kept his hand there for a moment. Something was going on. His hand was out of focus. Like the air was thicker there. Did it have something to do with Jace? Had he trapped himself in the dangerous goods compartment before his emulator generator was destroyed so that his swarm stayed with the ship?

As the minutes ticked by the situation became more real. Hiding in the closet might not have been a good idea. Mac was distracted by the fuzzy bits of space he had found and hadn't noticed that the walls were closing in around him. The little crack through which he had seen the stars was gone now. Every second there was another grind of metal on metal. Somewhere close by there was an explosion that made everything shake and made him wonder if there was any hope of surviving. The longer the pull went on the louder the noises got.

Wasn't the pull only supposed to last for three minutes? It felt like three hours had gone by. The luxury yacht was pushing its way deeper and closer to the pull point. Mac could hear the screaming of metal tearing as it uselessly tried to slow the progress of the triangular spear. That sound was the worst. That was the sound that was getting louder.

He didn't feel safe any more. If it stabbed through the door of the dangerous goods compartment there was nothing Mac could do to survive. There was nowhere else to go. With every crunch and explosion the walls scrunched tighter and tighter around him. Would he even be able to open the door after this?

The door slid open but only far enough for him to get the tips of his fingers out. That was enough. He strained. Maybe he yelled but no one would have been able to hear it even if they were standing right next to him. The strain of metal trying to stay strong and failing was louder than anything he could make with his body.

The door opened another couple inches and on the other side was more bad news. There was more room in the closet than there was out there on the control deck. Then the walls of garbage started to shift as something charged through from behind. The point of the luxury ship started out as something small but it didn't take long for it to become bigger than Mac. It charged right past him and slammed into the wall of the cargo bay, piercing it almost instantly. Air started hissing out of it. They were going to die in there!

Mac forced the door wide enough for him to get inside. No more messing around. The pull had stopped. He needed to inject those people in the next few minutes or they were going to die.

The door was blocked by wreckage but Mac had all kinds of adrenaline coursing through his veins now. With each effort, he yanked with everything his transformed strength would give him. Giving up meant they died. Not being able to move something because he wasn't strong enough was not something he even considered. There was no hesitation. The door was partially unobstructed now.

There was no point in worrying about them losing their air so he started kicking at the bottom seam of the door. It broke back almost immediately. Whatever air had been in the room was now gone for sure. Quickly he crawled inside and opened his first aid kit.

Everyone was inside, floating with a look of terror in their eyes. Most of them were still waving their arms like if they did that they could create some air for themselves. There were four people in space suits who were still breathing. They were trying to find a way to share their compressed air with the others around them but it wasn't going as fast as they hoped and was turning into a mess that would end up getting them killed. Mac saw that one of the men was Quentin. Amongst the floating people from Passage were several crates with the Earth Military insignia on them.

Mac started injecting people as he waved the space suited people over. Quentin bounced over and started helping. He couldn't communicate with Mac, but Mac showed him how to fill the syringes and then had him fill while Mac injected. The other three people in space suits saw what was happening and copied Mac. Quentin made sure they were all being supplied with liquefied rock.

Quentin did as he was told. Every time Mac held his hand out there was liquid rock there. But it was still going to be a while to get everyone. There were over a hundred people on the ship. Even under pristine conditions this would have been a chore for him. But there was no gravity and no air right now. There was no way he was going to be able to do this in the ten minutes and twenty two seconds they had until the next pull.

The tip of the triangle ship that had broken through the wall stood as a quiet reminder of what would happen if they failed. That thing was coming right through there and then they would all be dead. This was merely the tip of a ship that was designed to luxuriously carry thousands of passengers.

There was other trouble as well. The people he injected already weren't regaining consciousness. He expected more help as time went by but he wasn't getting any of that. Were the injections not working? The solution came to him suddenly and he felt like an idiot for not realizing it before. He remembered when he and Lynn injected themselves they didn't feel the full effects until they exposed themselves to the gas. How was Mac going to do that? He didn't know. He frantically kept injecting as many people as he could before the next pull. He wouldn't be able to get to everybody. Chances were these people were all dead anyway. How long could they survive without oxygen? He needed to find a way to get everyone to the surface, if anything to at least try to save the people who already had liquid rock mixing with their own blood. He noticed a change in the complexion of the people who he had injected. That gave him hope.

There was nothing Mac could do there to get down to the surface. None of the ships here had power. He tried reaching Scott on the com in his ear but there was no answer. Instead he looked right at Quentin and mouthed the words "We need to go to Ronos" very slowly and clearly. He did it two more times. Quentin stood doing nothing for a moment but looking around. Then he talked to one of the other people in a space suit and they went to retrieve some of the crates that were floating around. Mac didn't know what they were going to do but he kept injecting.

Time ticked by. Each injection made Mac more uneasy. It was taking too long. The pull was going to start at any moment. He didn't think even he would survive another pull.

Then there was an explosion. What remained of the transport ship was torn free of the luxury liner and sent spinning through space. Mac turned to see Quentin and another space suit man high five each other. The crates had been full of explosives. They were using them to propel the broken ship into the atmosphere.

Mac and the people in the space suits held on for dear life as the ship spun through space. Quentin waited until they got close to another derelict space ship and threw another explosive out the crack that Mac had used to get in. It served as a poor man's propulsion system. They were being moved away from the death area and towards Ronos, which, with its deadly gas and giant monsters, was the more appealing choice for survival. Mac hoped he wasn't making a mistake.

The junked ship was in the atmosphere now. The people who he had injected were being exposed to the gas through the multiple openings in the ship's hull. They had to still be alive because their bodies were glowing purple, some brighter than others.

How were they going to avoid dying when they reached the ground? Even with their new powers they wouldn't be able to withstand the force of falling for miles, but what would be able to stop them from hitting the ground?

The gargoyles. Mac regretted his thought pattern but knew at the same time that it was their only chance to survive.

Lynn, if you can hear me don't say anything for a few minutes while I try and trick some of those monster things into helping us. I'm bringing a bunch of people I've made like us down to the surface. We need to meet up so we can survive together. Raymond isn't down there anymore so maybe the caves are an option. If you are wondering where we are, look up for the falling shuttle. Hopefully we're on the same continent. I don't even know. I can't really see outside too well —

He didn't need to talk very long. Long sharp claws had dug into the ship. The air wasn't burning as much and there were now more people who were sitting up and looking around. There was also the hiss of burning foreign material. Mac looked around. He still had syringes and some liquid rock. There were still more people he could save.

"Everyone listen to me! If you are glowing then you are safe and you need to find someone who isn't glowing then and give them a bear hug. Only things inside the glow will be safe." He looked at how many syringes he had. Four. "I need four people to come here so I can show them how to help me."

Quickly he showed them how the liquid rock was what was keeping everyone alive and how to administer it. They had more time now because the gargoyle was taking them back to their nest or cave or burning pit or wherever gargoyles put things they wanted to eat. There were screams as some people started to get burned. Mac went as fast as he could and prodded others to do the same.

"Don't use too much rock. It doesn't take much and we need some for everybody," said Mac.

In the end they were able to save everybody except for twelve. Some had died in space from lack of oxygen and not being injected soon enough. Others died during the escape and while entering the atmosphere — broken necks and such. Each death weighed heavily on Mac and the others. They had all grown up together. They were each other's family and now they were dead. Mac felt particularly guilty because he was the one who had talked those twelve dead bodies into following him. Would the others still trust him?

"Where are we?" Quentin asked.

He, like many others, was standing so that he could look out one of the cracks in the hull. The whole world had a purple hue to it that blended into the background after a while. Mac stood beside them and looked to see if he was close to Lynn or not. They were too near the ground now to get a layout of the land, but he suspected there was trouble because he was seeing jungle mountains not forests. He hadn't seen any jungles on Ronos before.

"Ronos," answered Mac.

"So we made it?"

"Yes."

"Now what."

Making it was a very small but pivotal step in the plan.

Mac pointed up at the claw, "The thing that has us right now wants to eat us, so we are going to need to try and kill it before it kills us."

"What is it?"

"Think about a rhinoceros with an alligator head and giant bat wings."

"Are you serious?"

There were screams coming from the far side away from Mac and Quentin. They ran over to see what the problem was but they were told to stay back by someone Mac didn't recognize.

"The ship is breaking apart. Someone fell out," said a man who was looking down and had his arms out like he was balancing. He was wearing worn out jeans and a button up shirt that was filthy. He had to be one of the farmers or a farm worker.

That gave Mac an idea.

"We need to get out of the ship. Everybody needs to jump."

"There's no way I'm doing that!"

"We're too high, we'll die!"

"What about the bodies? We can't leave them here."

People were falling whether they wanted to or not. The floor was weakening. Once Mac got to the ground he was going to have to find a weapon against the gargoyles.

The people who still had their doubts about going to the planet immediately forgot about them when a section of the ceiling peeled back and revealed the full view of the demonic creature that was hauling them. Mac nudged Quentin and got him to follow his example and started stomping on the floor around the people that were still there.

"What are you doing?" John Summerset, the math teacher, yelled as he stumbled back and fell through the floor.

Mac ignored the questions and kept stomping. The gargoyle must have noticed that the tasty package he was carrying was getting suspiciously lighter and lighter. It looked back through the cracks and saw Mac and Quentin, the last of the people of Passage to leave the transport ship that had saved their lives, jump through the disintegrated bottom of the floor.

The monster didn't really know what to make of it and kept flying. It wouldn't be long before the shuttle disintegrated and it was carrying nothing. They needed weapons for when it came back. Or a cave to hide in. Mac needed Lynn. She was now the resident expert when it came to surviving on Ronos. It also didn't hurt that she knew a lot about biology, being a biological engineer. He wanted to call out to her but he knew that would be a mistake while the gargoyle was so close.

Mac had gotten so used to falling that he didn't feel the need to scream anymore. Quentin on the other hand looked like he might be peeing his pants. His voice was already hoarse and he flapped his arms and legs uselessly in an attempt to fly. Mac wasn't going to try and fly but he also wasn't going to make himself into a bullet and shoot to the ground. He spread himself out and when he reached the trees he closed his eyes and prayed that it wouldn't hurt too bad.

Nothing on him got speared, but that's not to say that he was super eager to do it again. He tore through the first few branches. When he got to thicker ones he started to bounce off of them. He felt one bone crack which was an accomplishment with his powers. When he hit the ground to say he was dizzy and hurting was an understatement. He moaned in pain.

He knew the gas would heal him so he waited until he felt better. It took a while. But he wasn't in nearly as much pain as when he had fallen back on Earth. The gas was thin down on the jungle floor. It made Mac a little suspicious of the types of things that would grow here. It was his arm that had broken. The gas was doing its work. His arm snapped back into place. After several minutes of letting the gas work through his body, Mac felt whole again and sat up. There was no one else around him. Too soon to mind speak. He shouted.

"Sneed!"

No answer

"Sneed! I mean Quinty! Or Quinton! Or whatever!"

Ever so faint he heard a reply.

"…Mac…"

Someone was yelling his name. Mac went crashing through the jungle to find him. The jungle was not like the jungle back on Earth. Not that Mac had a lot of experience there, but the military did do some survival training in the

Amazon. The leaves were not a normal shade of green. The veins were much darker, closer to a purple. The trees and plants were thriving on the gas and it was giving them exponential growth.

"Mac!"

It wasn't Quentin. It was a female voice. It was hard to pinpoint where the voice was coming from. The jungle was loud. The plant life wasn't the only thing that was thriving in the new environment. There were bugs chirping and larger animals moving through the growth. It felt like Mac was being stalked.

The footsteps sounded like they were coming from either side of him but when he looked there was nothing. The trees were thick; he couldn't wrap his arms around them. The foliage on the ground came half way up his shins. There was no way he could quietly move away from any predators. He couldn't move quietly anywhere.

What was stalking him? Was the gargoyle back? Mac didn't think so because it would have sounded louder, thrashing through the overhead leaves and branches. Those monsters couldn't break through that without Mac noticing. This noise was on the ground level and he wasn't stupid enough to think that the only predators were the ones that could fly, but he needed to get to the woman who was calling him.

"Hello!" Mac called out.

There was no response and he wasn't confident that his voice was even capable of penetrating the dense foliage that now surrounded him. He called out again, this time screaming it at the top of his lungs.

"Where are you?"

The leaves beside him parted and a woman emerged from behind them. She was dirty from head to toe and her clothes were tattered. Despite all the trials she'd been through, there was a smile on her face when she finally realized who she had found.

"Mac."

It was Lynn. Mac almost couldn't believe it. He ran over to her and hugged her. He wasn't usually a hugger, but he was so surprised and happy to see her. Leaving her behind hadn't been a death sentence, and the relief from that revelation couldn't be expressed with anything less than a hug.

"I'm sorry," said Mac.

"For what?" asked Lynn.

"For leaving you behind. Twice. I had no other choice."

"I know. I'm not going to hold anything against you. But help me get me back to my husband."

"No problem."

Mac said it like it wasn't a problem, but the only option they had was taming a gargoyle and flying it off the planet. Lynn was wise to it.

"Right. But first we need to find the others I saw falling out of the sky with you. Then I have something very strange I need to show you," said Lynn.

"Strange? Coming from you, that's saying something," said Mac.

Chapter 17
Descending Lights

It took a few hours to find the people of Passage. During that time Mac, Lynn, and their group were never once attacked by the gargoyles. They decided they would be fine as long as they used their voices instead of mind speaking.

The people from Passage looked shell-shocked. Who could blame them? They had almost died half a dozen times since Mac had shown up in Passage after being transformed. The only thing that kept them from going completely crazy was the transformation in themselves. The surge of energy they were experiencing for the first time dulled some of the shock, especially for the elderly people.

Mac's old babysitter, Claudia White — he was to refer to her as Miss White and still did to that day — looked especially excited about the change. It was like time had reversed for the elderly. The skin around her neck was already noticeable tighter. The crow's feet at the corner of her eyes were weaker than before and she had the annoying energy of a small child. Mac almost called her down from climbing a tree before he realized how ridiculous that would be.

He wasn't convinced that it was a return to youth that was happening. He had noticed slight changes in his own body. More so since he came back to Ronos than when he was away. There might have been changes before if he hadn't given so much blood to Nelson and the others. For him the changes made him feel and look mature. This led him to believe that their bodies were being changed to their full potential. For old people that meant they were being changed to look younger and to younger people that meant they were getting older.

Lynn herself looked dramatically different. Mac thought she looked fine before but now he realized she hadn't been in the best shape she could have been. She was going to look even more out of place when she was with her husband who was bald and a little overweight. He was going to appreciate the transformation.

The change must be a starting point. Mac couldn't wrap his head around it otherwise. Being in the military for a few years he was a firm believer in the law of the harvest. Reap what you sow. The more push-ups you did, the stronger you became. Maybe their bodies weren't transforming into the full potential they were capable of. Maybe they were transforming so that they could survive on Ronos.

There were sixty-seven people left. Some people did not survive the cold of space while Mac hurried to inject everyone, and not everyone survived the fall to Ronos. And back on Earth when Quentin had been loading people onto the ship, not everyone chose to leave Passage. Hopefully they weren't being interrogated by the military. Mac and the others would keep looking for the people who were missing since the fall, but right now they needed to find shelter.

Being from the prairie back on Earth, the people of Passage did not want to stay in the jungle. They were all within earshot of one other, but it was impossible to see all of them at one time. There were too many trees and bushes in the way, trees and bushes that were already noticeably taller than when they first got there. The supercharged growth was freaking everyone out.

Lynn led the way. As they walked Tayma Alon, the former soldier and one of the few people who didn't grow up in Passage, trotted up next to Mac.

"What's the plan?" she asked.

"Follow Lynn," said Mac.

"After that, I mean. You changed us to fight in the war. How do we get off the planet?"

"We'll figure that out soon."

Mac hoped, at least. That wasn't even the first thing they needed to accomplish. They needed to turn the beacon off that was pulling the *Lendrum* to Ronos or there was no point in getting off the planet.

Sitting behind his desk Zinger was barely able to look at what Raymond Tysons had become. Raymond stood in his office in the rags of his old uniform. He had been offered a new one but he turned it down. His skin was crispy in some spots and disturbingly mushy and black in others. Everywhere he went, an odor went with him. He looked like he was decomposing while he was still alive.

On the plus side he didn't actually have to look at Raymond. The charred man didn't have working vocal chords anymore so he had to bring in someone who could act as a translator. Raymond claimed all he had to do was drink a foul smelling liquid made by melting the rocks from the shuttle they found him on and then talking by thinking at someone was possible. Zinger decided to test it out on Spacer Quake. Quake had a canister of the liquid in his hand. Half of it was already drunk.

"Does that mean you're like Mac Narrad?" Zinger asked Raymond.

"He says it means he's better. Drinking this stuff will make soldiers like him," said Quake.

Raymond looked at Zinger with intensity. His eyes were wide. Zinger wondered if his eyelids got burned off. Raymond wasn't acting at all like he had been burned. He didn't even look like he was in any pain. He walked with confidence and strength, almost like he was happy it had happened.

Zinger choked back vomit. "They won't look like you, will they?"

Raymond smiled. Probably. What was left of his face moved around. His mouth scabs twitched upwards so a smile was a solid guess, but a frown was more logical. Zinger was beyond being sensitive. You don't order millions of people dead and then worry about the feelings of a man who now looks like a monster.

"They won't look like him. If they change before they go to the surface then they won't be burned," said Quake.

"Good."

"He wants to lead them."

"You?"

"He wants to kill Mac and Lynn for what they did to him."

"I guess that means you have a way of getting down to the planet."

Quake heard something but hesitated saying it.

"What?" asked Zinger. "Tell me exactly what he said."

"He said he knows a way down and that you would too if you weren't such an idi...busy person."

Zinger was always quick to take offense. He called out Raymond who only needed to take a few steps forward to keep the weighty general quiet. Then Raymond continued.

Raymond continued walking to the general until he was within reach of Zinger's computer console at his desk. He pushed some buttons and called up some information while the fat man struggled to find any fresh air in the room. While Raymond worked the console Quake repeated the words in his head. "He scanned the ships out there and found a small mining fleet. The ships look big, but they can only hold a dozen or so people each. The walls are surrounded by the hardest armor made by man. It's used to mine on dying suns and can withstand enough heat for multiple trips to the surface of Ronos. We use them one at a time until we don't have anymore. That should give Raymond enough material to make more soldiers like him. If the gas does burn through these then there is no hope to get to the surface unless we build something out of materials from the surface."

"Why would we build a space ship from the surface?"

"Because things from Ronos don't get burned."

"Okay. I will send soldiers to the docking bay. Your mission, Raymond, is to kill Mac, Lynn, and everyone with them, find a way to turn off this pull before we are all killed, and transform as many soldiers as you can."

"He agrees."

"Good. Get out of here."

Raymond stalled a little before he walked out and Zinger thought he knew why. The burned man was probably wondering why the general wasn't coming down with him. Of course Zinger wanted to take part in this great power but he couldn't get over the way Raymond looked. Zinger was willing to wait to make sure it was safe before committing himself to be changed. If it didn't work, he would rather be crushed by *Lendrum*.

Zinger had more questions for the smelly, scabby man but could not tolerate being around him anymore. Questions like why, if Raymond and Mac were equals, Raymond was severely burned and Mac was not. The general let the question slide because the answer obviously didn't matter. Mac wasn't willing to work with him but Raymond was, so it didn't matter if Raymond's way was different as long as it gave him the enhanced soldiers he needed before the

Lendrum came crashing into all of them and ruined their chance to win the war.

He checked the clock on his Imp while he sent out a message to the soldiers he had handpicked to be the first to go to Ronos. They had twenty-two hours until the space station was pulled into their space and obliterated all of them. It didn't matter if it was enough time for Raymond and his men to complete their mission. Either they could do it, or they all died.

Once the survivors from Passage got out of the jungle and onto the plains it was clear where they were going. The grass was almost three feet high, but it wasn't getting any taller. It had reached its maximum height. They could also see well into the distance and would be able to see even more if it weren't for the mountains jutting out of the horizon. But they weren't going to the mountains.

There was something else nestled among the grass: a glowing purple light coming from up ahead. Lynn was leading them toward it. The closer they got the more the Passage people slowed down. They were glad be out in the open, away from the claustrophobic jungle. They felt in their element and weren't eager to walk towards mysterious lights.

They all stayed behind, but Lynn kept walking. Mac, Quentin, and Tayma followed.

"What is that?" asked Mac.

"I'm not sure. I was hoping you would be able to fill in the blanks," said Lynn.

The lights swirled around in the air before settling on the ground. Once they landed the lights went out, but there were so many lights that the overall aperture never dimmed. Whatever particles were falling only lit up once they got close to the ground and there was almost a constant feed from the sky.

Lynn was right. Mac knew exactly what this was. It was Jace; it was the alien pretending to be Jace. Part of him had been in the transport ship when it had entered the atmosphere. Jace had said only a small part of him needed to be taken to Ronos and the rest would follow. This had to be the spot where the particle landed. The light it was generating could be compared to a roaring bonfire.

Mac moved closer to the ground to get a better look. There was a dark sticky substance on the grass around a jar. Poking it with his finger was an action he immediately regretted and started looking for a place to wipe his finger off. It was the twelve-year-old boy inside him that told him to poke where he shouldn't poke. Every light that touched the ground added another minuscule bit to the pile that was forming. Where they landed seemed random at first, but when he studied their pattern he realized it was anything but. When the lights got close to the ground they dashed to the proper space with a sense of urgency and excitement like they were finally home.

"This is amazing," said Tayma.

"It looks like millions of microscopic fireflies crashing to the earth," said Quentin.

"We're on another planet. I'm not sure Earth is accurate."

"Do you know what this is?" said Lynn.

Mac nodded his head. "It's one of the aliens."

"What?" all three of them said at the same time.

"Have any of you seen an alien?"

They all shook their heads.

"Their natural form is a swarm of millions or billions of imperceptible specks — imperceptible by themselves, but visible as a cloud when they are all together. I think that's what these lights are. Jace told me that if I brought even a little bit of him to the surface then the rest would follow. Who knows how far these little bits have travelled, but this is him gathering himself back up."

"Back up into what?" asked Tayma. She looked nervous. Her soldier instincts were kicking in. She sensed a possible threat.

"I don't know."

"Jace was an alien?" asked Quentin.

"Yeah. They can emulate humans. They actually have to emulate humans or their swarm forms drift apart. He wanted to come here to get his body back, I guess."

"Then all these little lights are going to build up into an alien body?"

"Yes."

"What do they look like?"

"I don't know."

"Is he a threat to us?" asked Tayma.

That was a tricky question for Mac to answer. Jace had insisted the whole time that he didn't want to hurt any humans and that he only wanted to get to Ronos. Who knew how the alien was going to react once he had his body back.

"I don't know. But we shouldn't wait around here to figure things out."

"What's the plan?" asked Lynn.

"We don't have a lot of time and only one option. The pull has been magnified somehow and it's pulling everything to one focal point. In a day or so a space station is going to be pulled here and destroy everything that's in orbit. We need to turn it off before that happens or we aren't getting off the planet."

"I know what happened," said Lynn. "It's the pull machine. It's acting like a beacon and pulling everything in. Raymond spewed liquid rock all over it."

"The beacon reacts to the Lynn Rock too?"

"I guess so. Could be some kind of organic machine?"

"Do you know how to turn it off?"

"I might. I can at least get us inside."

Mac smiled. Now they were on to something. Valtteri Happonen approached Mac.

"We heard you talking and the others made some decisions. We decided I would speak for the group and that we don't want to be anywhere near this light. If it is one of the aliens then staying here is not a good idea," he said.

"I agree. We are heading to some caves to try and save all those ships up there, and some other people from Passage. Lynn's been on the planet the longest, so the best idea might be for you folks to come with us."

"I'll present the idea to the others," said Valtteri.

Mac had no doubt about what they would end up choosing.

"Lynn, do you know the fastest way to the pull machine?"

"The easiest way is to go down the hole we created when we first got here. It's not too far from here. Maybe fifty miles or so," said Lynn.

"Fifty miles? Have you seen who we have with us? There are old people here. They won't be able to keep up. It will take all night to get there. Is there any shelter that's closer?" asked Tayma.

Lynn and Mac smiled. They knew she had no idea what their bodies could do now. Fifty miles was nothing to them. The entire group would easily be able to get there that night. After Valtteri had explained the situation to everyone he came to Mac and confirmed that the group agreed to travel with him.

"Then let's get going," said Mac.

Lynn started running. Some of the Passage people called out after her but Mac didn't bother slowing down to explain things to them. They had to have felt the changes already. They were probably vibrating with pent up energy. This was going to be something that was fun for them to figure out.

Some, the older people like Miss White, didn't need to be told they could run faster than they ever could before. She was right up there with Mac and Lynn. Others, Quentin's age and younger, had to work at it more. They were practiced at being tired and not having strength to keep going. It was a mental block they had to work through. Not a big block, but it was there. It didn't take long before everyone was running across the prairie towards the cave. The people of Passage were yelling, racing, and generally acting like children. The mood of the group had significantly changed. Mac doubted that any of them would regret coming to Ronos now.

There was a streak of fiery brilliance in the night sky. A ship had entered the atmosphere near the mountains and was streaking towards them at an alarming rate. There was an explosion of rock and dirt as it slammed into the base of one of the mountains.

The sound of it stopped everyone in their tracks.

"What was that?" asked Lynn. No one answered. If she didn't know then nobody did.

"Did anyone see what it looked like?" asked Mac.

There were several unhelpful replies.

"Comet."

"Fireball."

"It was one of those monsters! They're coming back."

"I think it was one of those aliens, again."

Mac turned to Lynn, "Will you stay here while I go check it out?"

She nodded and went to the others. Mac started walking towards the mountain and away from the group.

"Where do you think you're going?" said a voice behind him. It was Quentin.

"I'm going to go check it out. Won't take long. I'll be right back," said Mac.

"I'm coming with you."

"Sure."

Hearing that an expedition was moving out, Miss White joined the two men. She was getting younger by the hour. Her hair had gone from see-through white to light gray.

"If you're going anywhere then I'm going with you," she said.

"As my babysitter?" smiled Mac.

"Whatever you want to call me, as long as I'm included."

Valtteri morphed out of the darkness to voice his candidacy as well. "I want to go. If there are choices to be made then I need to be there."

"Sure, but it will be the four of us, no more."

There were a couple groans but no one argued. Miss White whispered in Mac's ear.

"He doesn't speak for me. I didn't even vote for the guy."

Lynn watched them walk away from the group. There was a nervous pit forming in her stomach. The *Lendrum* was coming and could potentially ruin everything. If there was no way to turn off the beacon than there was only one other thing she could think to do. But would using her power even help? Would she be doing anything more than buying them time? There was no point in worrying. Yet.

The Ryders did not talk about their power very often. Lynn had not heard her father talk about it from the time she was little, and her friend drowned in the ocean, until Lynn was eighteen years old when her father went to the hospital.

As she rushed in her hover car from the university to the hospital she didn't even once think about the power of Grenor. She had learned to train her mind not to think of such things. Mr. Ryder had been in a car accident and was severely injured. On the phone they had told her to get there as quickly as she could. There was no one else to drive her so she held back the tears and broke all the traffic laws she needed to in order to get there as fast as she could. Not once did it enter her mind that if her dad were to die then she would be able to use the family secret to go back and warn her father or stop the accident from happening.

Three days later Mr. Ryder woke up. Only Lynn was in his room. It was near midnight and she had sent her mother home to get some rest. She herself was droopy-eyed and fading in and out of sleep when she heard her father speak.

"Lynn…"

He struggled to find his voice, but she heard him and was immediately at his side.

"Dad."

"I need to tell you something," he said.

"You need to rest. You were almost killed. Do you have any idea how lucky you are to have all your limbs still intact?" said Lynn.

"That's what I need to talk to you about… If I die then you need to know how to use it."

"There will be time for that later, Dad," said Lynn.

"The time is now… If I die then it will be lost forever. You need to know so you can pass it on."

"Or use it."

"I've told you…"

"I know. You hope it never comes to that."

"It's important...you need to know that it can only be used when there is no other hope to survive..."

"Yes, I know. I'll be humanity's last chance."

"How is school? Have you learned...biological technology theories?"

"Dad, you need to rest. You're jumping all over the place."

"No...that's how it works. It will only respond to the thought patterns of the ancestors that activated the beacon."

"Beacon? What beacon?"

"It will read your thought patterns and follow your commands because you are a descendent...but you need to learn to develop the same wave length as the first Ryder or it will not work."

"Dad, this is crazy."

"I know. Please. Do as I ask."

So she did, and Mr. Ryder taught Lynn how to save everyone. She asked all the questions she could think of — "Time travel? Are you sure, Dad? Why can only our family do this? Where is Grenor? Why did I have to be born there?" — and then asked them again — "When should I use this? How is this possible? Why is this possible? Who made this possible?" when she either couldn't remember the answer or couldn't believe what her father was telling her.

There were a lot of questions that her father could not answer and he was honest with her about that. She was going to have to take as much of this on faith as he did. All he knew for sure was that there was a power out there and that he could feel it.

"What do you mean you can feel it?" asked Lynn?

"You can start the process of accessing the power and you can feel something out there that wasn't there before."

"Can you show me?"

271

"It's dangerous. If I show you then you will feel something that you never thought was even possible before."

"Why is that dangerous?"

"If you try to feel it over and over again you might get tempted to use the power to unleash the full force of what you are feeling. Or you could simply go too deep and unleash the power by accident."

"Does it hurt?"

"No. That's another reason why it's dangerous. Don't get fooled into thinking it's friendly because it feels good."

"Show me?"

"I can't show you. It all takes place in your mind. You have to close your eyes and then I'll talk you through it."

They were both tired and no doubt her father had reservations about doing something like this so late at night. Hadn't he been the one who said all his life that she needed to be in bed by midnight because nothing good ever happened past then? Hopefully he was wrong, because she was about to learn how to time travel.

"Close your eyes," her father said.

"What do you see?" her father asked.

"Nothing. My eyes are closed," said Lynn.

"It's completely dark?"

"No, my Imp. I can't turn off the feed. There will always be at least one indicator light."

"Try and make the display go as small as possible and make the light as dim as it will go."

Lynn thought the commands and the Imp responded. There was a dim green light in the lower corner of her mind's eye. It would be there for as long as she had her Imp. She couldn't even remember a time when it wasn't there. It was there even when she closed her eyes.

"What do I do now?" asked Lynn.

"Are your eyes closed?"

"Yes."

"And you can't see anything?"

"Except for one dim blinking green dot."

"Okay, that's fine. It's hard at first to make the connection. Try not to think about the green dot or even look at it. You need to be looking inside yourself to find the connection between you and Grenor, our home."

Lynn did as she was told. She tried not to think about the green light but that was going to be difficult. If you tell a person not to think about something, that's the first thing they'll think about. Plus the thing she was told to concentrate on was an abstract idea. She was supposed to find her connection to her home planet inside of herself? What did that mean?

"I'm not so sure..." Lynn started to say but her father stopped her.

"Talking isn't going to help. The less stimulation to your senses the easier it will be to concentrate. I will try to keep quiet while you look."

"I don't know what I'm looking for. It's obviously not something physical."

"No, of course not."

"Then what is it?"

"It's not tangible or measurable, but it exists and I've felt it. I don't know how to describe it other than it's a connection with Grenor and once you feel it you will know."

"Where do I start?"

"Start by emptying your mind and thinking of nothing and then noticing what is left."

One of the good things about it being so late was that it was relatively easy for her to clear her mind. The challenge came from trying not to fall asleep. She cleared her mind and concentrated. She wasn't supposed to think of anything but at the same time she was supposed to find her own connection to Grenor. It was a horrible tease.

It didn't help that her dad had told her not to spend time dwelling on the blinking green light that indicated she had an Imp. Now it was all she could think of or look at. Her mind suddenly became obsessed with it. Why did that light exist? Did they really need an indicator light to say that she had an Imp? She knew she had an Imp so why did she need a small green light in the corner of her mind's eye telling her she did. Why were the Imp companies so obsessed with displays and indicators and clouding up her vision?

Thinking about it wasn't going to help anything. Her tiredness was overtaking her. She needed to establish her connection to an ancient time traveling machine so that she could go to bed. Thinking it made her laugh a little. It sounded so ridiculous.

"Concentrate," her father said.

"Sorry."

Lynn rededicated herself. Focusing on the green light was unavoidable so she used it to focus on Grenor. In her mind, making sure not to activate her Imp but to use the part of her brain that thought independently of it, she pictured the blinking green light as a planet. Every time it blinked into existence she pictured it differently.

The first time she saw it she put it in space with stars forming constellations around it. She decided the space around it would be like how Earth was before space travel was discovered. Free of debris. Clean and pure.

The next time it blinked back she changed the color of the glowing green orb. She didn't think the planet would be completely green. It needed oceans and continents. As she formed these things in her mind she noticed something strange. The blinking had stopped. The planet was there, as vividly now as when it was an indicator light.

The continents were also forming outside of her willingness for them to do so. They were forming without her thinking about it and they were forming into very specific traits. This is what Grenor really looked like. She had found her connection with the planet. In her mind's eye she was looking down on the planet and, as strange as it sounded, she felt like the planet was looking back.

She almost started laughing again but stopped herself. Planets aren't alive. They have living things on them but they can't think for themselves. There had to be something on the planet that was noticing her noticing it. She was communicating with her mind. Not forming words or pictures but moving her consciousness from the hospital chair beside her father to a lost planet with mysterious powers. So how was she supposed to access that power now that she had the connection?

Time travel, she thought in her mind.

The planet started changing. Spinning. The atmosphere was losing some of its clarity. Unusual clouds were gathering.

"Lynn!"

Mr. Ryder reached out and whacked Lynn on the arm. That was enough to give her a jolt and break her concentration.

"What did you do?" he asked.

"Nothing. I found Grenor and then I was only trying to access the power like you told me."

"You took it too far."

"What's wrong? I thought I was doing what you told me to do," said Lynn.

"I didn't tell you to use the power," said Mr. Ryder.

Lynn's mouth dropped. Had she used the power? It could only be used once. Did that mean she had blown her opportunity already? Her heart filled with dread momentarily but then she took her Imp out of clear vision mode and looked at the date and time. It was 3:37 in the morning on the same day as when she closed her eyes. Either she had only gone in the future a few seconds or she didn't use up the power.

"What happened?" she asked.

"When you make your connection with Grenor all the other people who have made the connection can feel it as well. I knew when you made the connection and that's all I wanted you to do. I didn't think it would be so fast for you. You must have a natural talent."

"Did I screw it up?"

"No. I pulled you out in time. But you did something that I have never done before. You came within seconds of passing the point of no return."

"As far as you know."

"Yes," Mr. Ryder was quiet for a second. He closed his eyes and Lynn thought he might have fallen asleep but a couple minutes later he opened his eyes.

"It's still there. Everything's fine."

Lynn exhaled loudly. She didn't know she had been so worried. The sleep in her mind and eyes was completely gone now. She didn't know if she would ever sleep again.

"How do you feel?" asked Mr. Ryder.

"Amazing. How often can I go back there?" asked Lynn.

"You didn't go anywhere. You were here the entire time."

"My body was. But I wasn't. I went to a real place. I know it. I felt it. Don't you feel like that too?"

"No. I feel like it's all in my head. Like I'm seeing a representation of it in my mind."

"What about grandpa? How did he feel it?"

"Like me. He was the one who taught me and so I was a lot like him."

"But I'm different."

"You're special," said Mr. Ryder. "Make sure you find the right guy to marry so that you can pass this gift on to your kids."

"Good grief, Dad."

"And you are keeping the Ryder name. It's a reminder of your responsibilities."

"I know dad you told me."

"It also weeds out the weak men. If he doesn't love you enough to let you stay a Ryder then he probably won't be able to understand who we are and what we can do."

"I know."

"If it comes down to you to use the power then you are going to need a family who understands."

"Right," said Lynn.

The experience was one that Lynn would never forget. It excited her and frightened her at the same time. It also did very little to answer her questions. Again she opened the query gates and flooded her father with questions until the sun came up and he fell asleep exhausted. Lynn stayed by his side, wide eyed and wide awake. To be in a situation where she had to use her power was a situation without hope for humanity's survival — the worst situation that she could think of, yet she couldn't help but smile at the possibilities.

When she thought about time travel and the clouds started to swirl, an amazing energy coursed through her body that words needed to be invented to describe with any accuracy. She wanted to feel it again. Being afraid of being excited for the end of humanity was not something she ever thought she would be feeling.

The *Lendrum* was coming and would destroy all the ships orbiting the planet unless someone figured out how to turn off the beacon. Even if everyone in orbit were killed, there was still hope for humanity to win the war. Ronos still existed and they could still bring people here. Someone on the *Lendrum* would probably survive the collision.

As long as they knew where Ronos was and the aliens didn't, they could keep fighting for a very long time. She was able to put her mind at ease. As long as there was hope, she didn't have to use her power.

Chapter 18
Cubed

It was going to take a lot to get the smug look of knowing he was right off of Nelson's face. Aleeva and rest of the swarms who were opposed to the destruction of humanity had the same plan he did, but they were more informed than he was. They were going to take out key ships and cause mass panic in the fleet. While the panic was going on they would seize leadership of the civilization and lead their people peacefully to Ronos.

Phillip let Nelson have his moment. The young nephew didn't realize that there was something missing from their plan: the emulated prisoners. If the rebel alien's plan worked, then the prisoners would be released as soon as they got to Ronos. But if their plan didn't work, Phillip and his group were going to have to take matters into their own hands to free the prisoners. Without prisoners to emulate, the swarms would not be able to hold themselves together enough to use their ships, thus stranding them to drift uselessly in space.

The longer they stayed with the main fleet the worse Jazlyn got. It didn't help that the Searchers Sphere they were in was in the very center of the fleet. Phillip couldn't imagine the amount of noise that was going on in her head. She was once again on the floor in the fetal position. Phillip made sure to stay by her to protect her. Not that he thought anyone was going to try anything, but because she had no way to defend herself if something did happen.

Besides, he wasn't sure the rebel aliens could be trusted.

"This is good for us," Nelson kept saying. There were still aliens in the room but some of them had left and some of them could still be in swarm form listening in on their conversations.

Use mind speak, kid, said Phillip.

Why? We don't have to hide, said Nelson.

If the plan doesn't work we might have to do something that they don't agree with.

What's that?

Free the prisoners. Robbing them of their emulated bodies.

Why?

If what they are planning doesn't work then that will be our only choice.

Stop being a pessimist, said Nelson. *You haven't even given them a chance. We need to trust them. They are our best chance.*

Aleeva walked over to them. *We have reached the others and they are moving into position. The initial attack will have twelve targets. Three gathering ships, the lead collectors, the last Almic ship, and the Searchers Sphere.*

The Searcher's Sphere? You are going to destroy this ship? I thought that would be pointless now that you know where you guys are going, said Phillip.

That was the primary purpose of this ship. It was our leaders that inhabited the Searcher race and who were using them to find our home. They are revered among us and have a lot of influence. Ending their influence will help make our voice louder and move more people to our way of thinking. And we aren't destroying this ship entirely. We seek to cut off the leaders from their Searcher bodies.

Are you sure about that? asked Phillip. *Killing leaders isn't the way we would get people to agree with us.*

Correct. But we aren't killing them. We are keeping them quiet. Once we kill the searchers the leaders who control them will be left to disperse until they can be gathered at the appointed place. They will not be able to take control of a body or an emulator again.

Something about what she said sparked a connection in Phillip's mind. She said the leaders would be gathered once the searchers were killed. Before that she mentioned how three gathering ships were being targeted. Gathering ships must be like alien graveyards. Why were they being targeted by the rebels?

Can we trust you? asked Aleeva.

Yes, Phillip and Nelson said at the same time.

Aleeva looked down at Jazlyn on the floor as if noticing her for the first time. Looking for an explanation Phillip filled in the blanks.

She's in as well, said Phillip.

Why is she on the floor? asked Aleeva.

Human trouble. She'll be fine.

Aleeva must not have got very far in her acting-like-a-human training because Phillip's weak excuse was acceptable to her. She walked over to the other aliens to continue planning and communicating with the other rebel groups in the fleet.

Why did you lie? asked Nelson.

Because I don't trust them and I don't know how they would react to her being able to hear everything they are saying, said Phillip.

Phillip didn't think there was any way these alien rebels cared if they all lived or died, but they had to try something. If this plan worked then they would have some allies. They all wanted the same thing: to stop the swarm fleet from destroying all humans.

Aleeva walked back over to them with another alien. He was also a human emulator, freakishly tall and rail thin. His eyes were set deep in his head and his forehead was much smaller than average. His hairline was almost down to his eyebrows. His clothes indicated that the human was in the military, but he wasn't in combat gear so he must have been taken captive unexpectedly. Maybe he was sleeping when his ship was taken.

This is Durgan. He will be helping you with your part of the mission, said Aleeva.

Which part is that? asked Phillip.

Durgan spoke up. His voice perfectly matched his body, high and squeaky. It would have been comical under different circumstances. Did swarms have a sense of humor?

We will be taking an explosive charge to the center of the ship, said Durgan.

What's the escape plan? asked Phillip.

After the charge is set we make our way back to the docking bay. The rebels have taken control of one of the collector ships. We have been running our operations out of there. After everyone has completed their mission we will gather there.

Then what?

Then we will move on to our next objective. It will be a difficult journey but the results will be worth it. We will have redeemed our civilization and we will have saved yours.

While they talked, Aleeva and the other swarm aliens left the room. Now it was only the humans and Durgan. Durgan walked over to the wall and used thought speech to create two intersecting cylinders, one slightly shorter than the other. The package was small enough to be carried by one person. On the end of the shorter cylinder was a display and a red button. Although Phillip had never seen anything like it, he knew it was a bomb.

Did you create that out of the wall? asked Phillip.

No. The generators are not powerful enough to create something of this magnitude. This device was created elsewhere and then hidden on this ship until the appropriate time.

When are we setting this off?

One hour.

An hour came and went. It was time for them to make their move. They let Durgan lead the way. Jazlyn did her best to stand up straight and keep her face neutral but she still looked like a mess. The group was moving at a brisk pace so that they could get to the center of the ship to plant their bomb without anyone looking at them too closely.

There was no way for them to get from the room they were in to the center of the Searchers Sphere without going into one of the main hallways. Phillip was assigned with carrying the bomb. He was told that no one would question what he was carrying because it was disguised as part of an emulator generator. If anyone asked him about it he was to say that an emulator pad was on the fritz and he couldn't waste time stopping to talk about it. When Durgan handed over the bomb he also wisely informed Phillip that he shouldn't accidentally drop it.

The ship was still crowded with swarm aliens pretending to be human. This was going to cause a significant blow to the fleet. Phillip had to keep reminding himself that they were accomplishing all of this without anyone actually dying. When the bomb he was holding went off the beings around him wouldn't die.

The crowds didn't thin out as they got to the center of the ship. If anything they doubled. There was a major crowd forming. Phillip wasn't sure where everyone was going.

At the center of the ship the rooms and hallways became solid again. They would always be the size they were right now instead of adjusting to fit the number of people present. The hallway was large but not big enough for everyone who was present to fit comfortably. Durgan was trying to force his way to the front of the crowd.

Why not set it off here and make a run for it? asked Nelson.

We aren't close enough to the searchers, said Durgan.

What are all these people doing here? asked Phillip.

The searchers are our leaders. They have a greater connection to our home planet than anyone else in the fleet. Our people have gathered here for further instruction and insight.

The crowd was closing in around them. Phillip had the bomb pressed up against his chest and the farther they walked the closer it was pressed against him. He wanted to push people away but he wasn't sure if that would set anything off. He looked above the mob to see how close they were to getting to the door that would lead them to where the Searchers were.

They were still a ways away. The crowd was most dense right around the door, but no one was allowed to enter. Two guards stood in front of the door. Both of them held a strange looking cube in front of them. It was a perfect cube that was a foot in diameter and had handles on either side of it. It looked like it was made out of glass and inside there was a small blue light bouncing off the see-through walls. Was this an alien weapon of some kind? It had to be if it was stopping the crowd from getting the guards out of the way. The other aliens kept far enough away from the guards and the door that they wouldn't have to deal with the peculiar looking cubes.

Phillip guessed that he and the others hadn't seen any alien weapons that were used on other aliens before because they had never been close to something that needed this much protection.

There was no more forward progression. The crowd was too thick. Phillip did his best to protect the bomb he was holding but Nelson kept getting pushed into him from behind and that in turn squeezed Phillip closer to Durgan.

We aren't getting any closer, said Phillip.

The bomb isn't powerful enough to do damage from this far away. We need to get to the other side of the door, said Durgan.

Phillip wondered what would happen to the aliens closest to him if the bomb were to go off now. A human would be torn apart, but these swarm aliens were made to break into a million pieces and come back together. If a bomb went off in the hallway would the only people who got hurt be him, Nelson, and Jazlyn?

There was another abrupt push from behind and Phillip stumbled forward. His face bashed into Durgan's shoulder. Even though Durgan could flash into a swarm at any moment he was very much a solid then. The hit made Phillip drop the bomb. It hit the ground and almost immediately got kicked away, but not before Phillip noticed the display had turned on. It wasn't Earth Common Language but it didn't need to be in a familiar language for Phillip to know it had been activated.

The bomb! I dropped it! said Phillip.

Durgan turned around and looked at Phillip and then looked at Phillip's feet.

What do you mean? Where is it?

It got kicked away before I could do anything. I don't know where it is.

Idiot human.

I think it got activated when it hit the ground. How long was the timer?

Ten minutes. We have ten minutes to find it or this will all be for nothing. The Searchers need to be destroyed for our plan to have any success.

Phillip turned to the other humans. They had been in on the conversation and they were already looking around for where the bomb could be. It wasn't very big. It couldn't have gotten too far.

The fact that the aliens didn't talk out loud was a plus now. The only sounds that could be heard in the hallway were footsteps and the beeping sound of the bomb. They weren't the only ones who noticed. Other aliens were looking around for the source of the beeping.

Even the guards at the door knew something was up. They were looking at the feet of the people around them trying to find the source of the beeping. Phillip had to find that bomb. He was closer to the bomb than the guards were, but they had more control over the crowd. One of them took a step forward. The crowd immediately moved out of the way to accommodate him.

Five bodies away from where Phillip was he saw a man look down at the floor and then pick something up. It was the bomb. He had no idea what he was holding and turned it over until he found the display. Then he held it above his head. The man must have said something to the guard in a private thought speech conversation because the guard holding the cube in front of him cut through the crowd straight towards the man.

We need to get the bomb or we need to get out of here, said Durgan.

What do you mean? asked Phillip.

Once the countdown has been initiated there is nothing we can do to stop it.

What? How much time has gone past?

Two minutes, maybe a bit more. You humans have to do this. You are the only ones that are immune to the cube.

What is that thing?

It's a prison. The people who get caught in the cube will not be set free until we return to our home. Some of our people have been trapped in a cube for a very, very long time. I will not be able to help you if I get sucked in there.

Phillip got to see a prime example of what Durgan meant when he said *sucked in there.* The guard got to the man that held the bomb. The man with the bomb handed it over right away and then pointed to the display. Phillip wished he could hear their conversation but it was kept private.

Whatever the man was saying, the guard wasn't buying it. He held out the cube in front of him. There was no time for the man to run away. The small blue light left the confines of the cube and zipped all around the man freezing him in his tracks and then quickly taking away his ability to remain in solid form. As the light moved around the man he became particlized. Then the light went back into the cube and the man was forced to follow. He was trapped inside.

The crowd was thinning now. People were running away. No one else wanted to be cubed. The moment of chaos while everyone ran was going to be their only opportunity to get the bomb back.

Follow me! Phillip said to his human companions.

Phillip weaved through the crowd and made it to the guard. In one hand the guard had the cube. In the other he held the bomb. Phillip slapped the bomb out of his hand from behind and then started running so that no one could tell it was him.

The guard was so busy looking around for who hit him that he didn't notice Jazlyn, who had found a new reserve of strength, picking up the bomb and heading for the door. The problem was all four of them had forgotten about the other guard waiting there. He had seen the whole thing and was now moving in on Jazlyn.

The second guard held the cube out in front of him. What happened when they used that thing on a human? She threw the bomb into the crowd. Phillip went to where he thought he saw it land while the second guard tried to cube Jazlyn.

The light left the cube and flew around Jazlyn. Nothing happened. Jazlyn offered a weak smile and a shoulder shrug, trying to pretend she was as surprised as the guard. Clearly nothing like this had ever happened before. The swarm aliens that were still running around stopped to look. The blue light kept buzzing around Jazlyn in every direction but nothing was happening. The light returned to the cube and she took a couple involuntary steps forward but that was the only affect it had on her.

Phillip kept walking calmly to the bomb. Durgan had it in his hand.

Take it, said Durgan. *You place the bomb behind that door and I'll go and save your friend. If I can.*

If? asked Phillip.

She has exposed herself as a human. I'm not sure what we can do, but I'll try.

Before anyone could do anything there was a ripple in the ceiling and a long thin mechanical arm descended. It was exactly like the arm that had been used on the general and the crew of the *Bears Paw*. Jazlyn was being collected for emulation.

Phillip would get to her after he put this bomb where it was supposed to be. He looked at the display but there was no way to tell how much time was left. It couldn't have been very long. The door was close. All Durgan said was that it needed to be on the other side. Phillip wasn't going to waste any time.

The guard not trying to emulate Jazlyn noticed Phillip with the bomb and started walking towards him with the cube out in front of him. That wasn't going to do anything. Phillip ran to the door, put the bomb on the ground and slid it as far as he could. The blue light from the cube started buzzing around him as he closed the door. He stumbled backwards slightly as the cube tried to suck him in.

The room was starting to thin out as aliens ran out, some of them reverting to swarm form and leaving as quickly as they could. The guard looked at the ceiling and brought down another emulator needle. Phillip started running. As he ran he used his thoughts to try and order the needle back up into the ceiling. It wasn't working. At best it was slowing down. Jazlyn was already green and lying on the ground.

There are humans among us. Swarm forms will be mandatory until they are found. Only use your emulators as long as you need to.

The message was being broadcast so everyone could hear it. All the aliens who were left turned into swarms, including Durgan who, before changing, looked at Phillip but didn't say anything. There was nothing the alien could do.

Guys did you hear that? asked Ryan from elsewhere in the fleet.

You need to hide! said Nelson.

Everyone is in swarm form except for me. It might be too late.

Run!

Ryan didn't answer back. Was he dead? Had he been stuck with the green liquid feeding needle? Phillip couldn't worry about him now. He had to worry about what was happening on the Searchers Sphere. The guards were still in the room, albeit as swarms, and they were still calling down emulator needles to try and stop Phillip and Nelson.

What do we do? We have nothing to fight them with, said Nelson.

That was true. Phillip had no idea how to fight the aliens. The best he could hope for was to run away and maybe get to a ship. But even getting to a ship wasn't going to do them any good because they were in the middle of the fleet.

The answer came to him suddenly and he realized how stupid he was being. The cubes could be used against the aliens. He might be able to get the one from the guard but maybe he could make his own. As he ran he focused on the malleable part of the ceiling and called it out with his mind. It emerged and dropped into his hand. He did it again and tossed one to Nelson who was running nearby.

Now they had a way to fight back. While dodging emulator needles, Phillip turned and charged at the swarms with his hands out in front of him. Assuming that the cubes responded to mind speak like everything else he ordered the light to jump out and attack the clouds in the room. Nelson did the same thing. They each captured an attacking swarm. The rest were making a run for it. The emulator needles were retreating into the ceiling.

We did it! said Nelson.

Then the bomb went off. The room holding the searchers was unable to contain the explosion and the door blew off its hinges and slammed right into Phillip, throwing him to the ground. The shock wave was enough to knock Nelson off his feet. The fire storm from the other room ate all the oxygen in that room and swept over both of them. The sound was deafening. The ship shook violently. Both cubes were destroyed. If they hadn't been changed by Mac they would have definitely been killed but now they were only almost dead. The explosion ended but neither man could get up right away. Phillip didn't even have the mental power to wonder what happened let alone ask Nelson if he was okay.

The best Nelson was able to do was moan loudly. Phillip was able to roll over, which allowed him to see that the ceiling was rippling. It looked black from the flames but the more it rippled the more the metallic gray came back, like the ship was healing itself. Blinking was a trial. Each blink was long and he felt like passing out. When he opened his eyes the last time, he saw his end.

An emulator needle arm came down, quickly. It plunged deep into Phillip's stomach. He cried out but otherwise was too weak to do anything about it. Green liquid moved down the arm and entered his body. The same thing was happening to Nelson. Soon the aliens would learn everything about Mac, Ronos, and the human's only plan to win the war.

The mission had failed.

Chapter 19
What Happens When They Get to Ronos

Once Mac, Quentin, Valtteri, and Miss White were clear of the camp they broke into a full run. Watching Miss White run faster than a cheetah was one of the funniest things Mac had seen in his entire life. He never would have thought she would be tough competition in a foot race on an alien planet. *All part of growing up,* he laughed to himself.

The terrain had become hilly and they stopped at the top of each hill to assess their trajectory. For a while there was nothing much to see, but when they got closer to the mountains they heard their destination before they saw it. Something was tearing up the ground very near them.

They went over one more hill and then they saw it.

"Get down," said Mac.

"Why? It's dark. They can't see us," said Miss White.

"We glow in the dark, Miss White. Get down."

They all got on their stomachs at the top of the hill and looked down on what was happening below them. There were a dozen soldiers gathered around a hole in the ground where a great rumbling was coming from below the crust.

The soldiers were human and they were not being burned. Even weirder was they weren't glowing purple with power like the people from Passage. How was that possible? Mac looked closer and saw that one of them was burned. Raymond was down there madly pointing around. He wasn't yelling out loud, although that's what his movements indicated. There must have been some loud mind speaking going on. Was that guy ever going to stop being a thorn in Mac's side?

Raymond had obviously found a way to survive the gas without dying a horrible death, and he passed that knowledge on to Zinger and his men. Mac had no way of knowing whether Raymond's way was better or not, but either way this was bad news. There were only twelve men now. That was bound to change very quickly. What were they doing here? What was their mission?

Raymond was being very dramatic with his gesturing, but then he stopped and looked right at where Mac was hiding.

Aren't you going to come down and give me a proper welcome back? said Raymond in Mac's head.

What are you doing down here? What did you do to these men?

Nothing they didn't sign up for. We are here to find out what is keeping these ships here and to destroy it.

Mac saw the lie immediately. Raymond wasn't stupid. He knew the pull machine was the reason they were all there and he knew that Mac knew. He must be broadcasting to everyone. His men didn't know the full story and Raymond wasn't going to let them in on it. Mac doubted that the scab of a man even cared if everyone out in space died when the *Lendrum* came. Raymond was crazy and dangerous.

The ground started shaking and then a ship burst out of the hole that Raymond and the other soldiers were surrounding. Mac recognized it. His brother-in-law had shown him the schematics in a bit of technological amazement he wanted to share with everyone. It was a mining ship designed for the worst conditions humans could conceive.

The ship was a sphere with a protrusion that looked like a mouth if you thought of the round part as the head. The protrusion formed a box when the teeth were together, but when they were apart, laser cutters and mechanical arms were revealed. The lasers cut the rock, or whatever they were mining, and then the arms pulled it into the storage compartment.

The rest of the ball was armor except for the command deck which was not that big. Mac laughed at the thought of all twelve of the burly men around the hole crammed into such a tight space.

Mac knew he could use the ship for its armor not for its mining abilities, but it looked like Raymond was using it for both. What was he looking for? Even with all that armor it would only be good for one trip. Why were they wasting so much time mining?

"Let's get out of here," said Mac.

"What's going on down there?" asked Valtteri.

"I think those guys came to kill us. We need to go back to the others and find another way down to the beacon to turn off the pull."

"You said these guys are here to kill us. What are they waiting for?"

All twelve of the guys down below were facing towards the hill. If they were as fast as the people who glowed then they would be able to cover the distance in seconds. Raymond was holding them back for some purpose. Who knew what it was.

"Let's go."

Lynn was more than happy to lead the group away from Raymond to find another way into the cave system, but she did it with a warning.

"He knows where we are," she said.

"What?" asked Mac

"He can feel where we are anywhere on the planet. I don't know how he does it but that's one of his gifts, unfortunately."

"Then if he's not coming after us now he either doesn't want to kill us anymore or he's waiting for something."

"He still wants to kill us. We need to be careful."

"Will he be able to find us in the caves?"

"Not as easily. Once we are underground it's harder to mind speak and that has something to do with how he is able to tell where we are."

Lynn led the group to the mountains. She said that Raymond had attacked her in the mountains and to escape she had gone into the caves that linked up to the beacon. Everyone was told to be as quiet as possible and move quickly. There was no more child-like yelling and banter. Instead everyone focused on moving as fast as their new bodies were able.

Their pace slowed down a little once they got to the mountains. The group was big enough that someone could accidentally get lost, so Lynn made sure that everyone knew where they were going.

"There's the cave mouth. It's not much farther to the beacon," said Lynn.

"Gather everyone in the cave. I'll bring up the rear to make sure we have everyone. Once we are in deep enough I think we need to teach these guys to mind speak," said Mac.

"Good idea."

The people of Passage shuffled into the cave. Once everyone was inside and they had been walking for several minutes, Mac spoke in his mind broadcasting to everyone.

If you can hear me stop walking.

Even me? asked Lynn.

No. I'm testing if anyone can pick it up naturally.

Mac could hear some complaint up ahead.

"What's your problem?"

"I ran smack into you. Why did you stop?"

"This guy stopped. I didn't have a choice."

Say your name. Who stopped? asked Mac.

"Quentin Lenoch."

Try and reply in your mind.

Mac listened for Quentin's response. It didn't come right away but Mac kept encouraging him through mind speak. The first time he heard Quentin in his head it was too quiet for the message to be clearly understood but each time it was repeated it got louder and louder. Finally Mac was able to understand what Quentin was saying.

Have you been able to do this the whole time and didn't tell us?

Maybe, replied Mac.

It's almost like an organic Imp. Can you send pictures this way as well?

I've never tried. Before you start exploring your mind's potential I need your help teaching the others how to do this.

I don't know how I'm doing this.

Just get close to the person and say the same thing over and over again until you make a connection. Make sure you guys are focused on each other. Lynn, let's stop the group so we can work through this. Every one we teach will teach someone else so we can get this done quickly.

We should have done this before we got to the caves, Mac, said Quentin.

The mind speak attracts the gargoyles.

It didn't take long for everyone from Passage to learn to mind speak. Soon none of them were using their voices but they didn't all know the rules. Mac was overhearing some pretty private conversations. He didn't know everyone's voice so he couldn't tell where some of them were coming from.

Two young men were wondering about bodily functions.

I don't think we need to dump anymore.

Dump or pee?

Neither. I haven't felt the need to since we got here, and I'm not hungry. I haven't been hungry since we changed.

And you're always hungry.

Exactly.

But I think I peed a little when that creature caught us in the shuttle and then again when we were falling through the air.

Another guy didn't know how to take a hint and was trying to get a woman to go on a date with him. Where he thought they would go, or why he thought now was a good time, puzzled Mac.

I think it's fate that we survived. I think it means we are meant to be together.

My husband is still back on Earth.

But who knows when we will get back there. No one else has to know.

Mac started shouting to get everyone to stop talking. Several dirty looks were being thrown to a short man with long blond hair. He looked happy but that was likely because he didn't know everyone had heard him confess his love for a married woman.

"Now that everyone can mind speak you need to know a couple rules. First of all, if you don't focus on your audience then you are broadcasting to everyone. Most of you have been doing that accidentally. If you could hear us we could hear you. Learn to have a private conversation before you say anything you don't want everyone to hear."

Now the man with long blond hair understood. He stopped smiling and looked down at the ground.

Mac continued, "It's also important that you don't mind speak outside of the caves. Mind speaking attracts the gargoyles, so use your normal voice."

Mac.

"Does someone have a question?" asked Mac.

Can everyone hear this? asked one of the young guys who had been talking about bodily functions.

"We hear you Danny. I think he was asking about serious questions," said Mrs. White.

Mac.

Is someone trying to talk to me? I recognize the voice but you need to ask a question, said Mac.

The part of the cave they were in was long and the group was big enough that Mac couldn't see them all, except for a distant glow. The ones he could see were all giving each other strange looks. None of them had asked a question and none of them had heard anything.

Mac.

The voice was getting louder and it was easier for Mac to understand where he had heard it before. It was the alien Jace. He was close. Maybe not in the cave yet, but he was getting closer every second. Like Raymond, Jace must have been able to feel where Mac was.

"Run!" yelled Mac.

He had no intention of facing off with Jace on the alien's home planet. The Passage people didn't need to be told twice. They took off through the cave tunnels as fast as they could. The ground wasn't even and more than once someone tripped or smashed their head into the cave wall but Mac kept yelling from the rear for them to keep running.

There was a crashing noise behind them. Something big was trying to get through the cave. As he ran Mac looked around him. The cave was a foot over his head and if he reached his arms out straight on either side of him then his fingers could touch the walls. Whatever was smashing through the caves now was bigger than the caves and strong enough to still force his way in.

Suddenly Mac bashed his face into the person in front of him. The group had stopped running. There was a lot of yelling and confusion. The sound of the approaching monster only got louder.

Lynn! What's going on? asked Mac.

Dead end. I missed the tunnel that leads to the pull machine, she said.

Panic was taking over the crowd. They weren't fighters. They didn't know what they were supposed to do. Everyone was looking to Mac for guidance and he had none to give. They would need to back track to find the right tunnel but there was a beast hurling rocks in their way.

Mac Narrad! Jace yelled again. It was being broadcast. Everyone heard the yelling.

Now Mac could feel the walls and ground shaking. Dust was wafting towards them. Some Passage people were choking on it. One person even complained that they couldn't breathe. They hadn't figured out yet that they didn't need to breathe.

There was only one thing that Mac could do. If these people were going to make it to the pull machine, and if Lynn was going to turn off the beacon, then he was going to have to lead the monster away. Without any more thought than that he took off running from the group.

I'll take care of this. As soon as it's clear, take these people to the machine, Mac said to Lynn.

Be careful, Lynn said.

The change made Mac almost indestructible. He could go weeks and months without eating — maybe years for all he knew. He didn't need to breathe anymore. He had survived laser blasts and falls from incredible heights. Yet, he was still full of fear as he charged at his new foe.

Ahead Mac could see a massive creature smashing the walls of the tunnel in an effort to make it bigger. It looked like the monster had four arms but it was hard to tell in the dim light. It was so big that he wasn't sure that he would be able to run past him, but that didn't mean he was going to slow down his pace. Instead Mac pushed his legs faster. If he couldn't go around the leviathan then he was going to go through him.

Hold on, Mac, Jace said, but Mac didn't stop to listen.

Once he was close enough Mac jumped through the air and collided with Jace knocking them both over. Up close Mac was able to get a much better look at what Jace had become. He looked like a distant evolutionary relative of the gargoyles they had already been attacked by. His skin was gray and leathery and tightly covered the thick muscles that were all over his body. Instead of elephant stumps he had grown fingers and claws. The four arms that Mac had thought he'd seen before were actually two gargantuan arms and then two more fists and claws attached to the end of the wings. The wings themselves had changed. They were thick and looked like they might be made up of pure muscle. Seeing a creature like this flying through the air would be mesmerizing and terrifying at the same time. The mouth of the beast was very similar to the gargoyles. The teeth were still there with the elongated face. The eyes were large and set on either side of his head. Mac guessed he had 360° vision and was impossible to sneak up on. The way the mouth had evolved would make it impossible to communicate, so mind speak was necessary for intelligent conversation.

The tackle Mac initiated caught Jace off guard but not for very long. He let out a demonic cry through the jagged teeth and then reached down and flung Mac off of him. Mac flew through the air and landed with a thud among boulders on the tunnel floor. He had been thrown away from the Passage people and closer to the entrance to the caves. This was perfect. Gathering his legs under him he took off again.

Stop. Come back! Jace yelled.

Mac briefly wondered why Jace would ask him that. Jace was trying to kill them. Why would Mac stop and go back to him? As fast as Mac was, Jace's new body was equally as fast. And the cave had already been smashed to fit the creature's enormous form. The space between the two of them was closing.

In seconds they were at the cave entrance and Mac jumped out without slowing down. He was flying through the air. Below him was the rocky mountain side. He was on his descent but he never hit the ground.

Jace burst out of the cave and spread his massive wings. They were four times as long as he was tall. The farther he stretched them the thinner they got. The three-digit clawed hand was twice as big as his other hands. The monster's skin was a lighter gray than that of the gargoyles they had encountered. Jace was bigger and looked stronger than they were. He dove for Mac and plucked him out of the air with his feet that were exactly like his hands.

The wings flapped repeatedly causing massive lift and pulling the creature up into the air. Mac half suspected he would be ripped in half, but for some reason Jace was letting him live.

Jace flew to the top of a jagged peak and put Mac down.

You think I can't get down from here? asked Mac.

You could probably survive the fall, but I would recommend against it, said Jace.

What is this, Jace? A fight to the death on the top of a mountain?

My name isn't Jace.

What?

Jace was the name of the human I was emulating, but I have no need to be anyone but me now. This is who I really am. This is my body. I have finally come home.

If you aren't Jace then what am I supposed to call you?

My name is Vlamm.

Mac shook his head. He didn't want to be up here talking to an alien with a ridiculous name. Vlamm the gargoyle was hovering up above him while Mac looked around for an easy way down. It wasn't going to be easy to climb down, but Mac was done talking. He moved to the edge and started to lower himself down.

I'm sorry, said Vlamm.

For lying to me back on Earth or for playing a part in the planned extermination of mankind?

For everything. I didn't realize back in Northgate that you could be trusted. I was trying to find out if my people were really responsible for the destruction of Northgate. I wasn't looking for allies.

Don't try that with me. I'm not an idiot. You can mind speak. You could send a message back to your fleet and ask if any of them had anything to do with it.

I have no authority among the Almics. A message from me asking about the destruction of a human city would not be significant. The only companions I have on the front are the ones like me. The ones that seek to return home without destroying the humans.

How many of you are there?

Not very many.

You couldn't convert people to your cause?

Almics exists for only one purpose. To do whatever we can to return to our home.

And you really expect me to believe that you don't want to hurt any humans on your way here. It doesn't matter now because you're here. You got your body back. I'm going to go try to save humanity.

Mac started punching and kicking hand and foot holds into the side of the mountain and started climbing down. It was going to take forever, but he wasn't willing to rely on Jace or Vlamm or whatever the creature's name was.

Almics are driven by one thing. To get back here. If I talk to them and show them it's possible to get back here without killing anyone then maybe there can be peace, said Vlamm.

They won't stop because they found Ronos. I don't believe that and I doubt you're dumb enough to believe it either.

Vlamm didn't answer, but his silence said everything. The aliens, Almics as Vlamm called them, wouldn't stop their destructive ways because they had reached their goals. Humans and Almics had been fighting for over five years. That wasn't going to stop because they were neighbors.

After too long Vlamm finally said, *It's the only thing I can think to do. I'm the only one left with a body. It's possible that my words will have more weight.*

Possible. But not promising. I'll leave that to a last resort. We still have other things we can try.

They were both so focused on each other that neither of them noticed the ship that had entered the atmosphere until it was too late. Mac heard hissing and saw the damaged mining vessel streaking towards him. He doubted he'd be able to get out of the way, but that didn't mean he wasn't going to try. He pushed off the cliff face as hard as he could. The ship nicked the tip of the peak and then spiraled to the ground. Mac would have been hit if it hadn't been for Vlamm's quick thinking. The beast scooped Mac out of the air and dodged the hissing ship.

From the clutches of the winged creature, Mac watched the ship crash into the ground. He wondered if that was the same ship he had seen before.

Judging from how quickly the HAAS3 he had flown had burned up, he was able to guess at how many trips the mining ship could take. Two for sure. Three at the most. He had seen Jace with a dozen soldiers on the ground. There couldn't have been very many more than that. Those soldiers had been different. They didn't glow. Was there another transformation that could protect people from the new gas-filled Ronos? Mac figured that was important information to have. It might help him distribute power quicker or maybe that transformation had more potential. He needed to know what Raymond was capable of.

Take me to where that ship crashed, Mac said to Vlamm.

Raymond is on his way there. We should get back to the others. I had been trying to catch up with to you when you charged me in the tunnels.

You want to help us now?

Yes. I told you. We need to work together to save humanity.

Well, your plan might not be the best. I need to know what Raymond is capable of. It'll be a quick stop. If you really want to help then you will take me where I ask.

Just because I have agreed to help doesn't mean I take orders.

Just because you agreed to help doesn't mean I trust you.

The two of them had worked so well together on Earth when they were searching for answers in the rubble of Northgate. Now there was no trust, no unity, or clear way forward. Obviously Vlamm didn't want to argue further because he tucked his wings together and streaked to the ground, stopping by spreading his wings until they were at their thinnest. His claws opened and Mac fell. Vlamm took off without saying anything.

Mac landed on the mining ship, which was still sizzling as the armor was slowly burned away. For a moment Mac started panicking thinking the hissing sound was himself burning. Frantically he rolled off the ship and plopped onto the mountain valley floor. Once he did a quick check of his clothes and skin he realized he wasn't burning. Standing up he tentatively touched the side of the ship. He didn't feel a thing. He laughed to himself when he thought about how Lynn had done the same thing before their transformation and had been instantly burned.

Someone started pounding on the side of the ship. There were people trapped inside. Vlamm had said Raymond was on his way and Mac thought it would be easier to get the answers he was looking for without interference from him.

Mac started by punching the deteriorating shell of the ship. He was able to make a dent but that was it. He looked around for a jagged rock to use as a bashing tool. He found one that was three times as big as his head. He held it high above him and then slammed it down repeatedly. The force of each hit was so intense that the entire ship moved ever so slightly under each blow. The dent grew deeper and deeper. As the ship continued to disintegrate, chunks started to chip off.

After several blows a crack formed and soon it was wide enough for Mac to grip it's edges and pull it apart. Once he had put the rock aside and started trying with his hands he could hear some people talking inside.

"The door is blocked. We can't get out."

"Are you with Major Raymond Tysons or Mac Narrad?"

"Major Tysons. Who are you?"

"I'm the guy trying to get you out. How do I know that you are who you say you are?"

"Look man, get us out of here."

"I'm working on it. You can talk while I get it done."

Now that Mac could talk to them – he figured they didn't know yet that they could mind speak – he slowed down his freeing of the men. He could have easily pulled the sides farther apart but he pretended it was more of a trial than it was.

"How are we supposed to prove it? We were assigned to come down here and take out the hostiles and turn off whatever is causing that pull. We drank that disgusting black liquid and we have reserves on us so we don't get burned. That's all we know about this mission. How else can we prove that we are with you?"

Mac didn't get a chance to answer. A knife was plunged into his back. He screamed in pain and crumpled to the ground. It still hurt despite the change he had gone through. The blade wasn't plunged in and then pulled out. It stayed in, deep in the flesh, right up to the hilt. Mac could feel his body trying to heal itself instantly but it couldn't because the blade was in the way. He reached behind him to pull it out but it wasn't within reach.

If you remove it then I'll add another, said Raymond.

He was standing a little ways away, easily within throwing distance. There was a crowd of men with him. The dozen or so men had grown to fifty. Mac had to get out of there before they tore him to pieces. He got up, but two other men approached. One stabbed Mac in his leg. The other went for his heart.

Mac was still alive but he couldn't move. The blade in his heart made his whole body hurt. It was equivalent to the feeling when he fell out of the sky and landed on Earth. He couldn't move and could barely talk. His vision was cloudy.

"How…" was all Mac managed to choke out.

How what? How did we get so many people down here? Easy. We had a dozen mining ships to do with as we liked. Or were you asking how I survived down here after you left me to die? Turns out we stumbled onto the same secret. The liquefied rock on this planet is immune to the gas. If we drink it we survive. Or were you asking how I managed to kill you? That was easy. Guns don't work down here. But knives we can keep close to our skin and they don't get burned. You may be able to heal yourself, but we hit you right in the heart. You still need to circulate your life-giving blood.

The knives could survive on Ronos. They would only be flipped out when attacking was needed. That was short enough that the weapon could be used several times before becoming useless from overexposure to the gas. As Raymond spoke he took steps towards Mac until he was standing right over him. Then the man with the horribly disfigured face bent down and looked at Mac eye to eye.

I could end it all for you right now. No more worrying about how to rescue the ones you love. No more feeling guilty about the ones you left behind. No more trying to win this war and pretending to be the only human who cares about humanity. Is that what you want? Do you want me to give you your freedom?

It wasn't, but there wasn't much Mac could do to stop him. The pain was overwhelming but Mac did what he could to remove the knife from his chest. While Raymond was talking he managed to bring his hand up to the hilt but he didn't have the strength to pull it out.

Why do you fight so hard to do things your own way?

Raymond grabbed the knife and twisted it. Mac blacked out. He thought he was dead but soon his eyes opened. The knife had been pulled out of his chest and was now in a holster on Raymond's arm. Mac had only been out a moment.

You're lucky that you still have something I need.

"I won't help you," said Mac.

Don't be dramatic. I need your natural light. My men aren't as used to the dark as I am. Then to the other soldiers that were gathered he yelled in mind speak, *Get those guys out of the mining ship before the fuel ignites. We aren't going to wait for more reinforcements.*

The men smiled at each other, eager to get to the fighting and killing. Each man was armed with a long knife that they kept close to their bodies so that they weren't burnt up. They each had a canteen. Mac rightfully guessed that they were full of liquefied Lynn Rock. The mining ship was used to bring the rock up to the *Rundle* where it was melted down and distributed to the men. As long as they drank enough of it they would be safe on Ronos.

Mac remembered what the soldier in the mining ship had told him. The mission was to remove the hostiles — Mac, Lynn and the people from Passage — and then to turn off the beacon so that the *Lendrum* didn't kill everyone in orbit and strand everyone else on Ronos. Raymond stood Mac up and prodded him forward. Mac was already feeling better. His first few steps were cautious but as the healing gas flowed through him the torn flesh bound itself back together.

It's not going to be that easy, said Raymond.

From behind, Raymond stuck his blade between Mac's ribs. The pain was there but it wasn't as bad as the piercing of the heart. With the knife Raymond prodded Mac along to the cave entrance, using the knife like a steering wheel.

Let's go visit some old friends.

Chapter 20
Glow

Lynn was leading the group now, but she wasn't alone. Valtteri was right beside her. Quentin was there as well. When Mac had yelled for everyone to run, Lynn had no idea what was going on. They had to back track and find another tunnel and the speed they kept up helped them to get to the massive cavern with the beacon in it at a reasonable time. She knew they were getting close when the rocky tunnel they were crawling through was lit up by the pulsing red light on top of the machine.

"What is that?" asked Mrs. White. She was always near the front of the group. More than once she ran past Lynn to see what was up ahead. She would say she was scouting, but Lynn guessed that she was excited about being so quick and agile again.

"It's..." Lynn thought about it. How would she describe it? The reason they were all there? That sounded too profound. The reason they couldn't get off the planet? Maybe. To be more accurate she could say it was a colossal saucer shaped ship or machine that was more advanced than anything humans had ever built and it was in a cavern with ancient carvings from an unknown civilization, but she knew that would sound ridiculous. "It's hard to explain. You'll have to wait and see it for yourself."

Then they got to the cavern. Lynn was the only one who didn't hesitate jumping down to the cavern floor. She had been here before and the sense of awe she had felt when she first saw it was replaced by all the bad memories this beacon had caused. Quentin soon followed after her.

"This is the machine that's pulling all those starships in, right?" he asked.

"Yep," said Lynn.

"And you can turn it off?"

I'm going to try, she thought to herself. She already knew that she had access to the beacon's power of time travel and she didn't have to be in the cave to use it. While on the surface she had already tried to mentally turn off the pull. She could feel the presence of the beacon and the inkling to utilize its time traveling abilities, but she ignored those impulses and searched for a way to turn the pull off. It wasn't there. She couldn't feel it. It felt like there was a firm mental connection but nothing to do with the pull. All her commands went unnoticed. *Turn off the pull. Power down. Turn off the Reach. Disable Active Attraction.* She hadn't forgotten about the monitor she had seen in the control room. There had to be something they could do with that.

Lynn and Quentin found part of the ship they could climb up and started walking towards the door she had fallen through. The Passage people were still jumping and climbing down. Valtteri yelled to Lynn, "What are you guys doing?"

"Trying to turn the pull off. Stay here. You guys should be safe."

Valtteri didn't listen. He wanted to know what was going on and to be there in case a decision needed to be made. The spot he climbed up was where Raymond had been dumping liquefied rock. The hollowed out boulder he'd used was still sitting there. As Valtteri walked in certain places that were especially saturated he sunk down slightly with each step. He stopped walking.

"What is this thing? I thought it was metal, but up close it seems almost organic," he said.

"I think it is. That's the same liquefied rock that helps us survive on this planet without getting burned. Some idiot dumped a ton of it on this machine and that's when the pull started trapping Zinger and everyone else here," said Lynn.

Valtteri stepped lightly across the soggy section of the of the pull machine, leaving footprints behind him. Lynn waited to see if he would accidentally fall through, but that didn't happen. The structure was soggy but not structurally compromised. She led the two men to the door and into the ship. Then they started jogging to the control room she had found before.

"Who do you think made this ship?" asked Valtteri.

"I have no idea," said Lynn.

"Whoever it was, they weren't human. The hallways and doorways are massive. Plus everything works by mind speech. Humans also never made anything that could be abandoned for this long and still work," said Quentin.

"You're kind of observant," said Valtteri.

"Thank you. Lynn, if we can't turn the pull off, what are we going to do?"

"I have a plan B," Lynn said.

They got to the control room but most of it was a mess. The roof was completely black and the liquefied rock had dripped onto most of the monitors, including the one for the pull. As before, it did not respond to her touch or commands.

Valtteri was looking around at the other monitors when he saw the one that had been modified by someone from Earth. "Did you do this?"

"No," said Lynn.

"Well, whoever it was it was a human. And it looks like it used to work. I've done wiring on almost every house in Passage. I'll see if I can make something on this ship work."

311

Valtteri went onto his back and started poking and pulling from the wires under the monitor. Lynn was glad someone was able to try something, but she didn't have a lot of hope. Trying not to let it show, she sat in the oversized chair and waited for Valtteri to come up with something. Quentin came and stood beside her.

"What's your plan B?" he asked.

"It's...going to sound crazy," said Lynn.

"Crazier than injecting liquid rock into our blood stream so that we can survive on a planet that is covered in purple gas?"

"Time travel."

"What?"

"I can use this machine to time travel."

"How?"

"I don't know exactly. But somehow, before the planet was covered in the gas, my ancestors came here and programmed this beacon to respond only to them. When they did that one of the powers they controlled was the ability to go back in time."

"It's hard to believe that you've been able to go back in time during all of this and you never did."

"It only works once. I can't use it until we have no chance of winning."

"We are getting close to that, you know. There is a space station coming to obliterate everyone stuck in orbit resulting in us being stranded here. Not to mention that there is an alien fleet heading here with no way to stop them."

"There is still hope. Valtteri might be able to turn the pull off. Mac sent some men behind enemy lines to fight the aliens. Plus, even if we get trapped here we might be able to fight them off. Mac said we were immune to alien attacks."

"Oh wow. When you say no chance of winning you really mean it."

"It's our only free pass. We can't waste it."

"So where will you go?" asked Quentin.

"What?"

"If all else fails and you have to travel back in time, where will you go so that we have a chance at winning this war?"

"I would probably go back and stop Raymond from getting liquefied rock all over the pull machine. Then we would be able to turn the pull off and get out of here."

Quentin didn't say anything. Instead it looked like he was waiting for the punch line of a joke.

"What?" asked Lynn.

"You can go anywhere in time and you want to only go back days instead of years?"

"What would you do?"

"I would go way back. The further you go back the better chance the humans have at surviving. You could tell them about the invasion that's coming and prepare them. Society could be built around winning the war."

"Why would they believe me? As soon as I tell them I come from the future with a warning they will lock me up. Plus it doesn't matter how much we prepare for this war. Mac said that humans don't have any weapons that can hurt the aliens."

"Given enough time, years upon years with a concentrated effort in a single area, human ingenuity will be able to create what we need to survive. Maybe you wouldn't be able to convince everyone, but if you had a small group of people convinced and prepared for the war it would give us a better chance than we have now. Plus, after a few generations that group would grow and so would the humans' chances at survival."

"So you think I should bring a group of people over to Ronos and change them and build a society here to fight the war?"

"Yes…wait. I know exactly where you should go now. Did you study the generation ships in school?"

"Everyone did."

"Get yourself on one of those ships and change the course for Ronos. Change those people and build them up to fight a war. There were over two thousand people on each of the ships. Some had over five thousand. That's a huge head start."

Lynn was starting to get overwhelmed by the idea of humanity's fate resting on her actions. She hadn't even thought about where she was going to go, so how could she be expected to save the human race? There was no way she would be able to convince anyone to listen to her. Quentin was right, she needed to go as far back as she could and start some kind of a movement. In school she had learned a little about the massive, slow-moving colony ships called generation ships, but she wasn't sure that she knew enough to get herself aboard one and then to reprogram it to fly to Ronos. This was going to be impossible. She didn't want to do any of that. All she wanted to do was find Scott and be with him. That's all she ever wanted, right from the beginning. But that was also the reason she was in the thick of this mess to begin with. If she hadn't been looking for Scott in Northgate then she wouldn't have started the chain of events that led her here, trapped on Ronos, contemplating traveling to a time she knows very little about.

"Just relax," said Quentin.

"I am relaxed," lied Lynn.

Quentin laughed. "You are breathing like a horse in a race and you keep tapping your foot like you are impatiently waiting for someone to show up."

"I hadn't thought this time travel thing through all the way and it's starting to freak me out a little."

"Don't let that bother you right now. We need to focus on the problem at hand."

Valtteri got up from the floor and brushed the dust off of his pants.

"It's not good," he said. "Not only do I have no idea how any of this works, but I don't even think the wires are metal. Everything on this ship looks and feels organic. It's almost like this thing was grown somewhere and then moved here. I don't know how anyone can make a current go through these wires let alone find a way to fix it. Playing around down there I may have done more bad than good. I don't know."

"It's also possible that you did something good, eh?" said Quentin with a smile trying to lighten the situation.

"Anything's possible."

Lynn called out in her mind again, trying desperately to communicate with the ship. Again she could feel a connection, but it did not obey her. The only thing she could control was the parts of the ship that weren't affected by the liquid rock Raymond had foolishly slopped all over. She still had control of time travel but that was a decision that she couldn't make until she talked it over with Mac. There was also the promise she had made to her husband, but she didn't want to think about that. She was almost positive that no one else would be going back with her. There had to be another way.

Then the ground started shaking. The three of them looked at each other but no one knew what it was.

"An earthquake?" wondered Valtteri.

"Maybe the ship's engines turned on," said Quentin.

Lynn didn't think it was either of those things. She ran out of the room and down the hallway to the door leading out of the beacon. As soon as she hoisted herself onto the top of the ship she knew something was wrong. The rumbling wasn't coming from beneath them; there was something above them digging down. Dust and small rocks rained down on them. The people from Passage were all crowded together close to the pull machine, trying to use it as shelter.

Lynn jumped down. They were all standing too close to the crack in the cavern floor where she had fallen down into the river of liquid rock.

"Stand back. You don't want to fall down there," she told them.

The rumbling was getting louder. Bigger chunks of rock were falling. Now they were the size of hover cars. Every time one of them hit the cavern floor the fissure underneath the beacon got a little wider.

Finally the source of the destruction revealed itself. A ship burst through the wall of the cavern, destroying a section of hieroglyphs that may have been there for thousands of years. The ship was black and hissing from damaged caused by the Mac Gas. The front of it looked like a massive digging machine that rotated as it moved forward. She didn't know ships, but this looked like a mining machine. If it made it all the way down there without being destroyed, then it had to have massive amounts of shielding to it.

As soon as the ship punched through it tried to pull back out, but there were some strained mechanical noises coming from it and Lynn knew that it wouldn't be able to make the return trip. The mining ship's engine broke and the ship plummeted to the ground, right where Lynn and the others were standing.

Everyone was watching. Several people yelled "run" but most were already doing that. Lucky for them they already had incredible speed otherwise they wouldn't have made it. The mining ship wasn't very big, three times the size of a HAAS3, and looked down right minuscule next to the pull machine where it came crashing down. The force of it slamming into the side of the beacon made the mining ship crumple, but there was only a small dent in the larger ship. The mining ship rested atop the fissure in the ground. The gas was so concentrated there that Lynn could almost see it deteriorate before her eyes. Some of the Passage people were walking towards it.

"No, don't," she warned. But it was too late.

The mining ship exploded. The light was blinding so Lynn didn't get a good look at the full ramifications until it was already over. The explosion shot debris all over the cavern. She heard yells from the people of Passage as they were hit by shrapnel. Lynn herself felt incredible pain in her side that was so overwhelming it brought her to her knees. Looking down she saw a fist-sized hole in her torso.

"No," was all she could manage before she fell over and closed her eyes.

Mac saw the explosion. Raymond had orchestrated the whole thing. His plan was to crash the mining ship into the pull machine in an attempt to destroy it. That hadn't worked. Even from where Mac was, at one of the many tunnel entrances, he could see minimal damage to the beacon.

Get down there. I don't want any survivors, Raymond ordered his soldiers.

Raymond's fifty meat-headed, enhanced soldiers rushed into the cavern. Jumping down quickly, they were excited about the opportunity to inflict pain. Mac turned slightly to try and get away but all Raymond had to do was twist the knife ever so slightly and Mac was frozen in pain.

You'll get your turn. I want you to see this.

The two men waited at the cavern entrance and watched. The people of Passage were still shook up from the explosion but luckily they noticed before it was too late and most of them started running. Valtteri, Quentin, Mrs. White, Tayma, and others looked around for weapons of their own. There wasn't really anything other than boulders, so that's what they used.

Of course there were some people that didn't get up from the explosion. Mac saw a woman on the ground. It was Lynn. Her eyes were closed but Mac couldn't see any blood. He refused to believe the worst. After everything that happened she couldn't be gone now.

Lynn! he yelled to her.

Mac could have sworn that he saw her eyelids flutter. She was halfway between Mac and the pull machine. Raymond's men had reached her but they ignored her, thinking she was dead, and focused on dodging the incoming rocks the Passage people were throwing.

Lynn, if you can hear me then stay still.

I thought I was dead, said Lynn.

Me too. Was it shrapnel?

Yeah, went right through me.

Raymond has a knife in my back. If I try anything he'll cut my heart out. As amazing as what happened to you is, I still need my heart to stay alive.

Okay. I got this. Wait for my signal.

Lynn was still playing dead. The Passage people were putting up a good fight. There was yells of pain but they were coming mostly from Raymond's soldiers. Mrs. White looked over-the-top excited about being in the fight. Her current strategy was to bowl boulders at the charging men. They could dodge one but eventually they tripped up and then she pummeled them with rocks. Once they were disoriented she would pick the soldier up and throw him or her down the chasm that was under the beacon, down where the mining ship exploded. She had done it twice and both times she grabbed the attacker's knife and threw it to someone on her side. Now Quentin and Valtteri both had long knives to defend themselves with.

The soldiers weren't discouraged. One was enraged by the fact an old lady was effectively fighting back. He wanted to get her but targeted someone else instead. Tayma was turned away from the action picking up a particularly wide boulder when a knife entered her calf. She screamed and fell over.

It's not as bad as you think, said Mac to Tayma. *Pull it out. The gas will heal you.*

Tayma obeyed. It hurt but it wasn't more than a few seconds after she pulled it out that it was like it didn't happen. The soldier who threw the weapon didn't want to have his attack go to waste and jumped at Tayma before she could turn to stab at him. They both fell to the ground. She kicked him off and his leg was smashed by a rock thrown by Mrs. White. Tayma noticed his healing power wasn't instant like hers. He first had to take a swig of his canteen. That was an advantage for them. The knife was long enough and she was strong enough that she was able to knock the soldier to the ground and separate his head from the rest of his body. The soldier in her was coming out. She didn't even take a moment to revel in her victory; she charged at the next attacker. With a weapon in her grasp she was even more deadly than any of the people from Passage — she had been trained to be a killer. Half of the soldiers turned their attention to her. The other half made for the group of Passage people that were leaving the cavern and going into the tunnels. Mac could see John Summerset urging people to move faster and bringing up the rear.

Try and block up the tunnel way behind you. Try and buy time, said Mac.

Everyone was in the tunnel and John was now frantically pounding at the walls trying to cause a cave in. He kept yelling over his shoulder for the people to run. The soldiers closed in. One managed to get a knife into John's arm. John screamed and ran out of sight. The other soldiers streamed into the tunnel. Mac called after him but there was no answer. He didn't know if that was because the worst had happened or because John and the others were surrounded by Lynn Rock.

Mac! Duck!

Lynn had yelled the command at the last possible second and Mac didn't respond in time. The rock she threw while Raymond and the soldiers were distracted hit Mac square in the face. The force was so great that the back of his head crushed what was left of Raymond's nose. Both men fell to the ground. Mac's head was ringing but the gas was healing him already and he recovered sooner than Raymond. The knife was still there and it was in a spot that Mac couldn't reach. The best he could do was jump down to the cavern floor and stagger over to where Lynn was.

"I tried to warn you," said Lynn and she pulled the knife out of Mac's back. He took a deep breath and shook off the last of the pain the blade had caused.

"Don't worry about it," said Mac.

He grabbed Lynn's arm and started running towards the pull machine which. Raymond came to the edge of the tunnel holding his face and screaming out loud with what was left of his burned out vocal cords. It sounded like someone was dunking a cat slowly in acid.

The soldiers all turned his way, which allowed the Passage people who hadn't run off time to turn and climb up to the top of the beacon and higher ground. The mining ship had rained down so many boulders there was plenty of ammo for people who didn't have a knife yet. Mac and Lynn ran to where the others were.

"Good to see you again, Mac" said Quentin.

"Thanks, Sneed."

"Quentin."

"I might never get that right."

"Don't give up yet."

"We need to finish these guys off for good and then try and turn the pull off," said Mac as he hefted a boulder towards one of the men. It crushed the man and caused a chunk of the cavern floor to break loose making the chasm that much bigger.

Lynn filled in the gap, "We tried to turn it off. We don't know how."

That was not what Mac wanted to hear, but he wasn't going to give up hope.

The soldiers realized the flaw in their plan of attacking the last few people in the cavern head on. There was only Mac, Lynn, Quentin, Tayma, Valtteri, and Mrs. White left and there were still at least fifteen soldiers capable of killing them. The rest were dead or chasing after the other Passage people. The soldiers stopped their attack and talked to each other in mind speak. They spread out around the pull machine. Spread out like they were there was no way Mac and the others could stop all of them from coming up. There was a moment of silence while the Passage people waited to see what they should do. Mac thought that he could hear more crumbling rock. He looked up to see if there was another mining ship coming but couldn't find the source of the deterioration.

There's more of us than there are of you, said Raymond. He was sipping from a canteen of melted Lynn Rock as he walked along the top of the beacon to where Mac and the others were clustered together.

We shouldn't be fighting. We should be trying to turn off the pull, said Mac.

There is no way. We crashed a mining ship into this infernal machine and it did nothing. Not even a scratch. If there was a way to turn it off then we would have done it by now.

More of the men jumped up onto the beacon. All fifteen were up now. Mac and the others could only walk backwards across the pull machine away from them.

What do we do? asked Mrs. White.

We'll have to make a run for it, said Valtteri.

I'll stay and make a scene so you guys can get away, said Mac.

You are going to take them all on your own? said Tayma.

I was going to try.

The sound of crumbling rock grew louder and now everyone was looking up to see where it was coming from. Even Raymond looked confused so there couldn't be another mining ship digging down to them. Out of one of the tunnels exploded a creature with a massive wingspan and an ear-bleeding screech. That was the distraction that they needed. Mac knew it was Vlamm, the alien who had posed as Jace.

Run! Mac yelled.

The six of them took off away from the soldiers, across the pull machine. The soldiers didn't even notice.

"What is that thing?"

"It looks like one of those creatures we ran into up top."

"Don't be an idiot. It's different."

"It's bigger."

Vlamm took flight. He flew up as high as he could go in the cavern and then tucked his wings behind his back. It was like he was rocketing at the ground. The soldiers ran but Vlamm was still able to connect with one of them. The leathery leviathan slammed into the biggest guy there with such force the soldier no longer resembled a human being. No amount of liquid rock would heal his wounds. Vlamm didn't stop his attack. He took off again, digging his hands into another victim and clawing at another with the razor claws on the end of his wings. The soldiers were now fully focused on the new threat to them.

Mac stumbled in his stride. The beacon was shaking furiously. The section of the pull machine that they were running on was moving independently of the other broken parts. The gap between their section and the one next to it was increasing. The wires and tubes connecting the two were stretching.

"What's going on?" asked Quentin.

"It's that creature. When he slammed into the ship he broke open the cavern floor," said Lynn.

That was why Mac could still hear rocks crumbling. The cave floor was falling apart. The beacon was broken in five different pieces and now the one they were all on was falling into the crevasse.

Keep running! yelled Lynn.

That's exactly what they did, but it wasn't going to do them any good even with their exceptional speed. The beacon shifted under them again and they all fell over. They were at an angle now and Mac was so caught off guard that when he fell he even started rolling back the way they had come.

Vlamm had picked up another soldier and flown up into the cavern. Mac saw that the monster had four knives sticking out of his body but that wasn't slowing him down. These soldiers didn't stand a chance of stopping him. Vlamm made the situation for Mac worse when he slammed into another soldier. His section of the pull machine tilted into the giant opening in the cave floor. Mac had nothing to hold on to and was now tumbling end over end toward the pit.

There was a loud noise as the giant slab of ancient ship slid down into the cavernous unknown. Accompanying the grinding noise was the sound of the wires snapping and popping as the ship tore apart. Mac reached out to try and stop his descent and found a small nub to latch onto. Valtteri fell past him. Mrs. White wasn't far behind him. When Mac looked to see how the other people were doing, he saw that seven of the soldiers were still latched on to the ship. One of them was Raymond. He saw Valtteri falling and struck out with his knife slicing right through the meaty part of the leg of the Mayor of Passage. Mac wasn't going to let that happen to anyone else. He let go and slid down to where Raymond and the other soldiers were.

Be careful, said Lynn.

I've fallen from higher than this, said Mac as he approached Raymond.

There's nothing down there except for liquid rock.

Mac got what she was saying. If they went down there Raymond would be almost indestructible. As he fell he tried to come down right on Raymond, but the beacon continued to shift and fall. Mac was thrown off course. Not one to be caught off guard, Raymond was watching Mac coming the whole time. As Mac fell past, Raymond threw his knife and it impaled the falling man's arm.

The attack was enough to disorient Mac and prevent him from stopping his fall. Now he was free falling past the broken slab of the beacon. Below him he could see that Lynn was right. There was nothing down there but liquid rock. The cavern floor was rapidly losing its structural integrity. Knowing he would survive the fall he closed his eyes and waited for the impact.

When he hit the liquid he opened his eyes but couldn't see anything but blackness. Then he realized it was because he was in a lake of black liquid rock and swam to the surface. The blinking red light was still working and lit up enough of the lake area that Mac could tell that it was more of a river. He struggled to not get pulled away by the current but he had to dodge the falling rocks from above as well as swim to safety. In the shallow end of the liquid there was an island formed where the majority of the rocks fell. Mac swam there and pulled himself up. That was a bad idea. The reason there was an island there was because that's where most of the rocks were falling.

One of the rocks hit him in the head and knocked him to the ground. He practically landed right on top of Valtteri Happonen. His eyes were wide and lifeless. Half his body had been obliterated by boulders. The same thing was going to happen to Mac if he stayed there. He dove into the river again, only to be snatched out of the water by Vlamm.

You're a dead man if you stay down there, said Vlamm.

You saved me, but not Valtteri.

He got a rock to the head after losing a limb to Raymond. There was nothing I could do. There wasn't anything to save by the time I go there.

Why did you save me?

How many times do I have to tell you?

If we are on the same side then help me save the others.

Have you not seen what I've been doing?

Vlamm reached back and pulled a knife out of his back. With the one Raymond had used on him, Mac now had two. Using Mac as a missile he shot him out at the soldiers still trying to stay on the beacon.

Mac flew with both knives out in front of him and landed on one of the soldiers. Before the soldier fell Mac made sure he was in pieces so the liquid rock down below wouldn't heal him. Vlamm flew to try and pick up Lynn, Quentin, Tayma, and Mrs. White. He grabbed Lynn and Tayma and put them on solid ground. Mac stabbed at another soldier but then almost fell again. He ditched one of the knives and used the free hand to hold onto the beacon.

Raymond saw that Mac was back and yelled with his burned vocal cords. Their positions now reversed, Mac looked up as Raymond let go of the beacon and landed on Mac.

The knife entered Raymond's side, but it didn't slow down his rage. He pulled the knife out and swiped at Mac who then punched the yelling scab of a man in the face as hard as he could. Bones gave in and Raymond's swinging of the knife became more erratic. Mac hit him again and again while dodging the knife.

Raymond couldn't hold on any longer. He plummeted off the beacon and landed on the island of rocks. The beacon was now fully free of the rest of the pull machine and falling straight down into the liquid rock below. Mac braced himself for the impact and made sure the beacon wasn't going to land on him.

Scrambling to the edge of the rocky island Raymond drank fully from the filthy liquid hoping it would give him the power to heal himself. He laughed as his wounds closed around him, but when he looked up to find a way to get back to Mac all he saw was the edge of the beacon. It slammed into the liquid, obliterated the rock island and smeared Raymond into a blob that could never fully recover.

After one edge slammed into the water the other end dropped so that section of the pull machine was resting flat in the liquid. Mac was on top of it. He could see a few soldiers on the shore walking towards him, but Vlamm flew down and picked Mac up before there could be any confrontation.

Vlamm didn't drop Mac off in the cavern. Instead he picked up Lynn and continued flying up out of the caves, coming through the hole that the mining ship had created and heading for the surface.

Where are the others? Mac asked.

Tayma, Quentin, and Claudia went to help the others escape through the tunnels, said Lynn.

Then where are we going?

They broke free of the cave and now Vlamm could fully spread his wings and really gain some speed. Mac expected him to land and leave them on the ground, but he was definitely carrying them somewhere.

Where are we going? Mac asked again.

I thought that he was with you on this plan, Vlamm said to Lynn.

Mac didn't like the sound of this. *What plan?*

There's no way to turn the beacon off, Lynn said. *Raymond tried blowing it up and nothing happened. Valtteri tried messing around with the wiring and that didn't work. I tried using mind speak and that didn't work. The beacon itself is in several different pieces and not even all of it is in the same room anymore and the pull is still activated.*

What's your point?

The Lendrum *is coming. If it destroys everything in orbit then we are trapped here until the alien fleet gets here. We will have lost the war. There will be no way to build up an army. There is only one thing we can do. I have to use my power.*

Your power?

Remember when we were on Zinger's space yacht and he was interrogating me about Grenor and time travel.

You can't be serious.

I told you it was real.

You can't rely on time travel. That's crazy, said Mac.

Ronos is Grenor. My ancestors found the pull machine and programmed it to respond to them. I have that same power. I can use it to travel back in time, Lynn said.

Where — when would you go?

Back to the generation ships. Bring one of them here and prepare them for the war.

That was hundreds of years ago.

I know.

You'll never see me, or Scott, or your parents ever again.

Lynn didn't say anything back right away. She must have already thought of this but didn't want to admit how scary the thought was to her. They were so high up now that they couldn't see the tunnel entrance the mining ship had made. Mac wondered if Vlamm intended to fly them right out into space.

There is still hope. We aren't desperate enough for you to use your power, said Mac. *I have men on the other side trying to free the emulated prisoners. Plus we could still find a way to destroy the beacon. What about the* Rundle? *They have weapons. Zinger will help us. He wants it destroyed as much as we do.*

There's not enough time. Lendrum will be here soon. I don't have a choice, said Lynn.

Mac couldn't believe what he was hearing. Lynn couldn't do this. The power of the beacon was unpredictable, especially now that it had been torn apart and half of it was covered in liquefied rock. If Lynn used her power, there was no telling what it would do. It didn't matter if the *Lendrum* was coming. Being trapped on the planet was better than using something as dangerous as the beacon to time travel.

Vlamm! Stop! said Mac.

You wanted my help. So I'm helping you, said Vlamm.

Then stop helping us. This is crazy. Why are we flying out to space anyway?

Lynn thinks if she got into a ship before she goes back then she can take it with her.

Mac was starting to feel desperate. Lynn was actually going to go through with this. How could she? It was crazy.

Why did you bring me with you? asked Mac.

I wanted to say thank you. Thank you for coming back for me and doing everything you could to bring Scott back to me and I'm sorry it was all for nothing. If you see Scott again then tell him I love him and I didn't think there was any other way to save him and everybody else, said Lynn.

Don't do this, Lynn.

The atmosphere was starting to thin out. Vlamm flapped hard but his flying was becoming erratic and his breathing was frantic. Mac had seen the same thing in the gargoyle that had attacked him when he had the jet pack. Vlamm needed the corrupted air of Ronos to survive. He wouldn't be able to fly much higher. The sky was dark now and Mac could clearly see the stars and the mess of ships that the super pull had created. They were drifting free now so they must have been between pulls.

Vlamm grabbed Lynn with one of his arms, spun around, and then threw her as far as he could. He waited to make sure she made it out of the atmosphere before he did the same thing to Mac.

Wait! said Mac.

Vlamm stopped what he was doing and looked down at Mac.

I should have trusted you, said Mac.

I know, said Vlamm.

I'm sorry.

Vlamm didn't get a chance to respond. He was hit in the chest with laser fire. A small ship had seen the horrible beast with two human prisoners and opened fire. The sudden jolt shook Mac free of Vlamm's grasp and he was now plummeting to the ground. There was no way that he would be able to survive the fall from this height. It was all over for Mac.

More lasers rained down around Mac. He looked around to see what was going on. The initial laser blast hadn't been enough to kill Vlamm. He had a black mark on his chest but he was still flying and dodging lasers. He snatched up Mac again and flew straight up as fast as he could, higher than he had been with Lynn. His breath was haggard and his wings weren't coordinated. He barely had it together enough to duck out of the way of another onslaught of laser fire.

Quickly he chucked Mac into space as hard as he could. The moment the creature released his grip the ship locked on and assaulted Vlamm with a barrage of laser fire. He may have been able to survive one laser blast but there was nothing he could do now. The lasers decimated the alien. When he had been impersonating Jace Michaels it would have been a simple matter of breaking apart into a billion pieces, but it was impossible for Vlamm to survive. What was left of Vlamm — which was nothing more than ash — was whipped away in the windy upper atmosphere.

Lynn was quickly picked up by one of the ships nearby. It wasn't too damaged so it must have recently arrived to the party. She pulled herself along the ship until she got to the airlock and then they let her in.

"How on Earth are you still alive?" said the man inside. He was there with another woman. Both had blond hair and looked to be around the same age as Lynn.

"I'll explain later. Does this ship have an interplanetary drive?" she asked.

"Yes, but we are trapped here. It won't do you any good."

"Can I use your communications?"

They let her out of the air lock and she walked over to the terminal. Seeing her survive the vacuum of space they must have expected her to not have an Imp. They probably didn't even think she was human. Lynn had no idea who they were but they were going back with her. Either that or she would have to kill them.

"*Rundle* this is Lynn Ryder. Put Scott Ryder on the line."

One last time she wanted to hear her husband's voice. All the *Rundle* had to do was put her husband on the line and then she would use her power. The countdown clocks were mocking her. One labeled Pull displayed three minutes and thirty-seconds and counting. The other said five minutes. If the second clock was for the *Lendrum*'s arrival then she only had five minutes to talk to her husband before they would all be wiped out.

"Lynn Ryder, you do not have authority to order the military around," said the communications officer on the *Rundle*.

Lynn shook her head. None of this mattered. In a few minutes all of this will have never existed and she would save everyone. All she wanted to do was talk to the love of her life one last time.

I'm sorry, Scott. I tried. I love you. No matter what happens I will always love you. She thought the message with as much force of will as she could muster. If only he had been changed by Ronos, then the message would make it through. Now she would never hear his voice again.

Just as she thought this the pull clock ticked down to zero. Space became a mess of magnificent metal as ships crashed together without control, all of them being pulled to the same invisible place above Ronos. She pointed herself towards Ronos and hit full throttle. She was still within reach of the pull but she was far enough away that she could time travel without the interruption of crashing into other ships.

Just like when she had first made her connection to Grenor — as her family called it, or Ronos, as everyone else called it — she pictured the planet in her mind's eye with her eyes closed. The planet did not look the same as it did when she was eighteen. Even in her mind she couldn't help but picture the space garbage that now littered the space outside of the planet. The king of the garbage was Zinger's obnoxiously pearly white ship and it would be the king for at least another minute until *Lendrum* got there.

Once the connection was renewed in her mind's eye she did what she had done the first time. She opened her mind and spirit up to the planet and very deliberately and powerfully thought one phrase that would trigger everything.

Time Travel.

Change returned to Ronos. But it was different and more powerful than the cloud of Mac Gas that had emerged from the core. The atmosphere was getting thicker and somehow brighter, like it was now a light source of its own.

Her shipped moved into the upper atmosphere as the clouds of light fully cocooned the planet. Lynn didn't know what was going on but she gave herself over completely to the planet. It was the only way she would be able to save everyone.

What I Know

A lot of what I know hasn't changed since you guys read *Catalyst*. I am still in love and married to an amazing and beautiful woman, I still know that Joseph Smith was a prophet of God, that the Book of Mormon is a true book (and way better than what you just read so you should check it out), and that Jesus Christ has provided a way for all of us to be saved.

I also still know that I wouldn't have been able to finish this book if it wasn't for the help of other people. Rhonda Skinner at Words Nest did an amazing job editing this monster. The one and only Chris Pratt made another beautiful cover. Without these two it would have been a very different middle segment for *The Ronos Trilogy*.

Beacon was another book that I was able to write and produce quicker than normal. I know that is because I have the best part time job in Canada. Thank you Rod Kay for letting me work weird hours, Thank you Glenn Penman for making me a guru, and thank you Shane Trewin for ignoring the obvious nepotism.

Without the test readers I would not have seen the flaws in my first few drafts. I know that without them this book would have had an extra 20,000 words and I know that those words would have made this a less exciting book. I don't miss a single one of them.

I know that I wouldn't have had as much motivation to finish this book if it wasn't for all the feedback that *Catalyst* was given. Whether they were positive or negative, each time a review was posted I felt more motivated to make *Beacon* an even better story than *Catalyst*. I know that reviews are a huge help to independent authors like me so thank you for your thoughts. I'm looking forward to hearing what you thought of *Beacon*.

Lastly I would like to tell you that I know what happens in the final book in *The Ronos Trilogy*. It's all I can do to not spill the beans right now because it's so exciting. Did Lynn's time traveling plan work? What happened to Sneed and the people of Passage who were trapped on the surface or Ronos? Why did the planet turn into a glowing orb? Will Mac ever get to avenge his family? Will he ever see Janelle again? Are Phillip and the others doomed? Will Lynn and Scott ever be reunited? The story of Ronos and the humans battle for survival will definitely conclude in book 3.

About the Author

Tyler Rudd Hall is a member of the Church of Jesus Christ of Latter-day Saints. He grew up in the small farming community of Rosemary Alberta. Because of this he had to use his imagination and VHS copies *Star Wars* to keep himself entertained. After graduating from Rosemary High School he went into the Professional Writing program at McEwan University in Edmonton Alberta. There he met his beautiful and talented wife who was enrolled in the same program. Both of them are now graduates and pursuing their professional writing goals in Edmonton.

Twitter: @tylerruddhall
Website: www.chortleatmygirth.com
Facebook: www.facebook.com/author.tyler.rudd.hall